Awfully English

Faith Bretherick

Published in 2014 by FeedARead.com Publishing

Copyright © Faith Bretherick.

The author or authors assert their moral right under the Copyright, Designs and Patents Act, 1988, to be identified as the author or authors of this work.

All Rights reserved. No part of this publication may be reproduced, copied, stored in a retrieval system, or transmitted, in any form or by any means, without the prior written consent of the copyright holder, nor be otherwise circulated in any form of binding or cover other than that in which it is published and without a similar condition being imposed on the subsequent purchaser.

A CIP catalogue record for this title is available from the British Library.

Chapter One

Isobel studied her hands with some concern, and felt it was perhaps time for a visit to her manicurist. On her right hand the thumbnail had split, her index fingernail was truncated and the remainder of her nails were suffering minor degrees of disrepair. The damage had come about as a result of a mishap with the coffee grinder after one too many gin and tonics prior to the arrival of her cocktail party guests.

Whilst recalling events, she was reminded that she should send her silk cocktail gown to the dry cleaner to see whether the caviar and asparagus vol au vent remains could be removed without trace. Rupert Urquart had consumed rather too much of Isobel's special punch and it suddenly seemed very funny to him to attempt to insert the vol au vent into her cleavage. The manoeuvre was inexpertly executed and resulted in a messy and mildly embarrassing scene. Everybody laughed uproariously however, and Nigel Lamington-Krill, her husband, having landed a blow squarely upon Rupert's nose, thought no more of the incident.

If the thing was beyond salvation, she would donate it to the local aggrieved country folks' charity shop. After all, the fashion editor of Silk Scarf Trends incorporating Country Interiors with Hounds had indicated in recent issues that short but unstructured was out and that the season's colour scheme would be dominated by burnt umber and ultramarine. Maybe her unstructured cerise silk lace creation with exquisite detailing at the knees and shoulder straps could now be dispensed with.

As Isobel sat reflecting upon the weekend's events at Hake Hall her housekeeper, Mrs Tremble, was labouring over a stain on the cream shag pile in the en suite bathroom to one of the guest rooms in the east wing. As she sprayed, sponged and rinsed the carpet, her eye alighted upon a used prophylactic blocking the shower drain, and she sighed in dismay at the appalling behaviour of the week-end guests. She wondered whether she would have time to take her ailing Dachshund to the vet before joining the Hake on Spinach Ladies' Darts Team. This evening they would be competing with the formidable ladies from neighbouring Halibut under Endive and she needed to be focused. The match would be taking place at the Raddled Beanpole where, as fate would have it, Rupert Urquart's cousin Jolyon (considered to be the black sheep of the family) would be drinking with colleagues that evening.

"I'll be off now then, Mrs L-K. I think I've got the stain out of the carpet in the east wing en-suite but I'll check on it tomorrow when I change the flowers." Helena Ruby Tremble had an unexpected gift for floral artistry and had in fact been approached by the local Women's Group to promulgate her skills. She had declined however, being a very reserved character, and because she had had a falling out with the Treasurer over a personal matter some years before.

"Thank you, Mrs Tremble. I'm booked at Follicles tomorrow for a manicure and exfoliation and I thought I'd try a Japanese seaweed massage (Tilly Foxe said it's wonderful, her skin is so much improved, but then, I suppose, that's rather subjective, but if it makes her feel better ...), but anyway, the thing is, Cook will be here early to make a start planning for my Bavarian evening. Perhaps you two could have a chat and get things under way." Helena Ruby Tremble contemplated the prospect with dismay. She could already picture frankfurters jammed amusingly into the chandeliers and the inevitable beer stains on that hideous Chinese silk rug in the large drawing room. Still, she had no time to linger as she very much wanted to get Denholm to the vet before his skin condition deteriorated any further.

Hake Hall was an imposing pile, parts of which dated back to Elizabethan times. Its elegant frontage was pleasantly symmetrical with broad stone steps leading up to great glazed oak doors in the centre. The high stone mullioned windows were partly obscured by a vast and ancient wisteria which now almost formed part of the building. Various later red brick additions were for the most part hidden from initial view and in all, the building conveyed an impression of effortless grace and tranquillity.

A sweeping gravelled drive to the front was neatly edged with thick, square-cut hornbeam hedging, with acres of undulating lawns on either side. An ancient yew tree stood imposingly in the distance, as did several other magnificent specimens, giving a pleasing sense of balance to the view. Topiary bushes followed the line of the drive but with their increasingly vague definition, did give the impression of being over-ambitious, or at least half-hearted. Ron Tremble, Helena Ruby's husband, whose responsibility such matters were, was not renowned for his horticultural artistry and could only really relate to fairly straight lines and approximate right-angles. He was not deft with shears.

To the left of the Hall a wide stone arch within the remains of a weathered garden wall masked the entrance to the garage block which retained many features dating back to its original use as the coach–house. The clock in the bell-tower remained remarkably accurate, although the strident chimes had been disabled some years previously.

Helena Ruby Tremble glanced absent-mindedly up at the clock before setting off at a brisk pace down the length of the drive to reach the Lodge, which was available to her and her husband in their roles as housekeeper and groundsman. It took about five minutes to walk the distance and even in her haste, Helena Ruby noticed that the simple iron fencing which ran down either side of the drive was in need of repair and repainting, and imagined the complaining from Ron which this observation would reliably elicit.

She went in through the back door of the Lodge, which was built in the gothic Victorian style, compact but with pleasing proportions and particularly elegant arched windows (another inevitable source of complaint when painting was required). "You'll have to get your own meal this evening, Ron, I'm playing with the darts team and won't be back 'til late and I've got to get Denholm to the vet's before I go." Ron Tremble sat smoking, disgruntled in his worn armchair watching horseracing on the television: "Don't know why you bother with that mangey mutt."

'Because, you oaf,' she thought 'he's better company than you are. If I took you to the vet I'd ask him to put you down and do us all a favour.' Cheerfully, however, she said, "There's ham and cheese in the fridge, fresh bread and some nice salad but I've not washed it yet - that should do you."

"Oh you know I don't like salad, can't you ... oh don't bother. Well don't come in at all hours and wake me up. Is there any cake left?"

'If I had the opportunity,' thought Helena Ruby Tremble, 'I'd never come home again, you miserable old basket.' Instead she said brightly, "Yes it's in the round tin on the top shelf." She ran upstairs to the bedroom, changed into her darts team shirt and a pair of black trousers, went to the bathroom, brushed her hair and splashed her face with water then returned downstairs to collect the dog and depart. "Wish me and the ladies luck!" she called out.

"Yeah."

Denholm was scooped from his bed and Helena Ruby Tremble departed. Three years previously she had entered a competition sponsored by Golden Good Morning Weight Conscious Crunchy Breakfast Bites and to her astonishment, won a high performance hatchback which she enjoyed driving tremendously. Necessitated by this stroke of luck she took driving lessons, although practice outings with Ron had, predictably, been less than agreeable. However, happily all that was now past and Helena Ruby at least had the freedom afforded by her own means of transport.

Upon arrival at the vet's, Denholm began to display signs of anxiety. His small canine brain was probably registering his last visit when he was bitten by a hamster beside whose cage he sat too close, and the ignominy of the treatment which followed. His anxiety triggered a bout of nervous itching and he started to dislodge flakes of skin and hair when scratching vigorously with his rear leg. Helena Ruby realised that she should have sat him on his blanket as the plum and midnight blue upholstery in her car received a sprinkling of detritus. "Oh don't do that Denholm, come on, let's go and see the nice man who can make you better."

Once inside the surgery Helena Ruby sat with Denholm on her lap waiting to be seen. This gave the dog greater confidence than being at floor level (even though as a result her trousers received a light dusting), and in due course the weeping owner of a condemned pet came out and Denholm was next. Helena Ruby Tremble walked into the consulting room and placed the now trembling Dachshund on the examination table. His complaint was diagnosed as some kind of nervous dermatitis and he was prescribed soothing unguents. Helena Ruby was advised to return with the patient if his condition showed no sign of improvement. There wasn't time to return him home before setting out for the darts match, so she just resigned herself to the fact that she would have to give her upholstery a thorough vacuuming tomorrow, and set off for Halibut under Endive.

The road to the village was pleasant and tree-lined, and Helena Ruby's spirits lifted as she looked forward to the evening ahead, with the mellowing sunlight flickering through the leafy branches. She drew up in the car park of the Raddled Beanpole and decided it would probably be best if Denholm remained within the safety of the car, being diminutive as he was, and she promised to check on him regularly and bring him some water. She deduced from the vehicles already present that most of her team had arrived. The long-standing captain of the Hake on Spinach team, Pam Krenelli, whose husband died under suspect circumstances when on a business trip in Italy, had purchased a state of the art people mover with some of the consequent life insurance. It proved very useful for the Hake on Spinach Ladies' Darts Team when she was not transporting her five children, the youngest of which was born some time after Mr Krenelli's demise. This had caused many raised eyebrows at the time. Pam, being wise, had said nothing and in due course the rumours had subsided.

"Be a good boy, Denholm, and I'll bring you out some water - and try not to scratch too much. See you in a little while ..." Helena Ruby planted a kiss on his upturned head then shut the door, locked the car and looked forward to her evening ahead.

As she walked under the honeysuckle-laden arch over the door, and as Denholm gazed disconsolately after her, his attention was distracted by the sound of hoofs scuffing on the surrounding tarmac. He became acutely distressed at the inescapable fact that the car was surrounded by hounds eager to kill something, and not only did he start scratching furiously, but could not help himself doing what most animals in fear of their lives do. Suffice to say that the upholstery would require more than a mere vacuuming now.

The affable but anxious landlord, Corby, had suggested that the Leek over Partridge Hunt having exercised their hounds, and quite unable to prevent their accidental savaging of some unfortunate wildlife in their path, could not really be accommodated for post mortem drinks due to the darts match taking place that evening, and because Jolyon Urquart was providing corporate entertainment for his city friends within the delightful surroundings of the sixteenth century coaching inn. However Roger Whittingly-Beargarden, who took it upon himself to be master of ceremonies on this occasion, browbeat Corby into providing at least one snifter for his fellow huntsmen before moving on to the Goat and Crowbar. It was agreed that Gloria would serve drinks from a tray to the Leek over Partridge contingent in the car park in an attempt to maintain a modicum of order. Sherry, beer and wine was provided, but this could not satisfy the more strident members who demanded whisky - and what sort of a hostelry did this fellow think he was running anyway?

The hapless Denholm was by this time a quivering, scratching bundle of abject misery and the paintwork of Helena Ruby's car was rapidly losing its lustre as the hounds reared up and pressed their noses against the windows to eye up their potential prey.

Within the sixteenth century walls of the Raddled Beanpole bonhomie flowed freely, and although Helena Ruby Tremble had every intention of taking water out for Denholm, she was currently engrossed in a lively discussion with Martha Crenshaw of the opposing team about third world debt and the ethics of air-freighting exotic fruit and vegetables to supermarkets. It was announced that the match would commence in five minutes if the ladies would be good enough to rally themselves. This served as a timely reminder to Helena Ruby that she should check on Denholm and take him some water.

The scene which greeted her upon emerging into the car park with a bowl of water caused her to drop the thing. Not normally given to public displays of disapproval, Helena Ruby Tremble was consumed with rage at the sight of her car being subjected to canine vandalism and she could only guess at the distress being caused to Denholm. She inhaled deeply, and quivering with fury, yelled with all the force she could muster: "Get your bloody dogs off my car NOW."

Roger Whittingly-Beargarden sauntered over on his mount and said from his vantage point, "Good gracious, is that *your* car? I'll see if we can't get the hounds away." He half turned in the saddle and called - "I say, Purvis, call them off, would you." He turned back to Helena Ruby Tremble saying, "A trip to the carwash will soon put things right," then returned to join his colleagues, leaving Helena Ruby scarlet and speechless with impotent rage. She did not trust herself to speak and rushed to the car that she might comfort Denholm. The smell with which she was greeted confirmed her worst suspicions, but she did not hesitate in scooping up her pet and transporting him swiftly to the relative safety of the Raddled Beanpole. The Hake on Spinach Ladies' Darts Team were most supportive of their distressed colleague and insisted Corby supply a large vodka and lime to help calm her. The captain assured her that she could have a lift back to the lodge at Hake Hall in her spacious vehicle, and she was sure that they could find something for Denholm to sit on.

Murderous anger rendered Helena Ruby's aim straight and sure and her team emerged victorious. Denholm, feeling far more relaxed now, snoozed on a broad windowsill in remnants of late evening sunlight while the victors imbibed amiably with the cheerfully vanquished. The consensus of opinion amongst the ladies was that if only the idiot menfolk could conduct themselves with equal magnanimity, there would be an awful lot less unpleasantness in the world.

This convivial crowd gradually percolated into the part of the bar occupied by Jolyon Urquart and colleagues, who were by this time all in particularly mellow spirits and more than happy to engage in social intercourse with the ladies. Such diverse subjects as field drainage, haute couture, veterinary practise, inner city decay, financial markets, the European market, publishing, fast food, plumbing, horticulture, satellite television, wine tasting and solar panels arose during the evening, all very good-humoured. As the protagonists began to feel they knew each other better, it seemed quite natural that Damien Fitzherbert should have his arm around the waist of Mary Petherbridge and that Jolyon should have his arm around Helena Ruby's shoulders. Indeed, even though Pam was limited to drinking pineapple juice and sparkling mineral water, she found herself perched comfortably on the knee of Charles Enderby, who ventured to place his hand on her knee: he was not rejected.

Last orders were called and Jolyon, by now full of affection for his fellow humankind, instructed Corby to pour drinks for everyone in the Raddled Beanpole, and he should have one himself, together with the delightful Gloria. Jolyon would pay. The drinks were dispensed and Gloria was invited to join the assembled bon viveurs, while a mildly disgruntled Corby commenced clearing operations.

As the Hake on Spinach Ladies' Darts Team was rallied for the homeward journey, Jolyon leant into Helena Ruby's neck and said thickly in her ear, "I really think we should get together again soon, my dear - I think we could have a lot of fun." Helena Ruby had difficulty believing what she was hearing. She flushed and said breathlessly, "But - I - it's - well, there's my husband ..." (although if questioned closely she would be at a loss to explain quite what relevance Ron had to her life these days). Jolyon slipped his card into Helena Ruby's moistening palm and said, "Ring me if you get the chance - I mean it."

The rest of Helena Ruby Tremble's evening took on a dream-like quality, and it was only Pam's diligence which ensured the Dachshund's inclusion in the homeward journey.

As Denholm and his owner alighted from Pam's people-mover outside Hake Lodge, Pam offered to take Helena Ruby back to the Raddled Beanpole to collect her car at lunch-time tomorrow, as she had to drive to Mackerel for a dental appointment. There were muted but cheery goodbyes before Helena Ruby closed the car door firmly behind her. Even the thought of what awaited her in the car tomorrow could not dampen Helena Ruby's spirits as she attempted to get through the front door of the Lodge as quietly as possible. She inadvertently stepped on Denholm's front paw which caused him to yelp. "Oh, I'm so sorry my darling," she whispered.

Helena Ruby sat at the kitchen table cradling a cup of tea whilst Denholm settled himself in his basket. She was blissfully indifferent to the fish and chip wrappings screwed up on the draining board, and the squeezed tea bags sitting in a dark circle on the work-surface, itself sprinkled liberally with salt and vinegar. She breathed into the steam rising from the mug and kept running over the evening's events in her mind, and could not help but smile. She was still smiling as she trod carefully up the stairs, even though she was faced with the prospect of lying beside the man she must call her husband.

Chapter Two

Hake on Spinach and environs had several rather grand properties within its confines, not least of which was Lamprey Manse. Of a slightly later vintage than Hake Hall it nevertheless exuded a certain grandeur but of a more compact, red brick variety.

In the dining room of Lamprey Manse, Sonia de Souza consumed her third cup of coffee at the expansive rosewood dining table, which was speckled with fragrant petals from a central floral arrangement. She waited until her husband, Trevor, was safely off the premises, and watched through the French windows as his green Aston Martin rounded the curve of the drive, then she slowly stood up and strolled to the kitchen, her mule heels clicking across the Flemish-style black and white floor tiles in the hall.

The kitchen was fitted out with hand-crafted cabinetry imported exclusively from Mexico by a cosmopolitan city business contact (Trevor's choice, Sonia preferred clinical white); but it did offer, she conceded, useful storage space and gave a sort of non-functional warmth to the room. She removed from one of the custom-built spice drawers a small wallet, and proceeded to prepare her first and eagerly anticipated cigarette of the day. She jumped nervously at the noise of the mail dropping to the mat in the hall then muttered several curses as she proceeded to gather up her spilt 'tobacco' from the floor. Jupiter, their Labrador, made an energetic entrance through the open kitchen door having bidden his master farewell, and plunged his muzzle into the exciting-smelling stuff. "Oh get out of it, leave it, you tiresome beast," she said without much conviction. Sonia knew she had no control over the wilful black hound. Now he had dribbled in her 'tobacco', she was forced to throw what he had not eaten into the bin, secreting it within a discarded cereal box.

Having finally constructed a cigarette, her next problem was ignition. She frantically searched kitchen drawers for matches, with Jupiter contriving to stand in her way at every turn. In sheer exasperation she landed a light kick to his rump with her muled foot, but in the process parted company with the slipper which described a graceful arc and came to rest beside the range cooker right in the coal scuttle (a mere antique prop which nevertheless proved rather useful as a repository for rubbish). Sonia limped to the hob with a newspaper spill which she had torn in irritation from the discarded Times left on the side by the door, and lit her mis-shapen cigarette inexpertly from the flaming paper. The conflagration was such that she was obliged to drop the spill into the coal scuttle, and before she realised what she had done, her nostrils were greeted with the acrid smell of burning as the fur on her mule began to singe. Sonia's need for the cigarette was greater than her desire to save her mule, so she stood in the open kitchen doorway in her silk dressing gown, leaning against the frame and gazing across the sunny lawns to the twinkling water in the swimming pool beyond. She lazily dragged on her cigarette and contentment percolated through her veins.

Her reverie was interrupted by the shrill noise of the smoke detector activating in the hall. "Oh for chrissake," she muttered as she kicked off her remaining mule and padded furiously into the hall with the newspaper to dispel the fumes. Having silenced the thing, she turned and was greeted with the sight of Jupiter wandering unsteadily towards her. "What on earth ...," she began but then realised the cause of his unsteadiness. The dog had eaten her special 'tobacco' and was clearly now feeling the effects. "You dopey dog," she said before being seized with paroxysms of hilarity. She sat on the floor with him with her arms round his neck as he made feeble attempts to lick her affectionately.

Sonia left Jupiter dozing while she had a shower and

dressed for the day. She had been invited to join a ladies' lunch at the Mal de Mer, a happening new restaurant which had recently opened in Mackerel, so it had to be something chic. She finally decided upon an outfit, her self image rendering her blissfully unaware of the unsuitable length of her garments, even with the evidence plainly displayed in the full length mirror before her. By the time she had her hair just right and her make up applied (perhaps a little too much mascara, but she was not blessed with long eyelashes), and had whitened her teeth, she just had time for a pre-prandial gin and tonic whilst waiting for her taxi to arrive. She grimaced at the first sip, for, combined with the lingering effect of the tooth whitener, it was not an altogether pleasing taste. Jupiter was still sleeping but she supposed he would be alright when he awoke.

Sonia sipped her gin and tonic with the ice cubes tinkling in the glass as she sat by the dining table waiting to catch sight of the taxi. It was clearly going to be a very warm day and she began to wonder whether her outfit was entirely appropriate, and linen did crease so easily. Would she have time to change? She ran upstairs, threw her jacket on the bed, wriggled out of her dress which landed, and stayed, on the floor, and sorted frantically through her wardrobe. A revealing tight white tee-shirt and violet silk culottes seemed a winning combination.

Sonia scooped up her bag and door keys as the taxi arrived and walked jauntily out of the stained-glass panelled front door. Jupiter was still asleep, but she called to him anyway, "'Bye old thing, I'll see you later." The trip to Mackerel took about twenty minutes and by the time the taxi arrived outside Mal de Mer, the driver was relieved to deposit his overly-fragrant fare.

Manicured bay trees in pots delineated the alfresco eating area where some of the lunch party had already gathered. Diamonds and topaz glittered on fingers, chilled white wine shimmered in elegant glasses, fingernails and freshly coiffed hair gleamed, and genteel laughter mingled with a cacophony of expensive scent. The warm, still air fairly crackled with sideways glances from behind expensive sunglasses as outfits and accessories were silently appraised. Just as Sonia was oblivious to her sturdy legs and generous hips, so she was oblivious to the reaction of some of the assembled ladies upon her arrival. She pushed her Trent Cabernet demi-shade sunglasses carefully onto her head.

"Lucinda, Verity - how lovely to see you, how *are* you, darlings," she purred. "Oh and Petronella! Melanie - I *love* your handbag. Is it Agar? I keep meaning to replace mine. I'm going up to town later this week. I've seen a Tabitha Weinstock suit to die for, I think it was in Silk Scarf Trends, or was it Fashion Chic Week? Anyhow, I thought I'd pay her a visit too."

"Sonia, good to see you. Tell me, what is your scent - it's so - aromatic," breathed Simone Dawlish, as they air-kissed. "A Day in the Life, you know, SKB's latest fragrance. Trevor bought it for me at the airport when he came back from Singapore - we may be doing a six month stint out there while he establishes a marketing presence for the company. Only trouble is, it will be so hot, but we would of course be fully air conditioned and I believe it's a very civilized life. Do excuse me while I get a drink..." Looks were exchanged as Sonia went inside. "That must be six months' worth she's wearing today!" observed Melanie.

"Large gin and tonic please," Sonia requested of the barman.

"Ice and a slice?"

"Oh, yes please. In fact, make it a *very* large gin would you?" Now that her eyes had become accustomed to the cool, dim interior where ceiling fans rhythmically stirred the air, Sonia began to appreciate what a very fine visage the barman had, with appealing grey eyes and even, white teeth which he displayed to devastating effect when he smiled.

She appreciated too his well muscled forearms revealed by his rolled up shirt-sleeves. "You must be very busy - this place is *so* popular, Steven," (she read the name badge pinned to the lapel of his waistcoat) - "and I believe you had a very good write up from Ezekiel Trout in last week's supplement." Sonia leant onto the bar in order to emphasise her cleavage, amongst which was suspended a diamond pendant on a fine gold chain. "Indeed we did - and the quality of our cellar was highlighted in the article. Ah, and here's the author of our success – Charles..." As he sauntered from the doorway behind the bar, unseen by Sonia, Charles affectionately ran his hand across Steven's tightly-clad rear. "Hi, Charles - Sonia, Sonia de Souza." She extended her manicured hand, her wrist encircled by a heavy gold bangle, another gift from Trevor following a visit to Dubai earlier in the year. "Delighted. Is Steven attending to you?"

"He certainly is - would you care to join me?"

"That's good of you, but I'm off to visit one of my specialist suppliers now. Can I leave it all to you, Steven?" (The specialist supplier to which Charles referred was in fact not entirely relevant to his catering operation, but this was something of which Sonia really didn't need to be aware.) "Sure can, boss."

Sonia reluctantly left the bar and returned outside to join her fellow luncheon guests, Steven observing her exit with a wry smile. She had to replace her sunglasses as she emerged into the dazzling sunlight, and was unable to execute the manoeuvre quite as smoothly as she would have liked. Her hair had caught in one of the ornate hinges, and whilst concentrating on trying to release it before being observed, she tripped on the threshold, spilling some of her drink. A dark stain appeared on the violet silk, but she took comfort in the fact that it would soon dry in the warm air. She attempted to regain her composure, dabbing the damp patch with a tissue, before joining the twittering throng and hoping that nobody had been watching her.

"It was simply *awful*, I mean just how can you get chewing gum out of mink?" Penelope D'Arville was wondering. "Oh hello Sonia, how lovely to see you. You're looking well - I love your bangle."

"Penny - how nice to see you. You must give me the name of your colourist - your hair looks stunning and makes you look so much younger!"

"Oh, thank you, how kind. I decided to give Anthony Furnival-Pirouette a try. There was a feature on him in a recent Sunday supplement and I thought 'Why not!' - time to make a radical change to my wardrobe and my hair! I called in to the Hermione Shrubfest studio while I was in town and her collection really is most inventive. You really must go. Picked up a couple of lovely tops, but had to buy some slacks as they're not really the sort of thing you could wear with a skirt. Trouble is, when you start along those lines, you end up buying *far* more than you meant. My titanium card took a severe thrashing and when I got home Henry was a bit miffed and did suggest I might thin out my wardrobe, and he didn't even *notice* my hair."

All members of the lunch party were now assembled (with the exception of Jocasta Bentwood who was indisposed after a bibulous evening in the library at the Old Rectory with Lord Pith-Witherstock and his housekeeper). They took their seats at the tables which were laid out with crisp white table cloths, beautifully folded napkins, elegant glasses, highly polished cutlery and a single white rose in a glass tube at the centre of each table. Brenda and Michelle were their waitresses; Brenda glowered and Michelle simpered. Steven attended to the drinks orders and manoeuvred deftly between the lunching ladies, receiving many admiring glances as he did so. He smiled a lot.

Sonia's taxi arrived to collect her at four o'clock and she was not looking quite as fresh as she had earlier. There was a suggestion of dark rings below her eyes where her mascara had migrated a little in the heat and her lips were looking unfashionably pallid where her lipstick had not recently been replenished. What a blessing that she had used Tivoli's Supra-Guard Extra Protection Anti-Perspirant with extracts of sphagnum moss and elder berries.

When Sonia opened the front door and walked slightly unsteadily into the hall, she dropped her bag and keys on the circular table and was aware of an absence of greeting from Jupiter. This was because he was still asleep. She bent down and looked closely to ensure that he was still breathing, having to steady herself against the wall, then meandered upstairs to refresh herself and change into a more comfortable outfit before commencing upon preparations for the evening meal. Trevor normally arrived home at about 7.30 p.m. and as Sonia never really had become sufficiently acquainted with the vagaries of her state of the art range cooker, she always had to give herself plenty of culinary latitude (accompanied by several generous glasses of wine, naturally - it was the only way to cook and lent a certain panache to her otherwise unadventurous cuisine).

Unable to think up a convincing explanation for her fire damaged footwear, Sonia deposited the mule in the bin beneath several layers of household waste then went again to the spice drawer in order to roll herself a soothing cigarette, which she was able to light easily this time with matches retrieved from the bar at Mal de Mer. She opened the kitchen door, strolled across the terrace and sat half way down the steps. She leant her elbows on her knees and soaked up the tranquility as she gazed across the sunlit garden, blowing curls of smoke into the still air. Jupiter appeared sleepily at the top and lay down, apparently not sure-footed enough to tackle the steps. Sonia took a last drag on her cigarette, ground it out beneath her sandalled foot, then buried the remains in the loose earth beside her. She returned serenely to the kitchen, followed by Jupiter who now had the energy at least to wag his tail, and uncorked a bottle of white wine which had been chilling in the fridge. She filled herself a large glass and assembled some vegetables in anticipation of the evening meal.

Trevor arrived at about 8.00 p.m. and received a less than usually enthusiastic welcome from Jupiter, however he was sufficiently preoccupied not to give it much thought. He dropped his keys on the kitchen surface and kissed Sonia on the cheek as she was engaged in trying to crush the lumps out of a sauce she was attempting in a pan. He said, "I say darling, heard from Dick Neville today, you know, well-connected merchant banker, had Christmas drinks with him on his boat, and he said, strictly hush-hush, heard it from a minister, that old Lamington-Krill and his set-up might be heading for a bit of an investigation. Tried to head it off apparently, him donating so much to the party and all that, but now the Germans have got involved, it's going to be difficult. Looks like he's taken the piss once too often. Can't say anything, obviously, but a bit close to home isn't it?"

"You're in the clear aren't you?"

"Oh yes, not actually done any deals with him since helping finance that estate of his, you know, Buttercups, Bodewells, ah, Bullrushes, that's it. Never touched anything foreign, in fact haven't been in touch for some time. Best left that way for now if poss m'dear, under the circumstances." Sonia, exasperated with her efforts, tipped the contents of the pan down the sink, rinsed it, then tipped in a jar of ready-prepared sauce from the cupboard and stirred it absent-mindedly.

"Mmm, come to think of it, Isobel wasn't at the lunch today, but she never seems to know what he's up to anyway. Gin and tonic, darling?"

"Excellent. Large one please. Oh, and do remind me that I need to get the Aston serviced in the next week or so, old girl not running quite as smoothly as she should."

"Do you want me to arrange it?"

"That would be marvellous darling, thank you."

Chapter Three

As Hake on Spinach was home to several very grand properties, so it had also recently acquired a development of what were described in the sales literature as superbly appointed but modest executive-style homes. There were however, as far as it is possible to judge these things, no modest executives to be found living there.

In the master bedroom of Number 5, The Bullrushes, Neville Martin Painswick rolled over to silence the jarring alarm clock beside him. He was momentarily dazzled by the shafts of brilliant early morning sunshine which pierced the carelessly closed flimsy floral curtains. His wife, Donna, had insisted on fully co-ordinated furnishings. The finished effect made Neville feel as though he slept in a frilled, floral display case complete with authentically leaded bow window. It was difficult to tell quite where the soft furnishings ended and the wallpaper began. As he lay there adjusting to the new day, he noticed that the contrasting border running around the top of the wall was slightly torn. He would have to attend to that and the small crack in the ceiling before it was seized upon by his wife – after all, it had only been decorated two months ago. He sighed and wondered how he had been persuaded to move to the thoughtfully designed yet affordable luxury of The Bullrushes which sympathetically reflected the idyllic surrounding countryside. He had been perfectly happy in their terraced house in the centre of Great Roach – within walking distance of several good local hostelries, two curry houses, a chip shop and every amenity he ever really needed.

He realised they would need more room with their first baby expected in six months' time, and he gave in far too easily because Donna was pregnant and he didn't like to argue with her. She was at this moment retching in the en-suite bathroom and he did experience pangs of sympathy for her. She came back to bed looking very pale in her oyster silk nightdress and Neville stroked her head. "Never mind, love. It won't last for much longer. Can I get you anything?"

"No thanks – I'll just stay in bed 'til I feel less queasy. It's my day off. Will you be home for lunch?"

"I'll take sandwiches today as I've got Mr Lamington-Krill's Jensen in for a major service and I think Colonel Whipstock is bringing in his Bristol for me to look at – had a bit of a prang in the car park of the Startled Partridge. Don't worry, I'll make them before I go." With this, Neville Martin Painswick got out of bed, gently pulled the valanced duvet up to cover his wife and padded into the bathroom in his boxer shorts to make preparations for his day.

Having made himself beef paste and tomato sandwiches, Neville located his newly laundered overalls in the airing cupboard on the landing, looked in on Donna (now sleeping again), then went noiselessly downstairs so as not to disturb her. He cringed as one of the treads creaked loudly, and reflected that for a new house, this one was not very well finished and that no-one seemed to take a pride in their work any more. He took enormous pride in his, which was why he had such a surprisingly prestigious clientele and never any shortage of business. As if to compound these irritations, he had to pull the neo-Georgian front door to with greater force than should be necessary as it had never been a perfect fit from the day they moved in. The hanging baskets either side of the porch swayed as he made his exit and got into his car parked on the paved drive. His workshop was about ten miles away in a dilapidated light industrial unit situated on a farm. Donna had often urged him to consider moving premises to somewhere 'more fitting' – meaning light, bright, modern and expensive – but Neville was content in his rural surroundings and had no intention of moving.

He pulled up outside his unit and smiled as he saw Nigel Lamington-Krill's Jensen parked in the yard beside the Volvo and the Shogun also booked in for the day. His young assistant Melvin would be in later when his father dropped him off on his way to the hospital in Mackerel to visit Melvin's mother, who had recently given birth to twins. They were undeniably a source of some bewilderment to the Tredwell family. Neville was a kind-hearted employer however, and was prepared to accommodate Melvin's slightly irregular hours as he was showing great promise and was a very willing worker.

He unlocked the door to his workshop and stepped over three sets of keys which had been posted through the letterbox the evening before. He opened up the rolling shutters at the front of the unit and as the morning sunshine streamed in, he flicked on the switch to the radio and strains of Mozart filled the air. He pulled on his boiler suit, breathed in deeply then walked over to pick up the keys.

"Right, Volvo first," he said to himself as he walked to the kettle and switched it on. He got no further with making tea as he realised that the milk in the carton he picked up was solidifying, and he would have to wait until Melvin arrived with fresh supplies. He shrugged and walked out to Vanessa Fawcett's car, unlocked it and drove it on to the ramps. He was standing beside the hydraulic controls when the telephone rang, so he walked across the workshop, turned down the radio and picked up the phone. It was Mrs de Souza wishing to book in her husband's Aston Martin for a service. The necessary arrangements were made and Neville entered the details accordingly in the oily diary.

Neville was engrossed beneath the back axle when Colonel Whipstock arrived with his slightly dented Bristol. The Colonel never had displayed much inclination towards social graces and sounded the horn vigorously in order to gain Neville's attention. Neville climbed out from under the

Volvo, wiped his hands on a rag, and knowing the Colonel to be fairly deaf, said quietly, "That's alright you old bugger, I'll come to you, you just sit there ..." – then as he approached the Bristol and its occupant, called out, "Good morning, shall we have a look at the damage?" as the Colonel wound down his window.

"Bloody shame that idiot landlord decided to put bloody tubs of flowers in the car park – looks bloody ridiculous, I mean it's a car park for god's sake, not a bloody garden ..." Colonel Whipstock flung open the car door and levered himself out of the leather upholstery. Neville thought it best not to proffer assistance as he watched the overweight, wheezing and bewhiskered old goat.

"I think this can be beaten out without too much trouble, but I think we'll have to replace the ..." Neville Martin Painswick did not get to complete his sentence as Melvin's father drove around the end of the building at inadvisable speed and failed to take the necessary avoiding action before ploughing into the back of the Bristol and shunting it forward a few feet. The front caught the Colonel's knee and felled him like an oak. He lay in the oily dirt spluttering and wheezing, arms flailing, and Neville looked on aghast at the scene before him.

"What the ..." he began as Melvin's father got out of his Astra. William Tredwell was not normally a man given to much display of emotion, but trembling, he shouted hoarsely at Neville as he walked towards him, "What a bloody stupid place to leave a car ..." and then, in less abrasive tone and pointing at the Colonel, "Is he alright?" Still shocked, Neville stuttered "I, I don't know. You'd better bloody well help me with him. What d'you think you were doing? You were driving like a bloody moron – you could've killed someone."

The two men ran to Colonel Whipstock who had managed to manoeuvre himself onto his side, clutching his knee and groaning, and they heaved him upright taking one armpit each, and sat him on an overturned oil drum. William

Tredwell shouted to Melvin (who had been trying, ineffectually, to mop up the milk jettisoned into the footwell by the abrupt conclusion to their journey), to ring for an ambulance. This order was promptly countermanded by Neville who said he could drive the Colonel to the casualty department himself. The Colonel barked that he didn't need any bloody ambulances, hospitals, what a lot of fuss, but was overcome by the pain of his injury and slipped ashen, gasping and semi-conscious back into the dirt before Neville and William had the chance to prevent his descent.

"Christ, is he having a heart attack?"

"Melvin, ring an ambulance NOW" yelled Neville Martin Painswick. A tense twenty minutes ensued during which time Colonel Whipstock was not particularly lucid but he was made as comfortable as practicable under the circumstances. William and Neville decided he was safer on the floor, besides which, he was a not inconsiderable deadweight to attempt to raise.

The ambulance crew diagnosed shock and a broken leg and were to be congratulated upon the deftness with which they managed to lift the Colonel into the back of the ambulance, and not least, the diplomatic way in which they handled their irascible patient who was heard insisting forcefully as they fastened the doors that he have a private bed.

"You'll have to sort out insurance with the old bugger – I can't carry out these major bloody repairs without the insurance company's say-so now. You've really messed up my day – thanks a bloody lot."

"Ah, yes," faltered William Tredwell. "I'm, um, sort of between insurances at the moment, what with the twins and everything…"

"Jesus Christ, I don't believe it!" exploded Neville Martin Painswick, then, flatly, added "Oh too bad, it's not my problem, I wash my hands of it. You, mate, are in the shit. In fact, I wouldn't draw attention to myself in that car if I were you." William Tredwell was indeed in the mire.

"Look mate, couldn't you at least stick a new headlight in for me so I'm legal and I'll get it insured today. Melvin still needs a lift 'til he can afford a car and there's Deirdre and the twins. I'll be completely stuffed…" Neville Martin took a deep breath then said "Oh bloody hell alright, but you owe me big time and how're you going to sort things with the Colonel?"

"Don't know mate. D'you think he'll settle without involving the bloody insurance company? I haven't got any money anyway – what are we looking at – at least a thousand? Don't suppose Melvin could work it off in overtime?" Until this juncture, Melvin had foregone the opportunity to opine upon the situation, but now felt constrained to offer his point of view: "Thanks, Dad. P'raps I should become a rent boy – would that help? If you hadn't been driving too bloody fast none of this would have happened."

"Here we have doctor Melvin Tredwell MD, professor of the bleedin' obvious," retorted his father. Melvin cursed his parentage and stalked angrily into the workshop.

"Sorry, mate. Anyhow, if we can get this headlight sorted I'll be off."

"Yeah, right."

It took Neville half an hour to effect the necessary running repairs to the Astra, during which time William Tredwell decided to inspect the damage to the rear of the Bristol. He did not however confine himself to mere visual inspection and Neville became intensely irritated to find bits pulled off and a rear light half dismantled, with William Tredwell now sitting in the driver's seat fiddling with the controls and stroking the walnut veneer. "Get your bloody hands off that car," shouted Neville.

"Sorry mate, I was just looking. Keep your hair on…"

"Look – I've patched up your car. Just bugger off and get it insured and leave me in peace will you."

Neville Martin Painswick watched him reverse into an overgrown bank, shrug his shoulders then drive off with a clod of grassy earth embedded in his rear bumper. Neville shook his head, then running his fingers through his thick dark hair, sighed and walked back to the workshop, calling out to Melvin, "Make us some tea would you?"

"It'll have to be black – no milk mate," came the reply. Exasperated, through gritted teeth Neville said to Melvin, "Is there anything your father comes into contact with that *doesn't* go wrong?"

"Hopefully my job," replied Melvin.

"Hey, he's not your fault! I'll nip to the corner shop and get some milk. D'you want to get going on changing the oil in the Jensen? I'll be back in ten minutes then maybe we'll get some work done."

William Tredwell purchased a meagre and overpriced bunch of flowers from an opportunistic vendor outside the hospital entrance, then after several unrewarding circuits of the car park, came to rest in a bay marked 'Staff Only' telling himself that he'd only be ten minutes and it couldn't do any harm. He made his way to the maternity ward but Deirdre was not occupying the bed in which he expected to find her. "Ah, Mr Tredwell, isn't it?" William turned round to be greeted by an earnest member of staff who didn't appear to be a nurse. He glanced at the badge on her lapel which read 'Daphne Paddlewick, Senior Medical Social Worker'.

"We've been trying to contact you at home, but your telephone doesn't seem to be working. Would you like to come into my office?"

The news which Daphne Paddlewick imparted to William Tredwell left him perplexed. Deirdre had been apprehended at two o'clock that morning trying to hail a taxi along Mackerel Boulevard, wearing a coat over her night attire. Had it not been for the fact that she was wearing slippers and had a drip tube hanging from her sleeve, she may have got a lot further, but as it was, a sympathetic police constable returned her to the hospital, despite her pleas to the contrary. "So you see, Mr Tredwell, we will have to keep your wife in for a bit longer in our special unit until we can get her sorted out. Obviously the babies can stay with her, but we think it would be best for all concerned if you gave her a couple of days to settle down. Do you have any questions you'd like to ask me?"

"When can she come home? The freezer needs defrosting and we've eaten nearly all the ready meals. I need ironed shirts for my job and I don't know how the washing machine works. I think the milk needs paying an' all." Daphne Paddlewick was prepared to attribute this response to shock, but with thinly veiled irritation said, "You'll agree, Mr Tredwell, that it is most important to make sure your wife is well before she can be expected to return to domestic drudgery, don't you think? And don't forget the twins …" It would be true to say that William Tredwell was having the utmost difficulty in assimilating the concept of the presence of the twins in his life. Deirdre Tredwell meanwhile was quite unable to come to terms with the concept of the twins and Mr Tredwell in hers.

William Tredwell walked across the hospital car park disconsolately and was just about to get into his car when a tall, thick-necked porter accosted him: "Can't you read, mate? See those big letters on the floor? They say 'S T A F F   O N L Y'. They don't say 'RESERVED FOR LAZY GITS'. If I see your tatty vehicle here again, I'll let the air out of your tyres, alright?" William Tredwell nodded his head wearily and opened the car door to be greeted by the smell of milk on the turn. He slumped into the seat, wound down the window and started the engine.

Chapter Four

Helena Ruby Tremble sat at the scrubbed refectory table in the generously proportioned kitchen of Hake Hall, sipping coffee whilst discussing floral requirements for the Bavarian evening with Isobel Lamington-Krill. Isobel's intended extravaganza should, if indeed any title were required, more accurately have been entitled a Germanic evening, but Helena Ruby did not feel it her place to correct Isobel's geographical inaccuracies. If Mrs Lamington-Krill wanted Alpine cow bells hung from the swags of hops on the banisters, then cow bells hung from the swags there would be. It seemed that Nigel's contacts in the city could easily be relied upon to procure such adornments. On environmental grounds, Isobel was steered away from the charming notion of having gentians and edelweiss featuring heavily in the table centres. On the grounds of self respect, she was firmly assured that having waiting staff dressed in traditional Tyrolean garb complete with plaited hair coils for the ladies and lederhosen for the men, was a non-starter (for Helena Ruby would be among their number, and even she had her pride). "Oh very well, but I do think it's a shame – it would have been such fun. Anyway, I see an overall yellow theme for the main displays, Mrs Tremble. My Uncle Theobald is in possession of a stuffed bear which he is happy to lend me. I thought it would be fun to put him, the bear I mean, (Isobel giggled) in the dining hall. I don't know whether you could produce some sort of garland for the thing?"

"I'll order all the flowers I need next week. May I get them delivered here for the Friday, then they'll still be fresh for me to do on Saturday – it would be best if they could be left in the cellar. And while I'm here, is Turtle available to assist with removing the downstairs drapes? The cleaners are collecting them tomorrow so they'll be back by Friday."

"Go ahead with the flowers Mrs Tremble, and if you think of anything else we'll need, just let me know, won't you. Use the Floral Artists' Guild in Mackerel. They're so much more imaginative than Fenestra's Floristry, and more co-operative too." (There had been a falling out between the Lamington-Krill household and Fenestra Bingley-Schwarz, a hard-bitten northern woman who had disparate business interests in the most unlikely quarters.) "I have an account there and they know me."

"OK Mrs L-K."

"And I'll tell Turtle to see you about the drapes after lunch. Now I must get on. I have a hair appointment, then lunch and I promised India I'd get her the books on her reading list that she couldn't find."

"Will she be attending the Bavarian evening?" enquired Helena Ruby.

"I hope so, and I said she could bring some friends if she wanted. I do hope she brings that nice young Ferringby-Purcell lad. I believe his parents are big in laminates."

India Lamington-Krill, only daughter of Nigel and Isobel, was studying social sciences and media at the University of the North East Regions. Although neither parent would say as much, this was a disappointment to them as they had naturally assumed that their not unintelligent daughter, upon whom had been lavished a very expensive education, would aspire to Oxbridge where she could happily mix with her own kind. She had other ideas.

Helena Ruby Tremble drained her limited edition Bistra Blashworth coffee tankard, stood and smoothed her skirt. It occurred to her that she really could do with losing a little weight as her eyes fell upon the straining fibres encircling her midriff. "I'll be getting on then. I'll see Cook later to discuss the catering arrangements in detail."

"Right-oh Mrs T."

Helena Ruby opened the back door of the Lodge and stepped into the kitchen. "D'you want lunch Ron?" she called. Silence greeted her. Denholm trotted out with wagging tail and she scooped him up affectionately. "Where is the old bugger?" she said into his silky ear. "Ron?" she shouted again up the stairs, but still no response. Then Helena Ruby noticed the still warm tea-bag left steaming slightly on the draining board and assumed she had missed his lunch break, a suspicion confirmed by a sausage roll packet and sweet wrappers jammed into the overflowing bin. She took a deep breath, deposited Denholm, then heaved out the bin liner and its contents and went to drop the overladen sack into the dustbin , hidden behind a badly trimmed laurel hedge just outside the door.

Out of habit Helena Ruby felt her jacket pockets just to ensure that she had her keys, and having reassured herself, idly removed a card she found in the left pocket. It was Jolyon Urqhart's business card. It had a very strange effect upon her; she felt light-headed, there was an exaggerated pulse in her neck and her hand started trembling slightly. Images of that astonishing evening came back to her. She took several deep breaths to calm herself. Had he really meant what he said? "Don't be so stupid Helena Ruby," she said aloud. The inescapable conviction that she was a foolish, overweight, unremarkable woman crept upon her. Denholm looked up at her quizzically. In a grand gesture she crumpled the card and went to drop it into the kitchen bin only to realise that she hadn't replaced the liner. Thus, momentarily irritated, she dropped the card back into her pocket and went swiftly about her business in an effort to quell the feeling of humiliation which was beginning to envelop her. She sighed as she removed the general debris left carelessly, as always, by Ron, then made herself a piece of cheese on toast and put it under the grill. As Helena Ruby sat at the table sipping tea, her thought processes converged in a determination to improve her diet and to take herself and her life into hand. She had only taken a few bites of her toast when, looking down at Denholm sitting bright-eyed at her feet, she said "Right, young man. This is going into the bin. Things are going to change." She broke off a piece and gave it to Denholm as he stood on his hind legs in anticipation, then stepped to the newly lined bin and dropped in the remainder.

Still feeling hungry, (but this was something to which she was going to have to become accustomed she supposed), Helena Ruby returned to Hake Hall where her major task that afternoon was to clean and dust the glass cabinets in the large drawing room, hall and morning room. She had supervised the removal of the drapes with the assistance of Turtle, whom she always had the impression would rather be pressing the newspapers. The lad who arrived to take the drapes for cleaning rather alarmed them both. He was a young, thick-set fellow with nasal diction and studs embedded in his eyebrows. He had clearly not been in receipt of any effective customer service training. He also seemed to consider the company transport in which he arrived as some sort of high-performance vehicle and dislodged quantities of gravel upon his departure. Helena Ruby was more than a little concerned that the great expanses of velvet, silk and brocade just commended to his care might not be returned in good order, nor in good time.

It would have horrified Isobel and Nigel to know that this youth was a close acquaintance of India's and had a specifically engineered purpose for the visit. When he had followed the curve of the drive out of sight of the house, he pulled over, jumped out and opened the back doors of the van. Looking all around to ensure he was not being watched, he pulled out a large, heavy holdall and with difficulty, sprinted after a fashion across the grass and between ornamental shrubs, behind one of which he secreted the bag. Stooping low, he ran back to the van and drove off at a more sedate pace than previously in order not to draw unwarranted attention to himself.

With one cabinet still to do, Helena Ruby turned to look out of the window and noticed that the late summer afternoon had an almost tangible heaviness about it. She stretched her back and yawned then draped the duster over a chair back and went to visit Cook in the kitchen for a bit of lively conversation as much as anything. She strolled across the hall and whilst trying to picture the stairs bedecked with hops, her eye fell on a huge cobweb entwining the chandelier. "Someone's been busy," she said to herself.

"Ah, Mrs T!" Cook grinned as Helena Ruby walked into the kitchen. "Take a seat, tea in a jiffy!" Cook wiped his hands, then taking the kettle from its stand on the range cooker, made two mugs of tea, took them to the table and sat down opposite Helena Ruby.

"So, are we all set for the German extravaganza? I don't think the food will be too much of a problem. The butcher's got all the meat I need, but isn't wiener schnitzel Austrian anyway?"

"Mrs L-K doesn't seem to be bothered with letting minor details affect her plans, and I don't think anyone will care anyhow."

"I think you could be right there. And let's face it man, nobody could drink Blue Nun and eat frankfurters and sauerkraut all evening."

"Mmmm. Have we got final numbers, and I assume it will be a buffet. I *hope* it'll be a buffet – I hate having to do waitressing."

"Yep. Mrs L-K thought it would be more, now what was the word she used – convivial, that's it. I think that's her version of riotous, but I could be wrong. Will Ron be helping with the setting up?"

Ron and Cook tended to give each other a wide berth. Ron was convinced that Cook was an illegal immigrant and it was obvious to Cook that Ron was an appalling bigot, quite apart from the other less appealing aspects of his character. He liked Helena Ruby and never understood how the two of them could ever have had anything in common. Nobody knew that Helena Ruby Tremble had been obliged to marry Ron and that she was the mother of twin girls. They now both led their own lives well away from their parents. An annual Christmas card was the only indication for Helena Ruby that they were both well. It was a source of enormous sadness to her but she was unable to discuss it with Ron who never really acknowledged their existence these days.

Helena Ruby had attempted to broach the subject of the Bavarian evening with Ron yesterday, only to have her enquiry met with a depressingly predictable barrage of non co-operation and general spleen. Nigel and Isobel Lamington-Krill were fair employers, if a little self-absorbed, but when reminded would pay their staff for duties performed outwith their general employment terms. Ron it seemed felt the need to make a point of being as awkward as possible whatever the circumstances. Ostensibly it didn't make him any happier and merely caused intense frustration to those associated with him. Here was a man who seemed to enjoy being miserable. This thought lingered and did several circuits of Helena Ruby's mind whilst she drank her tea.

"Um, I'm not sure yet. I suppose it depends on how much he's got to do in the garden and I think they want the pool cleaned as well," replied Helena Ruby, not wanting to even think about it. Changing the subject, she said, "I think India might be coming. Didn't think it was her sort of thing."

"Ah, the lovely India," said Cook, raising his eyebrows and smiling. "I wonder who she'll have in tow this time. Oh well, on with the fancy fish fingers. We can finalise battle plans in a few days." He pushed his chair back which screeched across the hand-cut Bolivian slate flagstones. "I *wish* they'd get something put on those chair-legs. That drives me nuts. I mean, it's not like they can't afford it for chrissake!" Helena Ruby stood up too, pushing her chair back similarly, smiling at Cook and raising her arms in a gesture of helplessness.

"Back to the crystal ware," she sighed.

"Yeah, once more into the morning room Mrs T!"

"You really are wasted here you know."

"It does me for now. Ciao!" With a flourish, Cook turned on one heel and whistling, swaggered to the Aga. Helena Ruby, shaking her head and smiling, returned to the morning room, opened the ornate glass cabinet door and carefully lifted out a hideous semi-gilt punch bowl.

It had become unseasonally dark and begun to rain heavily, and Helena Ruby realised that she was going to get very damp walking back to the Lodge as she looked down with misgiving at her strappy summer sandals. At that moment, Isobel returned in a flurry of gravel as she braked hard by the front of Hake Hall. Turtle appeared from the large drawing room, walked to open the doors and took Isobel's wet jacket from her as she came in. "Oh dear, it's terrible out there! Thank you. Take the car round to the garage would you Turtle? I've left the keys in it. Could you bring the shopping from the back seat – oh and take a brolly or you'll get soaked!" Turtle silently acknowledged her instructions with a slight bow of his head and lifted the necessary item from the ebony and silver umbrella stand by the door.

"Pleasant day?" enquired Helena Ruby emerging from the morning room.

"Thank you Mrs Tremble, yes, although my hair is simply *ruined* ."

"Oh, what a shame. Did you manage to get the books for India?"

"Lunch went on longer than I expected and I couldn't miss the opportunity of the preview at the Adastra Gallery. Belle Winter-Heston took me as her guest. I only learnt today that it was her grandfather who founded Heston's House of Lingerie. He must have been quite a fellow."

"I suppose he was. Were the paintings interesting?"

"I really wouldn't know. I'm really not an artist you know, but it was fascinating to see who was there. And some of the outfits were quite frightful Mrs T. Have these women never heard of colour analysis?" Isobel walked to the kitchen and poured herself a glass of chilled wine from the refrigerator. She sat down on the leather couch by the doors to the terrace and kicked off her shoes.

"Aah, that's better. I say, something smells good!"

"Marine life for your delectation," responded Cook, very much hoping that she did not intend to take up residence in the kitchen. Helena Ruby followed her through the door and said, "I think I've got everything you wanted done today. The glass cabinets are clean, yours and Mr L-K's bathrooms have been given a thorough going over, and I thought I'd tidy the dressing rooms too."

"Splendid, you may as well call it a day then Mrs T, and I'll see you tomorrow morning." Considering the prevailing weather conditions, Helena Ruby flushed slightly when she asked whether she might borrow a brolly as she would be walking back to the Lodge.

"Oh Mrs T, I'll get Turtle to run you down there – silly of me, I didn't think. You'll be absolutely drowned, dear woman!" That was exactly what Helena Ruby did not want, but she knew she couldn't extricate herself from the arrangement, so steeled herself for a ride with Turtle, whom she knew on this occasion would definitely rather be pressing the papers.

Ron had returned to the Lodge early due to the inclemency and when Helena Ruby arrived breathless at the back door, she hurried in to find him leaning over Denholm whom he had by the collar, spraying him liberally with Superhold Ultrafirm Hair-o-sol with added shine and conditioning. Denholm, not unnaturally, found it most upsetting and was squealing and wriggling.

"What the hell do you think you're doing?" shouted Helena Ruby , barely able to believe the scene she witnessed before her.

"Damn' mutt keeps leaving hair and his disgusting bits of skin on my chair – this should cure it," responded Ron. "It did last time."

"You stupid, horrible man," she said in quiet rage. Helena Ruby pushed him away and scooped up the distressed Dachshund, making soothing noises as she walked into the sitting room with him. It was clear that the only way of restoring his coat was to bathe him, a pastime of which Denholm had never been overly fond. However, in due course, a very sorry Dachshund wrapped tightly in a towel emerged from the bathroom under Helena Ruby's arm. She was so furious with her idiot husband that she could not find the words to convey to him just how much she despised him. He by this time was sitting in his usual place watching a more than usually pointless game show on the television, oblivious to the rest of the world, so Helena Ruby, who now could not bear even to be in the same room, took Denholm to the kitchen where she proceeded solicitously to apply her hair dryer to the damp and trembling dog.

The words "I'm not carrying on like this, I'm not, I can't," were repeated over and over in Helena Ruby's mind. All manner of wild plans of escape emerged only to be discounted for a plethora of reasons, and Helena Ruby began to shed tears over Denholm as the suffocating hopelessness of her situation closed in around her. Oh how she wished she had her girls there. Their absence seemed like a great black chasm in her life. She took the bottle of Christmas vodka from the back of the cupboard, poured a generous measure into a tumbler depicting a palm-fringed beach, and finding only orange squash with which to mix it, ran some water into the glass and downed it in about four gulps.

In due course, Ron sauntered into the kitchen and with no real sign of contrition, enquired as to the likelihood of an evening meal. Helena Ruby was fairly numb by now, and knowing remonstration would be unproductive, said he could have sausage and egg, thinking that she would be delighted if it choked him. Denholm took refuge under the table, quivering then scratching. Twenty minutes later Helena Ruby thrust Ron's meal in front of him on a tray and without waiting for any response, left the room. She sat in the kitchen for some time, drinking another large vodka and nursing Denholm on her lap, then she settled him in his bed and went upstairs to have what she hoped would be a relaxing bath, and thence to bed hoping sleep would render her senseless before Ron came up to bed. Helena Ruby lay in bed rigid with exasperation and certainly no inclination to sleep. She tried very hard to make herself relax, but could feel the tension in her neck and shoulders. She lay on one side, then the other, then on her back, getting more and more furious. She sat up and punched her pillow hard several times, tears springing to her eyes. From downstairs she heard sounds of Ron moving around, then a yelp from the kitchen but her need to shut Ron out was greater than that to comfort Denholm, so feeling terribly guilty, she rolled over, planted her head in the pillow under her duvet of despair and made a passable impression of being deeply asleep.

Sleep did eventually take hold and the next thing Helena Ruby Tremble registered was the piercing tone of the alarm. Having given herself three minutes to make contact with her extremities, she got stiffly out of bed, pulled on her tired, rose-coloured candlewick dressing gown and made her way downstairs to the kitchen where she was greeted enthusiastically by Denholm. She picked him up and kissed him on his silky ear. She breathed in the fragrance of his shampooed pelt and held him close while she considered her prospects. Thoughts sparked and rebounded with increasing clarity in the sunny crispness of that morning which she welcomed in through the opened blind. "Here's your tea," said Helena Ruby as she planted a steaming mug beside Ron's bed. It was not time to disrupt her domestic routine just yet, and she knew that if Ron didn't get to work on time, his bad humour would only rebound on her and, it seemed, Denholm too. In a moment of optimism, she drew open the bedroom curtains to admit sunshine declaring, "It's a glorious morning!"

Chapter Five

Donna Painswick zipped up her pastel pink overall, inevitably getting tighter with every passing day, and it occurred to her that she should approach the management of Follicles regarding provision of maternity wear, as she intended to continue in her position as senior manicurist and facial therapist for as long as practicable. She aimed to finalise payments on their leather and mahogany three piece suite, upon which she had insisted for Number 5 The Bullrushes. The old velour suite just wouldn't have looked right in the practically proportioned yet airy sitting room, and because they were on special offer, it seemed only sensible to install a wide screen, slim line, high definition, low distortion television with integral movie-quality speakers, for which she also intended to conclude payments before becoming a full time mother.

She checked her hair and make-up in the bathroom mirror and looking at the crack which ran behind it, sighed peevishly - Neville really did need to pay more attention to the house. A spray of 'A Day in the Life' (which no longer prompted nausea) completed her preparations, and so she left Number 5, The Bullrushes, having to slam the front door hard, and caught the bus into Herring le Parterre, where Follicles had its main branch in the charming seventeenth century high street.

Donna checked the appointment diary having taken off her jacket and smiled as she noted that Mrs Penelope D'arville was booked in for 9.30 for a full facial, manicure and pedicure. She always gave generous tips.
"Is Shirley in today?" Donna asked Mandy. Shirley owned Follicles.
"I think she's coming in this afternoon. She said she had to go to Dean's school this morning – he's being picked on. Didn't think they allowed that sort of thing in expensive

places like that, and I thought he could handle himself anyway."

"Looks like our little one will be going to the local unless Nev ever gets his act together," remarked Donna wistfully. "Anyhow, have you got many in the diary for today? Did you see that thing on the telly last night ..." - and so the conversation continued aimlessly.

Ever more scent filled the salon as the day's beautification progressed. Sometimes conversation flowed, sometimes it did not. At 4.30p.m. having bid the redoubtable Mrs Olga Arkenplank a cheery farewell after a challenging manicure (which she felt essential for attending her grandson's christening), Donna approached Shirley who was attending to the accounts at her desk in an oak-beamed alcove.

"Er, excuse me Shirley, can I have a quick word?"

"Just a moment and I'll be with you," said Shirley as she ran her finger down a column of figures. It occurred to Donna as she observed her bowed head that Shirley really should get her own roots done. Having concluded her addition, Shirley looked up over her rimless spectacles and smiled at Donna.

"Yes, my dear, what can I do for you?"

"Well, you know, er, you know I'm pregnant. It's just that, well, my overall is getting too tight and I, er wondered if I could get something well, a bit more, um, maternity, really."

"Ah, yes, of course, we'll have to have a squint at the workwear catalogue – can't have you bursting at the seams. I'll look it out and you can choose something suitable. Is that alright?"

"Yes, great, thanks very much. Oh, and, um I was sorry to hear that Dean's not happy at school – you must be worried."

"They are a bunch of complete incompetents at St Herripole's and I intend to find somewhere a bit less stuffy. He's obviously too lively for them. Hah, call themselves an educational establishment. I told the head just what I thought of him and his school and if he can't do what I thought I was paying them to do, then I'll pay someone else. I'm going to look round the Arthur Trenchwarren Foundation tomorrow – I think he'd fit in well there. You've got all this to come of course, haven't you?"

"It seems a long way off. Oh, here's Mrs Dawlish for her facial. OK, well, thanks Shirley."

"No problem."

Sitting on the bus home to The Bullrushes, Donna Painswick considered the future and smiled as she pictured the nursery (which was yet to be decorated) and all the trappings of new motherhood. The state of the art pushchair would just about fit in under the stairs, although Neville would have to shift all his motoring magazines currently piled in the space. And he really would have to sort out the cracks and squeaks at Number 5 – she wanted it all to be perfect. She stepped from the bus and hummed quietly as she strolled home in the early evening sunshine.

She inserted her key in the front door lock but before she opened it, her attention was caught by a sizeable gap between the door frame and the brickwork. She was sure it hadn't been there that morning. She waved to Hazel and Barry Levinson whom she saw were gardening next door at Number 3, and invited them to come and have a look. After lengthy conversation during which Barry returned to his trowel, it transpired that the Levinsons were having similar problems with their house (although Donna and Neville had opted for 'The Everglade' whilst the Levinsons had chosen the rather more basic and less roomy 'Riverbank' which did not have feature stonework to the front façade). Hazel also told Donna that the Durcastles at Number 8 had mentioned difficulty with their panoramic sliding patio doors, and that the dog had narrowly missed having a length of guttering land on it only last weekend.

"D'you think we should get hold of the builder, after all, the houses are brand new and meant to be guaranteed, aren't they?" said Donna. "We should get one of the men to phone them as they'll be better at that sort of thing." Barry was summoned back and did have to agree that maybe it was time somebody brought the less than satisfactory standard of their homes to the builder's attention. Donna said she would send Neville round later to talk about it. She would probably have to go to bed as she got very tired in the evenings, what with work and everything. With her key in the lock, Donna applied her additional weight to get the front door open, sending the hanging baskets swaying again, and once inside took off her shoes, putting them in the rack strategically placed beside the front door, and with relief slipped puffy feet into her eye-catching sequinned slippers. She scuffed her way into the kitchen, opened the freezer door and took out two authentic Taiwanese fish suppers which could be prepared in the microwave in ten minutes. It had been recommended that she eat plenty of fish, thus a trip to the fish section of the local Supa Savas supermarket became inevitable. They did not cut corners, only prices, apparently.

While waiting for Neville to return, she settled on the sofa with her feet raised on velour cushions which really didn't match, and she wondered about having a look in the soft furnishing and interiors shop opposite Follicles tomorrow to find something that did. The last time she had tried to raise the subject with Neville, he was watching a Grand Prix motor race on the television and really didn't pay attention. She was flicking through the channels while waiting for her favourite early evening soap opera to commence when the telephone rang. That was something else they needed to get – a cordless telephone. She sighed, got up and went to the hall where the telephone sat on an ornately carved reproduction Raj table. It was Neville. He had been held up finishing off Mr de Souza's Aston Martin and as a friend had dropped Mrs de Souza off to collect it, he'd have to stay on. It was this sort of accommodating attitude which ensured no shortage of customers.

"You go ahead and eat love, I'll be back as soon as I can. Sorry."

"You know I don't like eating alone."

"Look, I'm really sorry, but I've got to get this finished. I'll be back soon, promise."

"But I told Barry you'd go and see him. Oh never mind, I'll talk to you later. 'Bye." And before Neville Martin Painswick had the opportunity to apologise further, she put the phone down and returned to the sofa.

Neville Martin suggested to Mrs de Souza that she go and sit in the office, but as it was a pleasant evening, she elected to stand outside and watch him finish, although her footwear was not entirely appropriate. Her stiletto heels would keep sinking into the earth, but she was more than content to gaze upon Neville Martin's lithe body evident even through his overalls as he worked under the bonnet of the car. She lit a cigarette, inhaled then blew smoky wisps into the still air. "Did Mrs Painswick mind you staying on?" she enquired, smiling at the view she beheld. Without lifting his head, Neville Martin replied that she wasn't too pleased, but in her present condition, she did take everything a bit too much to heart, and he was sure she would be fine. "Oh you're going to be a daddy, how marvellous!" she breathed.

Sonia trod her half-finished cigarette into the dirt, sauntered as best she could to the car, and gently caressing Neville Martin's overalled thigh, said "I guess that means you're not getting any sex at the moment then." Neville Martin Painswick dropped the spanner he was wielding and slowly turned and stood up straight to face Sonia, unsure that he can have interpreted correctly what she had just said. He was too perplexed to say or do anything and was easy prey for her as she grasped him around the back of the neck and pulled his head towards her for a passionate kiss. "Oh god, you've got a fantastic body – share it with me," she gasped. Neville Martin planted his oily hands around Sonia's not insubstantial waist in order to keep her at arm's length.

"P-lease, Mrs de Sou...."

"Call me Sonia," she said huskily as she pulled herself to him for another kiss. His arms relaxed a little as, quite against his will, he found himself enjoying the sensation, and he was almost unaware that his hands were moving down from her waist to her curvaceous rear as they lingered over an absorbing kiss. Reacting as if to an electric shock, when the telephone rang Neville sprang back muttering, "Oh god. Ah, oh. Blimey. I'd better answer that."

"Yeah, hello love, er, yeah, nearly finished. Well, say, about half an hour. No, please don't wait for me if you're hungry. Yeah, I will, I'll be as quick as I can, promise." Neville Martin Painswick was breathless and his heart was racing, and he replaced the phone with a trembling hand. He turned from the desk to find Sonia standing behind him with her blouse unbuttoned to reveal an impressive cleavage. He also could not fail to notice the black hand prints that clasped her waist.

"Oh my god, oh bloody hell," was all he could say before Sonia enveloped him in an irresistibly seductive embrace. She slid one hand inside his unbuttoned overalls and smothered any objection he may have had with another kiss. He was completely helpless and all thought of returning to Donna at Number 5, The Bullrushes was momentarily blanked from his fevered mind.

"Make love to me you fantastic fellow," she said softly in his ear, "it's quite safe my darling, I have the necessary. Come on, you know you want to...." After a few unconvincing denials, he did, there on the desk.

As Neville Martin was buttoning up his overalls after this moment of complete madness, feeling elated but ashamed and then just panic stricken, he looked up to see

Sonia smiling at him, dressed in nothing but her knickers and plunging bra, holding her oily clothes out with one hand.

"What am I to do with the evidence, Mr Painswick?"

"Oh my god, oh christ" was all he could say. She pouted at him and said with laughing eyes that luckily for them, she had jeans and a blouse that Trevor had collected from the laundry for her still in the back of the Aston, but she would leave her oily clothes there for him to dispose of. They were unceremoniously stuffed beside the filing cabinet.

Neville Martin Painswick had difficulty completing his work on Trevor's car. It was awkward to attempt everything at speed with shaking hands, knowing she was standing there watching him. His work finally completed, and not knowing now how to address Sonia, wiping his hands on a rag and looking at the ground, he said, "I'll um, send the bill on to you…"

"Darling, that was value added," said Sonia as she lifted his chin with a well manicured finger. She kissed her finger and placed it on his slightly parted lips. "If you ever feel like getting to know me better, here's my card – give me a ring. I have the house to myself all day." And without another word or a glance, she tottered to the car and drove off. Neville Martin Painswick slipped the card into his top pocket, looked at his watch and yet again uttered an expletive. He hurriedly pulled down the shutters, wiped his sweaty palms on his overalls, then realised he had to change into his shirt and jeans, the arms and legs of which seemed to have knotted themselves purposely in order to delay further his return to Number 5, The Bullrushes. He flung his overalls through the office door, locked it with shaking hands, climbed into his car and made a hasty exit.

"Hello love, sorry I'm late," called Neville Martin quietly as he came through the front door. There was no reply. Donna was asleep on the sofa with the television on, her empty plate and a glass on the floor. Neville Martin took the opportunity to go into the downstairs cloakroom and was horrified to see Sonia's crimson lipstick evident upon his forehead, and a scratch-mark down one side of his neck. Having hastily removed the crimson smudge, he emerged from the cloakroom muttering "Brambles, it was the brambles." Breathing deeply to calm himself, Neville Martin went into the beige-washed kitchen and grimaced at the sight of his Taiwanese fish supper waiting to go into the microwave. However he was feeling a bit light headed and decided food would probably help. After its allotted time rotating in the built-in eye-level compact microwave cooker, he spooned the steaming compilation onto a plate, poured over the thoughtfully provided sachet of sauce when at last he managed to get it open, and walked in to the sitting room to join his wife. Donna stirred as he slumped into the chair, spilling some sauce on his shirt, and as he uttered another expletive, she turned her head and yawning, said, "Oh, you're back then."

"Yeah, that car was trickier than I thought, but don't worry, I'll be charging overtime on the bill. This fish is delicious."

"It's too late for you to go next door now, but did you see the front door? One of you men is going to have to speak to the builders – these are meant to be brand new houses. And you'll have to get rid of your magazines from under the stairs – that's where the pushchair's going."

"I'll try to get that sorted out at the week-end love, I'll take them to the workshop I suppose. So what's wrong with the front door then?"

"Didn't you *see* when you came in?"

"Um, no, I'll have a look now as soon as I've finished this." Donna cast her eyes up.

As Neville got up and left the room she switched the channel to Celebrity Decorating Challenge. It was always an interesting source of design ideas for her to consider, and she was wondering about a theme for the baby's room. Lime? Metallic perhaps?

"Blimey, that's quite a gap isn't it?" said Neville as he came back into the room. "So what did next door say?"

"Nothing much, but they've had problems and you ought to talk to them, get stuff together for a complaint to the builders. What d'you think of that colour for the walls?"

"Mmmm. It's not too late, think I'll just nip round now." Neville Martin Painswick welcomed any distraction at the moment.

Barry and Hazel Levinson invited Neville into their sitting room which might itself have been the subject of some cutting-edge interior design experiment. Even with his almost total ignorance of interior decor matters, Neville wondered whether they were perhaps colour blind. Following the initial niceties and polite enquiries about work and family matters, a discussion of the quality of workmanship on their houses commenced. It was on the whole pretty shoddy, but cracks in the masonry were a bit more than just shoddy, and only yesterday Hazel had discovered a damp patch in the cloakroom. "So really, we need to contact the builders and get them to come and have a look then," summarised Neville. He found himself offering to undertake the task, following a second super-strength lager in which Barry insisted he join him, but the day thus far had been so bizarre, why not?

Chapter Six

Nigel Lamington-Krill loosened his tie as he leaned back in his leather swivel chair and admired the view afforded by his panoramic office windows. They overlooked an impressive section of London's skyline. A plain chrome frame containing studio posed pictures of Isobel and India smiling at anyone who cared to look sat facing him, and he tapped it saying, "This will do us very nicely girls!" He had just had an interesting conversation with the owner of a disused fertiliser factory upon which the housing development arm of his company, Harmony Homes, stood to make a sizeable profit. (That is, if he could get to know the local planners at Turbot as well, indeed, as he had those at Hake on Spinach.) They had agreed to meet for lunch as this sort of thing could not really be discussed over the telephone.

Taking into account the supposed provenance of Elliott Swardley (reluctant owner of the disused factory), Nigel felt that a meal in a booth at Banners, washed down with an ale or two perhaps, would fit the bill. The silver cutlery, champagne and damask table cloths could wait until the deal was clinched, perhaps. Nigel leaned across to the intercom.

"Alisha, book me my usual booth at Banners, yeh, for, say, er what is it now, yes, say one o'clock." Alisha brought in some letters for Nigel to sign and said that whilst he had been on the telephone, his agent's office in Hake had been in touch, in connection with the Bullrushes development. He frowned momentarily and said, "Well didn't they say what it was about?"

"All they said was that they have had several complaints from the residents recently and that they needed to speak to you."

"Oh is that all, what was it, wrong colour on the walls?"

"I really don't know, but they were quite insistent that you ring them back."

"Oh, after lunch, not now." And with that, Nigel imperiously waved the signed letters at Alisha who took them in an elegantly manicured hand, and with pursed lips, walked briskly from the room. Perhaps now was a good time to apply for the holiday which had been suggested by a charming man from the Serious Fraud Office who had called in to see her. She had his card somewhere safe.

Nigel thought he would walk to his lunch appointment as it was a nice day. What, he wondered, could the residents of the Bullrushes possibly have to complain about? He thought that sort of twee housing was precisely to what the lesser inhabitants of Hake would aspire. Not unduly perturbed he stood up, straightened his tie, and went to the wash-room to check his appearance. He washed his hands, applied a little cologne, ran his fingers through his hair and could not help grinning at himself in the mirror. He wondered whether that gorgeous little Hungarian waitress would be there today.

He arrived at Banners about ten minutes early and it occurred to him that it was a shame to be inside on such a glorious day, but then would Elliott Swardley really appreciate the continental ethos of lunching alfresco? He suspected not, but then he was apt to make arrogant assumptions about such things. He ordered a carbonated filter-purified ion-enhanced tap-water   (if only he knew it) as he needed to keep a clear head, and awaited the arrival of Mr Swardley. His favourite waitress was not in evidence, but a passable blonde with an Irish accent seemed most attentive and he smiled broadly as she leaned over the table with cutlery and a menu. "Ah, Elliott, over here!" called Nigel as his guest came through the door. They had only met once quite recently at a charity lunch hosted by an oil corporation on a brazen damage-limitation exercise, but he was easily recognisable from his build, his pony-tail and the fact that he was clearly uncomfortable in a shirt and tie. His fertiliser factory had gone out of business, he said, due to strangulation by EU rules, however both he and Nigel knew there was rather more to its demise than that. Nigel knew he needed to sell the premises and, literally, move on: and for the right price, Nigel could make that happen for him.

They shook hands, Elliott sat down and they ordered a traditional steak pie and chips at Nigel's suggestion. Elliott would have preferred the salad but did not wish to appear churlish. He had half a pint of ale as he was trying to get back into shape and Nigel had a bottled wheat beer. By the end of their lunch, the two men had made some progress towards reaching an understanding, although Elliott was a harder nut to crack than Nigel first supposed. However they parted company amiably enough, with the promise that Elliott would contact Nigel within a week having done some figure- work. Nigel was glad of the exercise on the way back to the office and was confident that Elliott would sell to him at a preferential price; he had to really, no-one else would touch his contaminated site. Upon his return to the office, Nigel told Alisha he didn't want to be disturbed, not even if his Hake agents rang again. He closed the door behind him, sat at his desk and dialled a sister company in Germany on his shiny desk phone.

"Guten Tag, Fischbacher Korporation," came a digitally remastered voice from the miniaturised loudspeaker.

"Guten Tag, Fritz Kennenspitz, bitte," responded Nigel.

"Ah, Fritz, wie gehts? Nigel here," he said, raising the wafer-thin handset as Fritz answered the phone.

"Fritz, I need to release some capital for a housing project and I wonder, is the Black Forest hunting lodge available in the next month or so? I may need to entertain some local dignitaries." Fritz's response caused Nigel to frown and sit up straight in his chair. "OK, so transfer from one of the offshore accounts – it will only be relatively short term and we stand to make one hell of a profit, trust me." Fritz needed to confer with colleagues and would contact Nigel shortly. He also thought Nigel should know that the German financial authorities were showing an interest in the joint dealings of the Fischbacher Korporation and Lamington-Krill International, particularly regarding various applications for obscure European Union grants. "They can prove nothing, and whilst I think of it Fritz, can you get hold of a consignment of Alpine cow bells, and send them to Hake Hall in the next week – we're having a bit of a do. An homage to your own country, in fact! Thanks, that will be excellent. Look, don't concern yourself, we're in the clear and if I can land this housing deal, we'll be fine. Chill, Fritz!"

Nigel Lamington-Krill got out of his chair and strolled to the window, rubbing his temple. Contemplating the human activity beneath him, he looked at his gold watch and felt he'd put in a sufficient day's work in the office. He needed to get back to his study at Hake Hall where some of his private papers needed further examination. He strolled to his reproduction Regency desk, pressed the intercom pad on the phone and said, "Alisha, get Terry to bring my car out will you, I'm leaving in two minutes. I may be in a bit later tomorrow, so just take messages .... Oh they can wait until tomorrow." Nigel tightened his tie before leaving, splashed cold water on his face in his wash room, dabbed it with a very white, very fluffy hand towel then combed his hair, smiled at his reflection and in jest saluted himself in the mirror, clicked his heels then turned and left for the lifts. Upon emerging from the revolving glass doors at the entrance to the building in the afternoon sunshine, he donned his Trent Cabernet zero reflection sunglasses and sauntered down the semi-circular slate steps to receive the keys to his Jensen from Terry.

"It's in bay 5, squire, lovely afternoon to give the old girl a bit of a work-out!"

"Indeed. No bad traffic to report then?"
"Nope, clear all the way last I heard."
"Excellent! See you tomorrow then."
"Good afternoon, sir."

Nigel Lamington-Krill opened the door of the Jensen, laid his jacket on the back seat, loosened his tie again then slid into the driver's seat and slipped the key into the ignition. He started the engine, opened the sun roof and took off into the London traffic with alacrity. Whilst stationary at traffic lights, he inserted a recording of a Mozart concerto into his surround-sound high end car hi fi system and felt he was at one with his world. He idly watched a girl with flowing blonde hair and an ample bosom totter across the road on high heels in a very short skirt, and smiled to himself. Mozart filled his surroundings and life was good.

As the suburbs began to give way to more open spaces and green fields, so Nigel picked up speed, for as Terry had rightly indicated earlier, it was a good opportunity to give the old girl a bit of a work-out. Mozart had been replaced by Beethoven and it was with particular annoyance that Nigel noticed the flashing lights of a police car some way behind him as he dashed along an inviting stretch of wide, straight and almost empty road to a particularly stirring passage. "Bollocks, damn!" he said through gritted teeth as he applied the brakes and pulled slowly to the side. The patrol car pulled up behind him and the occupants got out. One of them strolled purposefully to Nigel's side of the car, and he was momentarily taken aback to see that this was a female police officer. Blessed as he was with a certain inherant arrogance, especially where those he considered to be less well educated than him were concerned, Nigel, having removed his Trent Cabernets purposefully, tried the approach that the road was empty and he wasn't doing any harm and didn't they have bloody burglars and illegal immigrants to victimise instead? Nigel half intended this to be funny, but the police officers rather failed to appreciate the tone of his humour, and the WPC invited him to step out of his car while she commenced completion of the appropriate paperwork. Her colleague meanwhile sauntered around the front of the car and having looked at the tyres, glanced at the windscreen and said, "Do you intend to render your vehicle legal in the near future sir?"

"Now what have I done?" responded Nigel testily, starting to drum his fingers on the car bonnet.

"Driven a vehicle in considerable contravention of the prevailing speed limit on the Queen's Highway whilst not displaying a valid road fund licence disc sir," came the response.

"Oh bloody hell, it's only a few days out of date, what is your problem? My PA obviously forgot. I'll make sure she does it tomorrow."

"To whom is the vehicle registered sir?"

"Me of course, who else would it be?"

"It is the responsibility of the registered owner to ensure that the vehicle is legal and roadworthy, not that of the registered owner's PA, sir."

"Look I'll get it done tomorrow, alright? It was just an oversight. Do I look like an habitual criminal?"

"I don't believe I am qualified to say, what would one of those look like exactly, sir?"

"Now don't get cocky with me, just get this bloody paperwork done and let me go about my business, *if* you would be so kind, officer."

Nigel threw the completed paperwork on to the passenger seat. He got back into the car, replaced his Trent Cabernets and with a supreme effort, suppressed his towering annoyance and fought the natural urge to depart at speed, being mindful of the officers of the law eye-catchingly evident in his rear view mirror. When at last they turned off the road and out of sight, Nigel dialled his office on the mobile phone.

"Alisha, I've just been stopped by the bloody police and my car tax has run out. How did that happen? ....

Oh, didn't I? Are you sure? Well can you make sure it *is* entered into the system, I don't want to come into contact with those types again. Yeh, yeh, I'll see you tomorrow."

As he neared Hake on Spinach, Nigel decided a pint or two in a local hostelry before returning to Hake Hall was most definitely required, thus he drew into the Raddled Beanpole which, from the vehicles in the car park, already appeared to have quite a few visitors. He drew up beside Colonel Whipstock's old Bristol and remarked, "Hah, haven't seen the old boy in here for ages." He got out of the car, removed his tie altogether and strolled in. Gloria greeted him cheerfully as he removed his sunglasses in the beamed gloom and slid them into his shirt pocket.

"What can I get you, Mr L-K? A pint of your usual?"

"A pint of Roach Royal Ruby, yes, thanks Gloria. I see the Colonel's in this evening?"

"Yes, he's not been long out of hospital – the leg took a long time to heal and" (lowering her voice) "he wasn't a very co-operative patient I hear. He's over there." She gestured towards an upholstered corner seat where Colonel Whipstock sat with one leg outstretched and his walking stick on the table.

"Colonel – too early for another double?" called Nigel.

"Never too early dear boy, never too early!" Nigel walked over to join the Colonel with the drinks.

"I hear you had a bit of a prang – bad luck!"

"The bloody prang was nothing – I've had my sister staying at Herring Grange since the accident. I swear I'll be tidied to death – can't find a damn thing in the place. She insists on driving me as well – leg's still a bit stiff, y'know, but she'll do for my gearbox. She tidied her last husband to death three years ago, still, left her a packet, so she's alright."

"Where is she now, Colonel? I've never met her."

"Made her go and join the ladies in the garden – some charitable do-gooding going on – she'll sort them out, and I get ten minutes' peace. Anyhow, how's life in the city? Anything I should be investing in? Cheers!"

"Cheers! Mmmm..." Nigel took two great gulps of his ale. "Aaah, I needed that. Everything, old boy, was fine until I got stopped on my way back by bloody police with nothing better to do than victimise law-abiding citizens."

"Know what you mean old boy, where are they when some little bugger's stolen your garden statue? Cheers!"

Thus Nigel spent a very pleasant hour at the Raddled Beanpole before returning to Hake Hall in mellower mood than hitherto.

As he got up to leave, Colonel Whipstock's sister made an entrance via the stable door which led to the garden, requesting a tray of drinks for the ladies. "Ah, Amelia," bellowed the Colonel, "let me introduce you – Nigel Lamington-Krill, this is my sister, Amelia Strang-Wellow." Amelia strode over and grasped Nigel's hand, shaking it heartily. "Delighted, delighted," she enthused, as Nigel beheld a woman of robust proportions, sporting what could best be described as rustic-chic garb, with her grey hair piled upon her head and secured with an assortment of combs and clasps.

"If you're still in residence, you must come with the Colonel to Isobel's Bavarian evening we're holding at Hake Hall. You really would be most welcome, may I call you Amelia?"

"Oh I say, how kind. I can stay on as long as I like, and I know Peregrine can do with the company, and still isn't very steady with his bad leg – isn't that right old thing?" she enquired of the Colonel who responded with a barbed glance aimed at Nigel. Nigel smiled, wished them both a very pleasant evening, and took his leave.

Driving up to Hake Hall now in good spirits, Nigel left the Jensen by the garage block and left the keys in the ignition for Turtle to put it away later. Whistling, he gathered his jacket and tie from the back seat, stuffed the papers issued to him in his pocket and went in to the house via the conservatory. "Hello, anybody about?" he called. He could hear Cook preparing the evening meal in the kitchen, but he would not have been heard above the strains of Bob Marley, so he went up the elegantly curving stairs and to his dressing room to change his clothes. He heard a shower running and realised that Isobel was in her bathroom. He smiled, stripping naked and throwing his discarded clothes onto a chair. He walked noiselessly to Isobel's shower, pulled the door open, stepped inside and clasped his wife, smothering her shriek of surprise and feeble protestations with urgent kisses. They made slippery love in the steamy cubicle.

Wrapped in finest Egyptian cotton monogrammed bathrobes, Isobel and Nigel sat on the long stool at the end of their sizeable four poster bed: "So you've had a good day then, darling?" Nigel couldn't be bothered to recount his encounter with the officers of the law.

"I think I've got another housing deal in the offing. Oh, and better than that, I now know what Colonel Whipstock's first name is – it's Peregrine! I met his sister this evening and suggested she might like to come to the Bavarian evening too – she's a very, er, stout type, but good fun I think. Quite Germanic really. Ah, I may also need to invite a couple of key local authority types along too – don't know yet, all depends on whether any of them come to my project presentation lunch."

"I need to firm up arrangements with Cook and Mrs Tremble in the next few days, but a few extra won't make any difference."

"Oh, and Fritz is going to send over a box of cow bells – I asked him today." Nigel didn't feel he needed to share any more detail of his conversation with Fritz. Isobel wouldn't understand the niceties and otherwise of international finance anyway.

"Marvellous, thank you darling – it's going to be such fun. And India rang today – she'll be home next week and said she'd love to be at the Bavarian evening. I'm so pleased!" Isobel stood up, leant over and kissed Nigel on the forehead.

"Good, well let's get dressed and go down for a drink before dinner. Cook sounded as if he was having a good time in the kitchen – hope it tastes good!"

After dinner as Turtle cleared away the last of the dishes, Nigel said he needed to spend a couple of hours in his study, so Isobel took the opportunity to stroll around the grounds and make a note of jobs to be done by Mr Tremble.

At Hake Lodge, Helena Ruby Tremble sat on the edge of her not so sizeable bed, having just deposited a neat pile of ironing in the airing cupboard, and began to consider the logistics of packing her belongings, for she had concluded that it had to be soon. The sound from the television drifted up from the sitting room below and she sighed heavily. Yes, it had to be soon. She sat with her head bowed in her hands and hot tears dripped unbidden through her fingers. Although resolute she was still desperately miserable. She wanted to see her girls, she wanted to be happy. "OK Helena Ruby," she said quietly to herself, standing up, taking a deep breath and wiping her tears away with the back of her hand, "it's up to you, there's no-one else." She went into the bathroom and pressed a cold flannel to her eyes, blew her nose on the rose tinted super-soft quilted toilet paper and resolved to be out before her forty-eighth birthday which fell on 27th August. She forced a smile at herself in the mirror above the basin and said again, "It's up to you."

Helena Ruby Tremble slept fitfully and awoke before the alarm. She had dreamt of being pursued by a German chef wielding a cheese grater, she had seemed to be in an eternal quest to find her apron, and Denholm was somehow a guinea-pig and gave birth to so many babies that she was knee-deep in small, elongated rodents which all contrived to stop her fleeing the chef or finding her apron. Back to reality, Helena Ruby slipped out of bed, pulled on her dressing gown and left Ron snoring. It was, astonishingly, another glorious morning and upon opening the kitchen door she was greeted enthusiastically as always by Denholm. She yawned, ran her hand through her hair, stretched, then filled the kettle with water and switched it on. "Let's go out for an early morning walkies shall we my darling? This morning is too good to waste." Denholm, recognising that word, started performing a strange, fevered circular movement whilst wagging his tail vigorously and Helena Ruby scooped him up, laughing and buried her face in his silky ear. She drank her tea and took a mug upstairs and put it on the bedside table for Ron, who stirred and grunted. She gathered up the necessary clothes, said she was taking Denholm for an early walk as it was such a lovely morning, then before he could offer any opinion, went to the bathroom where she hastily washed and dressed.

Strolling along in the dazzling morning sunshine and listening to the birdsong, Helena Ruby's spirits lifted. On a morning like this, anything seemed possible. Today she would ask Cook whether he would consider taking a lodger and her dog. This would be the first step, to where she couldn't imagine, but it had to be in the right direction. She returned to the Lodge to encounter Ron in his vest and pyjama trousers complaining that he couldn't find a clean shirt. What a singularly unattractive proposition he was. She pursed her lips and said, "So you didn't manage to find one in the airing cupboard then – too much effort I suppose?"

"There weren't any hanging up, how am I supposed to know?"

'How indeed,' thought Helena Ruby Tremble, 'how indeed.' She stepped purposefully up the stairs, removed every ironed item from the airing cupboard, dropped them on the bed then proceeded to hang up every shirt, put every item of underwear in its correct drawer and the spare sheets in the top of the wardrobe. Then she walked downstairs and said "Right, I'm off to work." Without waiting for any response, she opened the back door and departed for Hake Hall. Today she was going to put all this behind her.

"Morning Mrs L-K," said Helena Ruby as she came through the kitchen door. "Anything special you want me to see to today?" Isobel was standing by the salt-glazed farmhouse sink cutting the stalk ends from a bunch of large, white daisies.

"Good morning Mrs Tremble. Just a general clean and tidy I think, but perhaps you could start in the laundry room. Some of Nigel's shirts have come back from the laundry rather creased. I think I need to have a word with them – they're becoming a bit slap dash. It's ever since that lout Craig was made manager. Standards are slipping. Oh, and if you could give India's room a good airing and make sure it's all nice for her, she's coming back for my Bavarian evening."

"Certainly Mrs L-K, you must be looking forward to it. It must be hard when you don't see her for so long." Helena Ruby was vaguely aware of the irony in this observation, seeing as how India had been sent away to boarding school at the earliest opportunity. It didn't seem to have done her any actual harm, but with the possible exception of the appalling Bartley-Grantwick twins, destined no doubt for the judiciary, she couldn't imagine why anybody would voluntarily send their children away.

"Oh it will be wonderful to see her, yes. And if you get a moment, you couldn't do these flowers for me could you? You know where all the vases are. I thought I'd put these in the main hall. They're such a cheerful greeting!"

"Of course," said Helena Ruby Tremble, anxious for Cook to arrive.

"I thought it would be a good idea for us to discuss the final details of my Bavarian evening with Cook today, if that's alright with you, Mrs T?" Disappointment descended upon Helena Ruby. She was hoping that Isobel would obligingly spend the day in pursuit of something vapid, however she clearly had other intentions perfectly suited to ruining anything Helena Ruby Tremble might have planned. There would be other opportunities; but today would have been good. It felt like Helena Ruby's perfect moment.

Chapter Seven

As Helena Ruby Tremble was tidying Nigel and Isobel's dressing rooms, placing discarded footwear into the appropriate pigeonholes, she considered her position. She had not had the opportunity to approach Cook with her proposition. Isobel seemed determined to pursue each detail of the catering arrangements to extremes, having purchased yet another recently published and highly acclaimed cookery book, this time fortuitously encompassing the ethos of German cuisine. However, Helena Ruby had another darts match to attend later and her thoughts turned to that.

She had been in such a state of anxiety and vague anticipation lately that she had rather lost her appetite, but Ron would be expecting his tea before she left and Helena Ruby could not stomach a confrontation at the moment. Pam had said she would collect Helena Ruby at seven o'clock, in two hours' time. She took Nigel's jacket from the balloon back chair and hung it in his wardrobe, then leant down and picked up his discarded trousers and placed them in the wicker laundry basket. The only laundry to which Helena Ruby was expected to attend was what Isobel coyly referred to as their 'delicates', for which an embroidered finest Irish linen bag was provided, discreetly hung inside Isobel's wardrobe door. Thus, Helena Ruby picked up Nigel's socks and underpants and placed them in the requisite receptacle. She noticed a business card lying on the large red rug, which she assumed had fallen from his trousers, and picked it up. It had the Harmony Homes blue and silver crest on it, with Nigel declared as Chairman in deep maroon print. Helena Ruby shrugged and placed it on the table beside the rest of the discarded contents of his pockets.

Having concluded her day's work, she turned and observed herself in the cheval mirror and sighed deeply, snatching a peacock blue silk tie draped across the frame and hanging it back on its rack in the wardrobe. She turned to the mirror again and said to her reflection, "Well Helena Ruby, is this all you amount to – tidying other people's lives for them?" Tears sprang up and just as she was searching for a tissue, Isobel came through the door.

"Ah, Mrs T, you haven't left yet. I thought I heard you in here. Oh dear, are you alright?"

"I think I've got a cold, I haven't been feeling too good," was all Helena Ruby could reply.

"Oh goodness, you must be alright for my Bavarian evening – I'm relying on you! Anyway, I wanted to catch you as I'm going to cancel our arrangement with Great Roach Laundry. They just don't press things properly and on several occasions the bed linen has come back with nasty marks on it. I thought we'd try Love Your Linens. It's in Mackerel, and Petronella Throck-Wallaby has particularly recommended them to me. Have you heard of them?"

"Um, no, but I'm sure it's worth giving them a try. It seems a shame to have to iron all the shirts twice," said Helena Ruby, having gathered herself together. "Will you excuse me if I go now, I have a darts match this evening."

"A darts match, Mrs T. That must be fun! Where is it?"

"The Startled Partridge."

"I don't think I've been there. Well have a good time and I hope you feel better soon."

"I'm sure I shall," responded Helena Ruby, raising a smile. 'I'm going to make sure I do,' she thought.

Helena Ruby returned to the Lodge and as always, Denholm was delighted to see her, and Ron was watching television. "Hello darling," she said to the dog, scooping him up affectionately, then she walked through to Ron, stroking Denholm's ear and said, "I've got darts tonight so egg on toast will have to do."

"That's not much – can't I have bacon and chips too? I've been working really hard today."

"Well so have I, so do you want egg on toast or not?" Helena Ruby was struggling to maintain any sort of civility, but just kept thinking to herself that soon all this would be behind her. "I'll do you some beans with it."

"Oh whatever, I'll probably go to the chip shop later." Helena Ruby had completely lost her appetite, so having provided food for her husband and refraining from tipping it upon his ungrateful head, she went to the bathroom to wash and change as Pam would be there in half an hour. "Well, at least make the effort," she said to her reflection as she brushed her hair, and glancing at a decorative bowl on the window sill containing a few unused cosmetic gifts, she picked up a container of mascara and gingerly applied it to her generous eyelashes. It did seem to lend the suggestion of a sparkle to her grey-green eyes. She smiled at the effect and went on to apply a hint of rebalancing, non-reflective pre-foundation crème which must have been at least three years old, but she shook it well, and once applied, it gave her complexion a certain smoothness, and she smiled to herself again. Helena Ruby went to the bedroom, took her jacket from the wardrobe and as she turned, saw in the window the reflection of Pam's car pulling in. She ran downstairs, told Ron expressionlessly that she was off now, rubbed Denholm's head affectionately, telling him it was best if he stayed behind this time, picked up her handbag and went out to join the Hake on Spinach ladies' darts team for their friendly match against the good ladies representing Trout Pennyford.

Pulling up in the car park, Pam remarked upon how much nicer the exterior looked since Terence, the landlord, had put large tubs of flowers around the edge, and her passengers all agreed. They disembarked and entered the cool, dim calm of the Startled Partridge. The dart board stood out like a beacon, illuminated as it was by a piercingly bright light at the far end. Most of the opposing team were already there, and introductions having been made and hands shaken, Helena Ruby paused to reflect, not for the first time, upon how civilised this all was. They all bought drinks while waiting for the last two ladies to arrive and Helena Ruby found herself feeling quite light headed after consuming the vodka and lime she thought she deserved. It was, she supposed, because she hadn't had much to eat.

The last two players having arrived, the match commenced and within an hour, the Hake on Spinach team conceded defeat. None of the ladies were really inclined to leave, thus more drinks were ordered and as the evening was still light and wonderfully warm, they decided to sit in the garden. In these delightful surroundings, Helena found herself relaxed and at ease, and realised she was laughing for the first time in months. She wondered what Jolyon might be doing at that moment, remembering her last darts match. Helena Ruby passed the pay phone on her way to the lavatories. On her way back, she was seized on a whim lent impetus by four vodka and limes, pulled the twisted business card out of her jacket pocket and dialled Jolyon Urquart's mobile telephone number. As it rang, she felt as though hot needles were pricking her scalp, her palms began to sweat and she was about to put the handset down with the word 'stupid, stupid, stupid' reverberating about her head, when Jolyon answered his phone. Helena Ruby Tremble's heart was beating so hard, she thought she would pass out. "Hi, Jolyon Urquart."

"Uh, I, um - it's Helena, d'you remember, from the darts match?"

"My dear, of course I remember, I've been waiting for you to ring. Where are you?"

"Er, I'm at the Startled Partridge, do you know it?"

"Sorry, you'll have to speak up – where, the speckled what?" (Helena Ruby's voice had dropped almost to a whisper for fear of being overheard.)

"Oh god, look, it doesn't matter. Sorry, I shouldn't have rung, the credit's run out…" Tears welled up as she replaced the handset and Helena Ruby felt her face turn crimson. She felt unutterably stupid. She took a deep breath, dabbed her eyes with her handkerchief and turned to rejoin her colleagues when the pay phone rang. A sensation akin an electric shock coursed up her spine, and Helena Ruby seized the phone. Despite her best efforts to sound controlled, the 'hello' she uttered was delivered in a high pitched, strangulated tone, full of anticipation.

"Did someone order a taxi for Limpet?" enquired a voice, "only our driver's wife has gone into labour and the replacement will take half an hour."

"Er, I don't know," said Helena, having difficulty responding to the enquiry. "I'll, um, pass the message on."

"Thanks love." Helena Ruby Tremble walked slowly to the bar and ordered another double vodka and lime. She was thinking: "You stupid, stupid, woman. You've just made a bloody fool of yourself. D'you honestly think that anyone would look twice at you, you stupid, talentless waste of space." She paid for her drink and in the time it took her to walk out to the garden, had finished it in several gulps. Not really caring now what anybody thought of her, Helena Ruby called out, "Is there anybody here called Limpet, only the taxi will be late – some poor woman has gone into labour."

The rest of Helena Ruby's evening was spent in a haze of mild intoxication and self loathing, and when asked by Pam when delivering her home whether she was alright, only she seemed a bit quiet, offered the standard lame excuse of being just a bit tired. She sat in the kitchen clasping Denholm and weeping into his neck, rocking gently back and forth. How she wished her girls were there. They were her only worthwhile achievement.

Despite her bleak mood, Helena Ruby Tremble had a thin thread of determination to which she was firmly anchored and she promised herself that she was going to take the chance and approach Cook at the first opportunity tomorrow. Automatically she picked up the plate and cup left by Ron and put them in the sink, threw two used teabags in the bin and heaved a big sigh, saying quietly, "Not for much longer." Thus she went resolutely upstairs to the bathroom, removed her now smudged eye make-up, splashed her face with water then slipped quietly to bed. Sleep evaded her for some time as she re-lived the evening, wishing she hadn't made that phone call. She wondered whether the taxi driver's wife had given birth yet and what sort of a life awaited the child. Helena Ruby still had a good portion of her life ahead and it was going to be better than hitherto, it had to be.

It was raining heavily when she awoke next morning and she had a dreadful headache. With some effort she got out of bed, wearily pulled on her dressing gown and went downstairs to the kitchen to make tea. As she bent down to Denholm's enthusiastic welcome, her head was pounding and she sat heavily on a chair, overcome by a wave of nausea. All Helena Ruby could manage was to get herself some water and swallow pain killers, then she sat with her head in her arms on the table, with Denholm sitting disconsolately at her feet. She felt as if the room were rotating about her and when she lifted her head, she could barely see Denholm for jagged lights spearing her vision. Crying hurt, but she could not stop herself. Helena Ruby dabbed her eyes with a tissue and knew that all she wanted to do was lie down, close her eyes and rest her pounding head. She had not had a migraine like this for years.

She didn't want to return to bed beside Ron, but the spare bed was not made up and so, with leaden limbs she wearily climbed the stairs, pushed the bedroom door open and said, "Ron, I've got a migraine, I can't go to work today." As she thankfully lay her head on the pillow, Ron sat up, pulling the duvet with him and said, "Can't you take some aspirin?" Helena Ruby could not be bothered to answer and just lay there in misery. "OK well I'll get my own tea then."

After what seemed an interminable succession of banging cupboard doors, yelps, running water, coughing, the creaky wardrobe door (which did nothing for Helena Ruby Tremble's wellbeing), Ron's ill-tempered search for clothes and his final grudging "Well *I'm* off to work now", peace finally descended upon the house and Helena Ruby dozed. Denholm, aware that all was not well, slunk up the stairs and pushed his way through the bedroom door. He was not normally allowed in the bedroom (the result of an edict by Ron) and was fascinated by all manner of new smells to investigate. He encountered Ron's moth-eaten slippers thrown in the corner, and having examined them for some time, lifted his short back leg and urinated on them. Having left his mark, he trotted back round the bed and, standing on his hind legs, drew himself up level with Helena Ruby's relaxed hand and began licking it affectionately. Helena Ruby stirred, opened her eyes and smiled. At least her vision was a little clearer now. She scooped Denholm's rump up on to the bed and the two lay there together, momentarily content.

Having dozed for another two or so hours and receiving much solicitous licking and nuzzling from Denholm, Helena Ruby felt much improved and lay looking at the ceiling wondering about her future. The events of the evening before ran idly through her mind and that same inspiration, devilment, call it what you will, began to take hold of her again and despite all that she had beaten herself up about, and the self-belittlement evoked, she was suddenly overwhelmed with the need to make contact with Jolyon, and what better opportunity than now in peace and calm with Ron off the premises. She glanced at the clock and realised that he would be home in about half an hour. That gave her enough time. She slowly sat up, making sure that her head wouldn't start pounding again, and Denholm jumped up, tail wagging frantically.

"I've got terrible butterflies old thing, your mum is about to do something ridiculous, but at the moment she doesn't care!" Helena Ruby kissed Denholm on the head then gingerly got out of bed, found to her relief that she had shaken off the worst effects of her migraine and went to the bathroom to freshen up before making the telephone call. Denholm trotted happily behind her. With familiarly shaking hand, Helena Ruby lifted the telephone and taking a deep breath, dialled Jolyon's number from his increasingly dog-eared card. Again, her heart felt as if it was about to burst through her ribs as she anticipated his voice answering the call. What she was going to say, what if anything was to be arranged, she hadn't the faintest idea.

"Hi, Jolyon's phone," came the unexpected response from a velvet-voiced woman, oh god, clearly from a more suitable background than Helena Ruby Tremble. She felt as though her veins had been filled with hot treacle and heard herself say, "Oh dear, I'm sorry, that isn't Janet's number is it," in exaggeratedly clumsy tones.

"No dear, there's no Janet here;" purred the velvet voice, "better luck next time." Helena Ruby gulped back a sob as she put the phone down and right on cue, Ron barged through the back door, his only response being, "Oh, you're up then. I told the boss I didn't know when you'd be back." In a vain effort to take her mind off the excruciating humiliation she felt, Helena Ruby Tremble made Ron sandwiches, claimed a relapse and returned to bed taking her own personal miasma of misery with her. Denholm knew better than to follow her on this occasion and installed himself in his own bed and hopefully out of Ron's sight.

Chapter Eight

As Helena Ruby entered Hake Hall on the morning of Isobel's Bavarian evening, she was greeted with the sight of Turtle manhandling a startled-looking stuffed bear from the entrance hall to the dining room. She smiled as she walked to the kitchen where she found Cook un-stacking cases of food associated one way or another with Germany. Her arrival elicited a grin and the cheerful offer of tea (English) which she happily accepted. They perched at the edge of the table, which was laden with cutlery, crockery and table linen, ready for Helena Ruby to set out in the dining room. "Mrs L-K's not started the day in a good mood," Cook said. "Nigel had to go out this morning and won't be back until early evening – I heard raised voices. And flying gravel as he left. I guess that will need raking before this evening."

"Ah, yes, not the best day to go absent. Still, I don't think Mr L-K's likely to be a lot of help setting up. Ooh, I know what I meant to tell you, while I think of it - did you know that it's his company who built the estate you live on? I found a business card in the dressing room."

"No I didn't, but I happen to know there's a lot of discontent about the, shall we say, workmanship, and I think the residents are forming some sort of action group. I've had to get my front door re-hung once already, my mate's very handy like that, and he doesn't think much of the building. Cowboys everywhere, eh? Ha, cowboys and cowbells!"

"Mmmmm." Not wanting to waste any more time, and with a tide of hopes and intentions rising up inside her, Helena Ruby finally seized the moment to ask Cook what she had been summoning up the courage to ask for what felt like an eternity. She inhaled with some deliberation, then without allowing herself any more leeway, said "Um, I don't know how to ask you this, but, er, would you have a spare room for a lodger and small dog?" She felt the heat and colour rise in her cheeks as she raised her eyes to look at Cook who was returning to the table with two mugs of tea.

"Er, would I be correct in thinking, am I completely wrong ... do you mean *you*? I, er, well ... Blimey Mrs T, you've rather caught me by surprise. I mean, *why*, well, er, you know ..." Taking a deep breath, Helena Ruby launched into an explanation. "I'm leaving Ron. Living with him is making me completely miserable, I can't bear it any more. But I don't want to find another job just yet. It would only be for a few months until I can get myself sorted out. I know it's a terrible imposition, but I'd earn my keep, pay you rent, stay out of your way. And .... I, ... oh dear, would you object to the dog? I can't leave him." Accompanied by the sound of scraping legs, Cook pulled out the chair to sit down and handed a mug of tea to Helena Ruby. Having put down his own mug, he rubbed his chin thoughtfully.

"Er, I'm not always alone in the house you know."

"Oh, of course, I didn't expect you not to have any friends, and like I said, I'd stay out of your way."

"I've got, ahem, shall we say, one very special friend who often stays, but hey, it wouldn't affect the spare room I suppose Mrs T." Cook grinned broadly and Helena Ruby couldn't help but respond likewise. "I'm really pleased for you, I'm sorry, it was thoughtless of me not to consider, I shouldn't have asked, I just didn't think .... I don't want to cramp your style." Helena Ruby's cheeks began to colour up again and she really wished she hadn't started this conversation. "Look, I'm sorry, I really shouldn't have put you in this position, please forget I asked. It was a stupid idea anyway." Helena Ruby decided she'd have to find another job. "Hey, not so fast. If I can help you out I will Mrs T – you know, I think we'll all get along just fine. Yeah, in fact, I'm sure it will work." Helen Ruby's eyes filled with tears of relief and gratitude. She reached across the table and squeezed Cook's hand as she was now unable to speak.

Having finished her tea and composed herself, Helena Ruby Tremble set about her day's tasks with renewed enthusiasm. She carried her floral displays up from the cellar with a spring in her step, and humming quietly to herself, arranged them variously on tables, sideboards and window sills. She placed a stray yellow rosebud behind the left ear of the stuffed bear which upon close inspection, proved to be a rather moth-eaten affair with two broken teeth and a cracked eye. "You could do with a good vacuuming," she said to it, then laughed as she envisaged the balding pelt being sucked into the hose. "Maybe not, old thing."

Swags of hops were draped along the stair banisters and across the gallery with odd-sized cow bells hung here and there. Ron Tremble and Turtle had been given the job of applying this particular touch and the end result was no great surprise. Helena Ruby made a mental note to vacuum the floor where vegetation had fallen and been ground underfoot, then went to the kitchen to see if she could make a sandwich as she didn't really have time or the inclination to go back to the Lodge for lunch.

She found Cook unpacking cold meats from the state of the art fridge, and he looked up with a smile as Helena Ruby Tremble came into the kitchen. "Hey, Mrs T – I need your artistic input with all this dead flesh!"

"Anything, Cook, anything to help as long as I can have something to eat. It's going to be a very, very long day." Still apprehensive about their earlier conversation, she added, "You know, you're perfectly free to change your mind if you feel I've sort of manoeuvred you into a corner."

"Not necessary my friend, it's not a problem. Like I said, we'll get on just fine. Give the neighbours something else to talk about."

"Oh goodness, thank you, thank you so much. It's just that I ... ah ...oh dear, I'm welling up again."

"Make us both a sandwich and pull yourself together woman! We've got a lot of work to do." At this moment in her day Helena Ruby allowed herself to start believing that everything might just work out alright.

Isobel Lamington-Krill however was beginning at the same time to feel that her evening was going to be anything but alright. She had returned from her manicure and collagen-rich facial to find that the wrong sparkling wine had been delivered. It should, of course, have been German. "Bloody hell – Nigel should be here sorting this out," she fumed. She tried contacting his mobile phone but it was switched off. "I haven't time to sort this out now. Serena is coming to do my hair for me. Damn and blast," she said to anyone who cared to listen, as she stamped upstairs, unaware that Serena had the appointment in her diary for the following week-end. As it was, Turtle merely raised an eyebrow as he stood sampling a particularly fine malt from the cabinet in the large drawing room. He had been having a tiresome day thus far supervising deliveries and ensuring domestic good order, and he needed something to buoy him up for the evening's activities. Then he took a deep breath, smiled and strolled to the kitchen. With Turtle's rather more than usually energetic assistance, Helena Ruby transported the glasses, crockery, cutlery and table linen to the dining room and installed it as indicated in a rough sketch hastily produced that morning by Isobel, but on the understanding that Helena Ruby must do what she thought best; she had, after all, a better eye for this sort of thing. Numerous cold dishes, beautifully presented and garnished and encased in acres of plastic film were then arranged between candlesticks and a magnificent floral table centre on the ivory damask-covered table and along the vast sideboard. Helena Ruby and Cook stood back to observe. "Doesn't really look very German does it?" said Cook.

"No. Maybe what it needs is some of those beer drinking jug things," said Helena Ruby with her hands on her hips.

"Couple of Panzer tanks too perhaps," muttered Turtle as he went out through the door.

"Well we've done all we were asked Mrs T, now we have the evening to get through."

Turtle was planning his own particular wry touch to the evening's events. In a past career he had acquired an iron cross, and he was also in possession of a disarmed hand grenade and several other items which he thought it might be amusing to deploy at some time during the evening. A long-standing financial venture of his had weathered all manner of ill omens and had now come to fruition. This was to be his parting gesture. He need be obsequious no longer.

Helena Ruby took a last tour of inspection, straightening a couple of stalks in her arrangements, picking up a few fallen hops and dropping them in her apron pocket, then walked across the landing and knocked on Isobel's bedroom door where she supposed her to be, in order to confirm that she had checked all the rooms, provided fresh towels and that she would be returning to the Lodge to change shortly. Isobel was inconsolable in her bedroom. She still couldn't get in touch with Nigel, India was going to be late and that stupid, stupid girl Serena had got the date wrong for doing her hair. "Everything's a complete mess Mrs T," wailed Isobel. Looking at Isobel's blotchy, mascara-stained face Helena Ruby could not help but concur. In a half-hearted attempt to buck up Isobel, Helena Ruby suggested that she have a shower, wash her hair then Helena Ruby could at least blow dry it for her – something she had always longed to do for her own daughters, both blessed with thick, glossy locks of chestnut hair. Isobel was surprisingly grateful for Helena Ruby's offer, and so it was agreed that she would return to the Lodge, wash and change and then return to help Isobel and have something to eat. Even Ron's perpetual bad-tempered grumbling could not dampen Helena Ruby Tremble's newly found spirit of bonhomie. He was to be in charge of car parking that evening, so they would see very little of each other.

Isobel Lamington-Krill insisted Helena Ruby share a glass or two of the 'wrong champagne' with her as the hairdressing got under way, and just as the finishing touches were being applied to a now beaming and impressively coiffed Isobel, Nigel was heard to slam his dressing room door and turn on the shower. "Better late than never," said Isobel, smiling at Helena Ruby in the mirror.

Whatever passed between Nigel and Isobel upstairs, when they descended in preparation to greet their guests who would be arriving shortly, they were arm in arm and presenting a united front. Isobel's coiffure was a little less sleek than half an hour previously, but she looked presentable enough in leather trousers and an off-the-shoulder chemise. As if to complete the moment, India burst in to the hall with a large khaki duffle bag over her shoulder, beaded dreadlocks cascading. "Mum, Dad – sorry I'm late – stopped to help out at a protest on the way down."
"Darling, were you hurt, what's the wound over your eye?"
"Oh, my stud went septic, but it's clearing up now."
"Darling, you never told me about that, and what's happened to your hair? It looks as though you haven't washed it for months."
"Mum, you know how you fuss and they're dreadlocks."
"Oh, well, come and give us a hug. Welcome home darling! I want to hear all about how you're getting on." Having given a potted summary of her course, her friends and financial status to her parents, India went upstairs to prepare for what she anticipated would be a very successful evening. Her father had naturally promised her additional funds, but then he did every time she came home.

About half an hour after the appointed time guests, not wishing to be first, began to arrive. In a state of nervousness and excited anticipation Isobel spent the time checking on the buffet table (which looked absolutely splendid), sipping the sparkling wine and checking her appearance every five minutes in the vast mirror hanging in the entrance hall. Nigel sat pondering in the huge leather chair in his study, carefully considering his next manoeuvre in securing the necessary permission for Harmony Homes to build on the factory site, upon which he now knew he had clinched a very favourable deal. He had to find a friendly soil analyst, a willing worm. Nigel was disturbed from his reverie as he caught sight of the first guests arriving from his window. He sighed, got up, placed the documents from his desk in the safe, then went to join Isobel in the hall. There was much air kissing, the air was soon laden with expensive, pungent scents, double-barrelled ladies of leisure shrieked in recognition and ostensible delight, husbands and partners shook hands and slapped backs, and Isobel's Bavarian evening had begun. She could now relax as she had the feeling that it was clearly going to be an enormous success. India, wearing an astonishing burnt orange diaphanous affair looked almost exotic, but Isobel did think it was a shame that she wore black leggings and baseball boots underneath. However she was so grateful that her daughter was there that she really couldn't complain.

Nobody noticed that the sparkling wine was not in fact German and the carefully selected scene-setting disks laboriously composed by one of Nigel's eager young IT fellows were very swiftly tossed aside in favour of more transatlantic tunes. These were extracted from a vast selection of CDs in the large drawing room housed in a purpose-built faux Jacobean cabinet with slightly faulty hinges. "She's here somewhere," Isobel responded to yet another enquiry about her daughter, and it occurred to her that India really hadn't been much in evidence for the last hour at least. It was too bad, she really could have made a bit more of an effort.

Drink and food was consumed eagerly as Helena Ruby, Cook and Turtle replenished, circulated and observed. A couple of local girls had agreed to assist in the kitchen (for a fee) and Helena Ruby glanced enviously at the lithe young girl in a very short, tight skirt who was collecting plates and glasses. There she was, Helena Ruby Tremble, wearing over her black skirt and white blouse her token pinny which only served to emphasise her sturdy stature, when who should catch her eye from the hall but Jolyon Urquart. She felt the heat rise in her cheeks and shifted her gaze to the floor, then the table to which she turned, wiping her suddenly clammy hands on her crisp white pinny with exquisitely embroidered edelweiss on the pocket. She started moving dishes on the table and primped the displays as a distraction. As she passed the stuffed bear she noticed it still had the rosebud balanced behind its ear, and that it was also now sporting some sort of medal round its neck. Jolyon sauntered to the dining table, walked up behind Helena Ruby Tremble and spoke into her ear over her shoulder. "The flowers look fine to me. How about a break and a breath of fresh air my dear?" Helena Ruby nearly shed her skin. "I shouldn't, I can't, I've got ......" Jolyon took her by the elbow and steered her firmly through the French doors, across the terrace and behind the pool house, a haven of dark anonymity amongst the glare and twinkle of garden lighting.

"Why didn't you ring me back, I was so pleased to hear from you," he said softly as he held her at arm's length. Jolyon put his hand under Helena Ruby's chin and lifted her bowed head. Her big dark eyes glistened in the gloom.

"I just felt so, so... stupid," she whispered, finally plucking up the courage to look directly into his eyes, "- and the second time I tried, I thought it was your girlfriend answering." Jolyon drew her towards him and kissed her. She closed her eyes, not quite being able to believe that this was happening to her. In fact, she couldn't remember the last time she'd kissed anyone except the dog. Just as Helena Ruby was being transported to a different plane of existence, she was plucked unexpectedly back to reality. A youth in combat gear complete with balaclava and walking backwards hugging the wall, reversed into them, but was clearly as nonplussed as Helena Ruby and Jolyon. "Oh I say, frightfully sorry, didn't expect anyone down here. Don't mind me, bit of night manoeuvres. Carry on," and he slipped away into the darkness, crouching low. Bizarre though this was, having more pressing matters on his mind, Jolyon said, "Yes, let us carry on," undoing Helena Ruby's top buttons and kissing her cleavage. She became helpless as desire took hold of them both. They kissed tenderly, first clinging to each other then running their fingers through each others' hair. They fumbled as they somehow sank to the ground together, but suddenly, Helena Ruby was seized with the desire to laugh helplessly. She couldn't contain herself, it was as if a coiled spring had suddenly been released from its box, everything was glorious, hilarious and she lay with Jolyon in the long grass convulsed with laughter. It was infectious and soon Jolyon was laughing until the tears ran down his cheeks. They lay in the darkness embraced, dishevelled and euphoric. Jolyon was kissing Helena Ruby's neck and she was running her fingers through his hair as the laughter subsided.

The noise of what sounded like breaking glass somewhere outside broke the spell, and Helena Ruby Tremble sat up, mildly alarmed and brought back to the reality of the Bavarian evening, saying "Did you hear that? I really should go back and see what's going on."

"Hear what, oh come back, it's so cosy...."

"I really ought to go and see, I'm meant to be working, but look, thank you, I mean, well, you know, I ..." With a long kiss and the promise to get in touch again very soon they parted unwillingly, hurriedly brushing the grass off their clothes. Having re-assembled each others' appearance as best they could, Helena Ruby returned breathlessly to the house via the kitchen door, smoothing her apron. Jolyon sauntered back through the French doors and into the hall smiling and distracted, and returned to join the bibulous throng, hoping he would catch sight of Helena Ruby returned to her duties.

Cook was sitting with his feet up on the table drinking his own special blend of herbal tea and raised a friendly eyebrow upon Helena Ruby's return. She grinned expansively at him. "Just taking the weight off, as, I suppose you have been Mrs T?"

"Er yes, needed some fresh air, you know..." Not very convincing. "But I heard a noise, sounded like it came from the front, glass breaking. Has anybody been to see?

"Probably the girls throwing out some bottles, I'm sure it's nothing, blimey they've got enough security equipment and I assume Ron is in charge. You've er, got a daisy in the back of your hair by the way."

Turtle meanwhile was nowhere to be found, for, wearing an SAS officer's cap acquired many years previously, he was by the garages plying Ron with a cocktail of remainders and regaling him with tales of the war. Having bedecked the bear with the iron cross, Turtle had also half buried his hand grenade in the dish of pot pourri in the main cloakroom, and wondered whether it had yet been noticed. Ron meanwhile, not an experienced bon viveur, was becoming reckless and incoherent, cynically encouraged by Turtle who really had no time for the man.

Cook and Helena Ruby were checking on the sweets and replenishing the drinks table, and as might be imagined, Helena Ruby was not really paying attention to the Black Forest gateau and apple strudel trodden into the rug, and somehow adorning an elaborate candle-stick. She did however find the sight of half a frankfurter pushed between the bear's teeth highly amusing.

Isobel glanced past several guests at her reflection in the hall mirror, then made her way to the kitchen in search of ice-cubes. She was surprised to find that the girls she had hired were nowhere to be seen, and the kitchen strewn with debris. However, she was too busy socialising and just made a mental note not to employ them again. Mrs Tremble and

Cook could cope. She walked back towards the large drawing room carrying the replenished ice bucket. Looking again rather more closely in the mirror on the way back, seeing that her eye make-up was looking a little tired, she made a detour to the cloakroom in order to effect some repairs. She handed the ice bucket to Cook, who was on his way back to the kitchen and said, "You couldn't just take that through to the drinks table could you? Oh, and have you seen those two girls, the kitchen's in an awful state."

"Can do, and they were there half an hour ago. I suspect they might have gone outside for a smoke, it's what girls of that age do."

"Maybe, but I shall have to speak to them about it, I mean, what are we paying them for?" With that, Isobel lurched very slightly into the cloakroom, bolted the door and exhaling heavily, flopped inelegantly onto the closed lavatory seat. Her pointed lizard-skin boots were squeezing her feet terribly and it was such a relief to take the pressure off. As she sat massaging her temples, she caught sight of the hand grenade in the pot pourri dish and muttered "What's that doing ...." Isobel quickly tidied up her eye make-up, ran her fingers through her hair to restore a little more body, then even with her feet throbbing, went hurriedly in search of Nigel. He was eventually to be found in the conservatory, deep in conversation with Vernon Starling, an unpopular local figure who owned a vast cement works on the outskirts of Great Roach. Mr Starling was currently embroiled in major confrontation with councillors ('petty officialdom') and neighbours ('whingers, all of them') over his plans to excavate a gravel pit. He was an undeniably unpleasant character, but it seemed he might be able to put Nigel in touch with the willing worm he sought.

"Darling I ..."

"Give me five minutes Izzy, this is important business!"

"But darling, there's something you must see now, really!"

"Can't it wait? Nobody's dying are they?" Vernon was enjoying all this hugely and chimed in, "Found an unexploded bomb in the garden?" Isobel ignored the dreadful man and just said, "Nigel, pleeease."

"Oh OK, Vernon excuse me, pour another scotch and I'll be back."

"So what the bloody hell is so important then?" Nigel asked Isobel testily.

"There's something you should see in the cloakroom."

"What, a severed limb, a leaking pipe?" Isobel and Nigel got to the cloakroom only to find it occupied. Isobel became agitated and just as she was about to try to describe to Nigel the source of her concern, Miles Kent-Burrowes emerged, slightly bemused at the welcoming committee the other side of the door and holding the offending bowl in his hand.

"I say, latest sort of air freshener old thing?" he asked.

"Bloody hell, how did that get there?"

"Don't worry old boy, as far as I can tell it's harmless, used to be in the bomb squad y'know. German. See? You can tell from the maker's name round the top. Not seen one of those for years. Where did you find it?" Nigel really wished he would keep his voice down.

"I, I really don't know, someone's idea of a joke I guess," stuttered Nigel. His mouth had suddenly gone dry and he had a very uneasy feeling.

"Bloody clever to find that Iron Cross too, what a laugh old boy! No detail left out. Good party old chap, bloody good."

Nigel might have guessed where he would find this particular offending article, and was not disappointed. He angrily pulled the frankfurter from the bear's jaws, which was accompanied by several teeth, then roughly removed the Iron Cross, ignoring Isobel's plea that that he be more careful with her uncle's bear, as a result of which one of its ears became detached. Isobel disconsolately bent down and picked up a couple of teeth and the ear and for want of anywhere better to put them, dropped them into the cutlery drawer of the sideboard amongst the fish knives. Nigel dropped the medal into his pocket and wondered just who had been responsible for this. He would examine it more closely later in the privacy of his study. Luckily the guests were unaware of Nigel's discomfiture and he continued as if nothing had happened. Well, what had happened? Nothing. Some joker had bunged a grenade in the pot-pourri and given that bloody bear a German medal. That was all. But still he was uneasy. Isobel threw herself back into the party with renewed vigour, determined not to let Nigel's behaviour spoil her evening. It was not Nigel's behaviour about which Isobel should really have been concerning herself.

Whilst the merriment continued, India had slipped upstairs, removed her eye-catching outfit and donned black top, combat trousers and gloves, and a black knitted hat into which, with difficulty, she stuffed her dreadlocks. She ran down the back stairs which usefully, led to the old washhouse where she met several eager accomplices from university together with Perpetua Tenby and Lucy Farlow-Pitt (the kitchen absentees). Two of the lads were sporting balaclavas, although they were finding them a little on the warm side, and Perpetua, giggling, suggested they try stockings instead. Terence told India of an encounter with an amorous middle-aged couple behind the pool-house, but that they didn't seem to take much notice of him and he had mentioned night manoeuvres, so he thought it was OK. Muffled laughter rose through a grate near the garages, but the occupants above ground were by this time a little too inebriate to notice, or care. India had managed earlier in the evening to remove the fuse controlling the security floodlights which were thankfully, clearly labelled. She had, in a moment of panic when her father unexpectedly emerged from his study, dropped it into a huge pot standing in a corner of the entrance hall containing a palm. She couldn't risk being found with that in her possession. "Hello darling, enjoying the party?"

"Ooh, er, yes, it's great, thanks. I, er, just found some rubbish in the pot, I'll put it in the bin, must go to the loo...." Nigel was sufficiently distracted by general events not really to notice just how very insincere his daughter's explanation of loitering by the potted palm was. There was no way in which that fuse would ever be located.

Terence had retrieved the holdall secreted last week in the shrubbery by the studded youth, and within the old wash-house the assembled conspirators, all now wearing their gloves, began sharing out the contents. There were paint sprays, screwdrivers, knives, a canister of fake blood, spray-glue, cans of expanding foam and torches. Walking quietly with this array of equipment jammed into pockets and pouches was not going to be easy. "OK, this is it gang, keep it as quiet as you possibly can and at the first sign of trouble, scarper. You two, if you can't make it back up to my room there's a rendezvous at Paddy's parents' place, it's just down the road past the post box, and they're on holiday, right?" She turned to Paddy Figglestarch for confirmation. "Yep, the old folks are in Mustique for a month so I'm in charge. I've stuck a ski stick with a bottle on it by the side entrance. The alarm's not on and you can get in through the pool house, but pleeeease take your shoes off!"

"OK, great, so are we all ready then? (gloved thumbs up) Brilliant! Tally ho!"

The motley crew slunk around the front of the house and did not in fact need their torches as the moon produced sufficient illumination for their task, which was a relief as it now left both hands free. Cars known to belong to Roger Whittingly-Beargarden and his cohorts were identified by India with a sprayed red cross on the bonnet. The others circulated amongst the gleaming vehicles and as carefully as they could, sliced tyres, sprayed expanding foam into exhaust pipes and sprayed glue onto windows followed by handfuls of dirt, grass and leaves (akin to Easter card construction so beloved of infant schools, minus the cotton-wool Easter chick). Perpetua spelled out 'CARNAGE IN THE COUNTRYSIDE' in fake blood across the bonnet of Mr Whittingly-Beargarden's Bentley while Lucy etched some interesting designs in the paintwork of the door with a screwdriver. Terence, not blessed with verbal dexterity, scratched along the side of Purvis Mallard's black four-wheel-drive country pursuits 'Thermonuclear Terminator' the words 'SKUM WAGGON' and sprayed expanding foam into both exhaust pipes, then with a spray-can of blue paint wrote 'BASTED' across the back. He had some difficulty piercing the tyres so contented himself with just a front one then moved on to help India throw grit and grass onto a huge silver BMW, which she had prepared earlier.

Whilst spraying 'ASSHOLE' on the roof of a low sporty number, Perpetua overstretched herself, lost her balance and fell through the fabric roof which gave way with a curiously satisfying rending noise. Whatever satisfaction there was to be had from this was instantaneously dispelled as the car alarm started in deafening fashion and the game was up. "Shit, scarper!" called India in a loud, hoarse whisper. As she was retrieving Perpetua from her sprawl across the car, the front door was thrown open and light from the hall spilled out onto the steps, closely followed by agitated guests wondering if it was their vehicle registering distress.

Nigel was amongst their number and was struck almost speechless as his eyes adjusted to register the enormity of what lay before them. "What the ....." he mouthed, but was elbowed aside by Roger Whittingly-Beargarden yelling customary abuse and demanding to know why someone didn't switch the bloody lights on. Mr Whittingly-Beargarden caught sight of a retreating shadowy figure behind a large shrub by the steps, leapt upon them from there and a brief scuffle ensued. He was rather winded by this manoeuvre and not a little unsteady on his feet anyway, and when the terrorist in the bushes grabbed him by the hair, he fell forward as his hair-piece parted company with his scalp. It was flung into full view of everybody now emerging from the front doors, squawking and hollering, and Roger Whittingly-Beargarden's intended victim managed, in the surrounding inebriated chaos and patchy darkness, to make a panic-stricken escape while barely stifled giggles started breaking out from some spectators on the steps. India and the two girls had managed to run back around the side of the house unseen, thence into the wash-room, where doubled up and gasping, they gradually got their breath back.

"Christ .. that .. was close," whispered India. "Better .... get back ..... upstairs and .... change bloody fast." With leaden legs, the girls returned up the stairs as fast as they were able and once in the safety of India's neo-gothic room, rapidly changed back into their earlier attire, washed in her en-suite bathroom, brushed their hair, tried to stop trembling, then put all incriminating evidence into a black plastic sack which would be secreted in the bins amongst the rest of the party debris. The two girls managed to get down the main stairs unnoticed and hurried to the kitchen which, thankfully, was empty as everybody was by now observing the fracas at the front. They started clearing and cleaning with a vengeance. It helped steady their nerves.

Meanwhile, uproar ensued amongst the topiary and gravel as aggrieved guests discovered their vandalised vehicles, and more voices were raised demanding that somebody turn some bloody lights on. Helena Ruby ventured out, and buoyed up by her recent amorous encounter, upon seeing Roger Whittingly-Beargarden's vandalised car, laughing, said, "Never mind, a quick trip to the carwash will soon put that right, squire!" Nigel, by now in a state of rage and frustration, had just discovered the reason for the non-functioning of the floodlights and was cursing Turtle for not being around to address the problem, although he had a dreadful uneasy feeling about Turtle's role in all this.

Taking advantage of the uproar, Jolyon had sought out Helena Ruby whom he saw in magnificent moonlit silhouette standing to the edge of the top step beside a pillar. He was eager to continue with their liaison. He sidled up to her and she jumped slightly as he slipped his arm through hers, but did not hesitate to follow him as he suggested. It felt as though all her internal organs were fluttering. Everybody's attention was focused on the scene of the crime and they slipped back into the hall and dived into the cloakroom, being the nearest bolt-hole (with a bolt). Jolyon leant against the secured door and pulled Helena Ruby to him, and kissed her tenderly. There was something about her that he simply could not resist. Helena Ruby felt light-headed yet on fire inside, and slid her arms around Jolyon inside his jacket and then, overcome with a fierce desire which had started coursing through her veins, was fumbling for the fastening of his trousers. Jolyon's braces momentarily foiled her efforts so she slid her hand inside his zip and was not disappointed. Within the limited space among the gold-plated accessories and between passionate bouts of grappling, they managed to remove each other's clothes and there, in the downstairs cloakroom of Hake Hall, made love against the door, Jolyon's buttocks slapping against the carved wood and Helena Ruby standing on tip toe.

Isobel, as might be imagined, was in a terrible state of nervous agitation and her voice rose almost to squeaking pitch as she tried to make sense of what was going on. She would never be able to hold another party after this. Having returned indoors, not knowing what to say to her guests, she glanced up the stairs and saw India descending and demanded to know where she'd been, and did she know what was going on outside?

"Oh dear, no, sorry Mum, I've been laying down in my room, I got a terrible headache," (she clasped her palm to her forehead better to illustrate her malaise). "I don't think my piercing is healing as fast as it should... So what's happening?"

"Oh it's just awful, ghastly..." Isobel's voice began to falter as tears sprang to her eyes. "Some mindless thugs have vandalised the cars outside, it's .... I ... oh this is *dreadful* ..." and Isobel sat on the bottom stair and started to cry. India sat beside her and put her arm around her shoulders.

"Oh mum, that's awful, don't cry, but why..... I mean, who...?" Isobel looked up at India with smudged black, bloodshot eyes. She dabbed her nose with a napkin she was still holding. "Your father says it's an anti-hunt lot . Oh but why would they pick on us? What have we ever done?" India began to feel decidedly uncomfortable, but was soon distracted as Roger Whittingly-Beargarden came blundering in through the front door, hairpiece slightly askance, very red in the face, demanding that somebody call the bloody police immediately. Isobel started to cry again. Nigel followed behind and suggested they go to his study, where he would call the police as requested. He suggested to Isobel that she go upstairs and 'freshen up'. India felt she should go with her, hoping to get the opportunity to check her room, and left the men to it. She should have guessed that the police would become involved and just prayed that the girls had already put the incriminating sack in the bins.

Breathless and blissful, Helena Ruby and Jolyon clung together, Helena Ruby listening to Jolyon's now steady heartbeat with her head resting against his chest. Jolyon whispered, "I think we need to formulate some sort of exit strategy my dear, don't you?" Helena wanted to stay there like that forever but could see it was not a practical proposition.

"Clothes first my dear?" Helena Ruby had not really been aware of her nakedness until Jolyon prised her away from him and she suddenly became terribly self conscious, and was aware of a distressing amount of wobbling as she scrabbled around on the floor seeking out her bra and knickers. Her mood plummeted from euphoria to self-loathing and Jolyon, sensing her distress, placed a warm, reassuring hand gently on her back as she leant down to pick up her blouse and whispered, "You are a lovely woman you know, you have nothing to be ashamed of my dear." Tears sprang up in Helena Ruby's eyes. She felt so foolish. When she stood up, Jolyon kissed her gently and wiped away her tears with his thumbs. "Enough of that my dear, couldn't help me with my braces could you?" They smiled at each other, Helena Ruby not daring to trust her emotions, just as a bit of a commotion erupted in the hall upon the arrival of the police. "Oh dear, this is going to take some careful manoeuvring," observed Jolyon. Helena Ruby smoothed her hair as best she could in front of the mirror, splashed her face with cold water while Jolyon stood behind her with his arms around her waist, then patted it dry with a towel. She would go out first and Jolyon would exit five minutes or so later. One last kiss, and Helena Ruby Tremble took a very deep breath and made her exit from the cloakroom, trying to look as nonchalant as possible, but not really trusting her legs to convey her in a straight line. However they did, so she made straight for the kitchen as she couldn't think where else to go, in fact she couldn't string together one coherent thought. Helena Ruby was not aware of it, but her eyes were sparkling. All she wanted was to go back to Jolyon but knew for the present that she could not, and it was agony for her to know that he was so near.

Two young policeman pulled up in the drive and were barely out of the car before Roger Whittingly-Beargarden confronted them.

"I was expecting someone a bit more experienced than this, what's happened to Inspector Struthers?" he barked.

"Inspector Struthers was retired on health grounds, sir."

"He was bloody alright at our last lodge meeting."

"That's as may be sir, however he is no longer in uniform. Now did anybody see or hear anything?....." With that, the police constable took out his notepad while surveying the scene before him. He was not at liberty to divulge the reason for Inspector Struthers' absence, however it would be true to say that he had rather forfeited his pension rights and was facing enforced retirement in penury after a spell behind bars.

The realisation dawned upon Nigel that this was the self-same constable with whom he had had the encounter in his Jensen. "Hello again sir, this is a bit of a mess isn't it?" Nigel overcame the desire to congratulate him on his observance of the bloody obvious as he had not actually got round to taxing his car yet. In the background guests could be heard on their mobile 'phones furiously trying to arrange for taxis, or pleading with unwilling offspring, some because their method of transport had been well and truly disabled, and most being over the limit and recognising the folly of attempting to drive in the presence of police officers. They all faced a long wait.

Inside Hake Hall Cook sauntered into the kitchen from the large sitting room where, in the sudden absence of guests, he had taken the opportunity to sit down in comfort and sip a crisp, refreshing Entre Deux Mers. He just had a feeling that the girls knew something about what was going on. They had been missing for a very long time, and he had caught sight of them coming downstairs in a hurry earlier, but it was not for him to become embroiled and he had very little sympathy for the wronged parties anyway. The kitchen was at least clear now, so they had done their job as far as he was concerned. Perpetua and Lucy had gone to bring through more dishes from the dining room but were currently steadying their nerves with a stiff vodka and tonic in the morning room. "Oh, shit," exclaimed Lucy "we've left the bloody bag upstairs and now the police are here. What if they search the place?"

"Aaah, yes, oh crikey, we'll have to get it out down the back somehow," replied Perpetua, putting her damp glass down on a hideous marquetry-topped table depicting a hunting scene. The stag at bay would henceforth have a white halo. "They'd only search the place if someone had been murdered or something wouldn't they?"

"Don't know, but you know what it's like around here..." Lucy trailed off as Helena Ruby came in and said, "Come on girls, what are you two up to? There's still a lot to clear from the dining room and could one of you go round collecting glasses, oh, and don't forget the conservatory."

"Sorry, er, yes, we were just taking a break..." said Lucy as evenly as she could, hoping that none of their recent conversation had been overheard. Helena Ruby would not have cared, she was borne along in a euphoric bubble through which everything was rendered wonderful. She did not care about the dessert trodden into the rug, nor the red wine stains on the drapes. It appeared somebody had mistaken the magazine rack for a bin and that would need a thorough cleaning out, but she didn't care. She did feel a momentary twinge of sympathy for the bear which, in addition to its missing teeth and ear, had had a cocktail stick complete with olive pushed into its posterior, but she just laughed and went back to the kitchen with several plates full of remains. It was necessary for her to occupy herself and focus.

"Not a very auspicious end to the evening wouldn't you say Mrs T?" said Cook, grinning broadly as he registered her sparkling eyes and clearly altered demeanour, despite her best efforts to appear normal. Cook was an astute observer of human behaviour and, bearing in mind she did have a daisy in her hair earlier, had a pretty shrewd idea of how Helena Ruby Tremble's evening may have developed. Who would have thought it?

"Er no, bit of a mess. Where was Ron though? The idiot was meant to be looking after the parking. Sorry Mrs T, no disrespect, but Mr & Mrs L-K will be furious." The very mention of Ron caused a dark cloud to materialise on her hitherto sunny horizon, and with good reason.

Even in his inebriate state, Ron had repaired hastily to the scene upon hearing the car alarm, for it had been his responsibility to oversee guests' cars, but after being harangued at length for his inattention by Isobel and Nigel, he stalked off to the garages in black humour and plotted his revenge. After a while, fired up with more alcohol, towering indignation and Turtle's encouragement, wearing the SS officer's cap, Ron got into Isobel's BMW, for he had the keys. After some wrenching and swearing, having managed to engage the automatic gearbox in forward mode, Ron uncertainly drove the thing at alarming speed, lurching past the squawking throng and spraying the police officers taking notes with gravel. He was unable to find the brake and the vehicle glanced off the rear of the patrol car pulled up on the drive, then careered around the side of the house, across the velvet lawn, over the terrace and thence into the swimming pool. It began to dawn upon Ron just what a reckless manoeuvre this had been as he watched the blue pool water rise across the car windows. He really wasn't feeling very well.

Chapter Nine

Helena Ruby Tremble hastily pressed the contents of her wardrobe into two careworn carry-alls, then went into the bathroom to remove her few toiletries. She had written, after four attempts, an explanatory note to Ron regarding her departure:

'I think you'll agree that our life together is not happy. I don't know what you expect out of it, but I would like some happiness before I'm too old to care and I miss the girls so much, I can't describe it. I don't know what makes you happy, we don't communicate, I don't know what you really feel but I have come to the stage where I need to make something of the life I have left.

I am so sorry for messing things up for you, but like I said, I have some life left and I want to live it. Maybe this is what you want, I really don't know.

Forgive me

Ron would find this on the kitchen table upon his return from hospital, having been questioned by the local constabulary before his release. The timing was appalling, but Helena Ruby had made up her mind.

At Hake Hall, Isobel and Nigel sat disconsolately at the kitchen table breathing into their steaming coffee, not sure whether they felt worse because of the previous night's over-indulgence or because of the effrontery of some narrow-minded anti-hunt campaigners who had landed them in a very unpleasant situation. Roger Whittingly-Beargarden had left the previous evening's proceedings in bellicose mood threatening legal action and worse besides. Isobel was hurt beyond words by the fickleness of some of their guests and their readiness to take sides, but then she always had been naïve. Nigel was furious with Turtle for having left them in such a manner and was also mildly unsettled by his hitherto undisclosed German connections. It was probably not possible to reinstate the BMW after its immersion, but that was the least of their concerns currently. It would, however, prove a major additional headache for Ron as Nigel was all ready in no uncertain terms to terminate his employment. "He can't be trusted, and I've never particularly liked the man," seethed Nigel. "I hold him personally responsible for this bloody mess. If he'd been doing his job instead of getting pissed...."

"But Mrs T is invaluable darling, we can't let her go."

"Gross dereliction of duty, that man is a bloody menace - can't think what the woman sees in him."

The front door bell clanged before they had the opportunity to pursue the conversation further. Isobel rose from her chair and walked gingerly to the hall. She didn't even check her appearance in the mirror on this occasion. Several recovery trucks were pulled up on the drive and there was no mistaking a distinct smirk on the face of the overalled man standing at the door. "Hullo love, we've been asked to come and remove the, er, damage. Blimey, this is going to cost someone's insurance. Party get out of hand did it?" The smirk had now developed into a full-blown grin as he took off his baseball cap and scratched his shaven head with oily fingers. "It was particularly nasty, criminal vandalism," snapped Isobel. "Whatever, we'll take this lot off your drive." With that, he turned and went down the steps and yelled to his colleagues, "OK guys, let's shift this lot of shit!" Isobel watched in dismay as several of the trucks manoeuvred on the lawn, flattening her shrubs, then saw a police car pull up. She was particularly wounded to see ill-disguised amusement on the part of the constable during his brief exchange with one of the truck drivers. The constable who had been in attendance only the night before assumed a rather more sober visage as he came up the steps, and Isobel viewed him through narrowed eyes. "Found the culprits yet?" she said with no small amount of sarcasm.

"Er, no madam, I actually wanted to talk to you about Ronald Arthur Tremble whom I believe is in your employ."

"Not for much longer if Nigel has his way," said Isobel. "I suppose you'd better come through, my husband's in the kitchen."

"Oh, it's you again," said Nigel as he looked up to see Constable Berwick being shown into the kitchen by Isobel.

"Yes sir, it's just the way our shifts work, nothing personal."

"Oh good, I was beginning to wonder whether you'd been personally assigned." Constable Berwick chose to ignore the tone of Nigel's remark and asked him whether he intended to pursue any charges against Ronald Arthur Tremble for the criminal damage occasioned by his drive to the swimming pool. "There's probably no point, he'll only get five minutes' community service, the man's an idiot and I doubt he's got the money to pay any fine. He's not going to have a job for much longer unless of course I haven't issued him with sufficient written warnings or offered him counselling," retorted Nigel.

"Won't be pressing charges," Constable Berwick mouthed as he duly entered it in his notebook. Looking up, he continued, "And do you have any reason to believe that Mr Tremble may in any way have been connected with the criminal activity which took place last night?"

"What, other than driving my wife's bloody car into my swimming pool?"

"Darling, please," interjected Isobel. "The constable is only doing his job."

"Er, as I said, the man's an idiot, I think he must have a drink problem and he's very soon going to have an unemployment problem too. No, in answer to your question, I don't think he has the wit to organise anything like that and I have in the past loaned him out to the Leek over Partridge hunt and he never objected. Still, that game's all over now too isn't it?" Constable Berwick declined to opine, for his colleagues were currently investigating Mr Whittingly-Beargarden and his own particular style of countryside pursuits.

India waited upstairs until she saw the police car leave then came down and sauntered into the kitchen, and on seeing her parents said, "Hi you two, how are you feeling this morning? Pretty awful I suppose. What a night!"

"Bloody awful, sweet of you to ask," sighed Nigel.

"I, ah, was thinking of going back to uni later today if you don't mind. It's just that one of my mates can pick me up," said India as she attempted to extract a cup of coffee from the multi-function stainless steel coffee maker. "Er how do you just get an ordinary coffee out of this - don't s'pose you've got any fair trade stuff have you Mum?"

"No darling, here let me help you, and can't you stay a bit longer, we've hardly seen you?"

"Look Mum, I'd only get in your way and all my friends are at uni. Hey, all this will blow over. Blimey, Grandma Olberspitz survived far worse than this, come on, you know you can manage."

"Yes, but she had ..... oh never mind," finished Isobel, knowing that she was not going to persuade her only daughter to stay any longer. Nigel, who had wandered outside to do some thinking and only to discover the swimming pool virtually empty, came storming in through the back door. "OK, that bloody man has done it, he's not getting any more employment within a twenty mile radius of this place, within this bloody county," he fumed.

"Oh darling, what's wrong now?" asked Isobel, not really wanting to know.

"His underwater stunt in your car is what's bloody wrong now."

"Don't yell darling, calm down."

"I feel like bloody yelling and I can't calm down. He's wrecked the sodding swimming pool. Maybe I will press charges, or maybe I'll just commit murder instead - far more satisfying. And what the bloody hell are all those bloody tyre marks on the front lawn? Looks like the bloody Somme." Isobel started to cry. She hated it when Nigel became angry and felt in no state to cope with anything much this morning. Nigel stalked off to his study, slamming the kitchen door behind him. "Oh don't cry Mum, you know what he's like when he gets wound up. Here, let me get you some more coffee, or wouldn't you like tea instead?"

Having put her luggage, the dog, the dog's bed and one or two favourite bits of ornamentation in the car, Helena Ruby Tremble had been most anxious to leave swiftly that morning prior to Ron's return. She had wondered whether she should have accompanied him to hospital, but he had been so inebriate, he probably wouldn't have noticed, wouldn't have appreciated it anyway, and she couldn't put off her escape any longer. She knew she would have to encounter him some time, but that was a bridge to be crossed at another time.

Just as she had shut the back door of the Lodge and dropped the keys in her pocket as she always did, Helena Ruby Tremble froze as she heard the sound of a car pulling up to the front of the house. Her heart started pounding. Why did life contrive to arrange things so? If only she had left her mother's vase and that floristry book, she would have been away by now. She edged her way towards the front of the house, commando-style, keeping close against the wall, and beheld Ronald Arthur Tremble being returned to the Lodge in a police car. To compound matters, Denholm started barking from within the safe confines of Helena Ruby's car, and for the first time in her life, Helena Ruby would happily have strangled him. "Oh bloody hell, no," she cursed under her breath.

"We will be talking to Mr and Mrs Lamington-Krill," she overheard the policewoman say to Ron, "and you may be hearing further if they wish to press charges. Good morning Mr Tremble."

"Yeah," was his only response, then he turned to Helena Ruby's car and yelled spitefully, "Shut up you stupid little bugger." Helena was transfixed in panic, as Ron let himself in through the front door, this time shouting, "Anybody bloody home? I've had a bloody awful night. Where are you?" The police car seemed to take forever to manoeuvre out of the drive, the policewoman glancing at the still excited occupant of Helena Ruby's car as she finally drove off. "Oh just *go, please*," she whispered, desperate to get to her car and away. Ron would find the note any second now and she couldn't be there. As soon as the police car was out of sight, Helena Ruby made a run for her car, but jabbed her knee painfully on a bracket protruding from the corner of the wall. She gasped but continued to hobble at speed, blood running down her leg. The pain was beginning to balloon and she felt slightly sick, as with sweating and trembling hand she opened the door, and with an involuntary cry of pain, got in to the driver's seat. "Denholm shut UP," she said through gritted teeth as she started the car. It was difficult to concentrate on driving, but adrenaline was coursing through her veins by now and gripping the steering wheel fiercely, Helena Ruby took off at speed, heading for the promise of a new beginning at The Bullrushes. Had she been inclined to look in her rear view mirror, she would have caught sight of Ron standing open-mouthed in the front door with her note in his hand.

The momentous nature of her exit began to dawn on Helena Ruby Tremble and tears started to prick her eyes. She had to pull in to a bus-stop as her vision began to blur, then broke down in great sobs, rocking in her seat and clutching her now excruciatingly painful knee while Denholm attempted to lick his mistress better. "Oh Denholm, what am I doing?" she whispered as her tears plopped on to his head. She pulled a tissue from her pocket, took a very deep breath, blew her nose, and looked in dismay at her blotchy visage in the mirror. "Helena Ruby stop being so stupid," she said sternly to her reflection, "just look at the state of you." She dabbed her eyes, ran her fingers through her hair, sat Denzil firmly back on the passenger seat and bent down to look at her knee. At least it had stopped bleeding, but it was still throbbing painfully and looked quite swollen. "I hope Cook has some frozen peas," she said to Denholm, whose tail was wagging furiously.

Helena Ruby arrived at number fourteen, The Bullrushes and was rather hesitant about getting out of the car. She felt awkward. "You must promise to behave," she said to the dog who was now agitating to get out of the car, sensing they had reached their destination. She pushed open the door and got gingerly out of her seat, taking the weight on her undamaged leg and then straightening her back. She was moving like a geriatric patient. "What *have* you been doing?" came Cook's familiar voice from behind her.

"Oh, er, hello, oh this is *so* silly of me, but I've bashed my knee and I think I need to clean it up. It was during my getaway, you might say," she added, smiling for the first time as she turned to face Cook. "Well let's get you in and have a look at it. Welcome to my modest home!" Denholm was not entirely sure about getting out of the car now, but Helena Ruby picked him up and said, "Can I introduce you to Denholm, I've told him he's got to behave. I'm sorry, this is awful of me, but I've only ever known you as Cook, and please, call me Helena." Cook's laugh boomed out as he clasped Helena Ruby's hand and said, "You can call me Denzil , for that is my name!" At the sound of laughter, the dog was now relaxing, and was very glad to be away from the sight, scent and feel of Ron's antipathy, for his recent statement in the bedroom had not gone unacknowledged. He started wagging his tail vigorously.

At Hake Lodge Ron was rapidly becoming acquainted with Nigel's antipathy. "Have you any idea of the trouble you've caused us, not to mention the damage you've done to our property?"

"Er, yeah."

"Is that all you've got to say man, bearing in mind the police wanted to know whether I intend to press charges?"

"Um, yeah."

"Well you might not be surprised to learn that you've lost your job."

"Oh christ," said Ron, dropping on to the kitchen chair, running his hand over his thinning hair.

"I was all for kicking you out, but Isobel is particularly keen for Mrs Tremble to continue with her employment, so I suppose you'll have to sort it out with her, but believe me, I don't want you anywhere near Hake Hall again. Is that clear?"

"She's left me," said Ron flatly, staring straight ahead, " What am I going to do now?" This rather took Nigel aback. He was momentarily angry with Mrs Tremble for having placed him in this awkward position, but then in some respects it made everything so much more clear cut.

"Ah .... I see. Well hard luck, but you're still looking for another job, and, well, I suppose you'd better start looking for somewhere else to live then, under the circumstances. Good day." Then Nigel Lamington-Krill turned on his heel and left through the front door.

"Bastard," muttered Ron, banging his fist on the table. He started to cry uncontrollably. So this was what it felt like to be kicked as he lay helpless in the mire. He picked up a jar of marmalade left on the table and hurled it in fury against the wall. It smashed then plopped onto the side, the marmalade sticking to the broken glass. Ron walked out of the kitchen and left it, wiping his eyes with the back of his hand, then flopped into his armchair in the sitting room and pressed on the television remote control. A pearly-toothed presenter was introducing 'Vegetarian Cooking for Your Pets' on the first channel, but luckily racing from Cheltenham was on another and he sat gazing at the screen, temporarily removed from his predicament. Ronald Arthur Tremble awoke in his chair some two hours later. He was almost unable to move with a stiff neck where he had been sleeping with his head to one side, exacerbating the minor injury sustained during his drive into the pool. "Aaah, bloody hell!" he shouted. Then he thought that Helena Ruby should be back to get lunch as he was very hungry, but awful reality settled upon him and he repeated quietly "Oh bloody hell," and bowed his head stiffly into his hands. Had he been paying attention to the television, he would have heard the lunch-time business news presenter refer briefly to questions over the European business dealings of Lamington-Krill International.

Chapter Ten

Nigel arrived at his office much earlier than usual on Monday. He was in a bad mood as he had received several urgent e-mail messages to his private address from his financial director and the chief executive. They were being asked awkward questions by officials from the Department of Trade and Industry and felt an urgent meeting was indicated. He had sent a curt e-mail to Alisha at the office instructing her to set it up, forgetting that she was taking two weeks' holiday. Thus he was momentarily taken aback when he strode up to her desk and found an impostor sitting in her seat. "Who the bloody hell are you?"

"I'm filling in for your PA while she's on holiday sir, I'm Amy Creswell, pleased to meet you."

"Can you spell? Last time the agency sent a complete bloody bird-brain."

"My English is excellent, I am computer literate and I can type at seventy-five words per minute sir," she responded sweetly, thinking to herself that this one deserved everything that was coming his way.

"Yes well we'll see. I wanted a meeting set up today with a couple of my directors, can you manage that?"

"I noticed your e-mail this morning sir and have sent messages to the gentlemen concerned, I found their details on the system. I hope that was alright?"

"Just let me know as soon as they respond, and *please* stop calling me sir."

"OK - Mr Lamington-Krill."

"Oh and you might go and get my car taxed before the bloody police are after me for that," said Nigel as he dropped the necessary documents on the desk. "I'll have coffee when you're ready." Nigel went into his office and slammed the door behind him. He went straight to his desk and rang Fritz, only to be told he would not be in until later. "Damn!" said Nigel as he put the phone down. He was beginning to feel very uneasy about the way things were going. He jumped when the intercom buzzed, and snapped "Yes?"

"Just to confirm that Mr Fallowburton and Mr Carmichael will see you in the meeting room at 11.30 this morning, and I have a gentleman by the name of Hockley on the telephone, he says it's to do with bullrushes."

"Oh bloody hell not him again. Look, tell him I'll ring him back this afternoon, I've got an important meeting I need to prepare for this morning." The intercom buzzed again.

"No more calls," barked Nigel.

"But, er, Mr Hockley is most insistent and says it really is urgent that he speak to you, to do with the planning authority....." said Amy hesitantly.

"No, he'll have to wait." Nigel sat back in his chair rubbing his temples. Amy made discreet notes of names and times. She also sent a brief e-mail saying 'Check out Hockley, director of co. resp for Bullrushes devpt in Hake - planning authority connections.'

Messrs Fallowburton and Carmichael arrived, nodded an acknowledgement to Amy then walked into the meeting room which led off the reception area, where Amy provided coffee for them, having alerted Nigel to their arrival. She noticed that they were both wearing strident aftershave and knitted brows. Hugh Fallowburton was short and stocky and wore large tortoiseshell-framed glasses which had a tendency to migrate down the bridge of his broad nose. Beads of sweat glistened on his forehead and Amy thought he probably dyed his hair which seemed unnaturally black. Somehow he just didn't look like a financial director, even in a pinstripe suit. Louis Carmichael on the other hand looked every inch the chief executive being tall and slim with his distinguished grey, slightly receding hair. As if to counterbalance his colleague's appearance, he wore a pale grey suit and sported a pair of gold-rimmed half-moon reading spectacles which sat well on his aquiline nose and gave him a sagacious air.

Although Amy was unable to distinguish the exact detail of the conversation in the meeting room, there were raised voices and it was clear that all was not well in the upper echelons of Lamington-Krill International. After an hour or so the protagonists emerged, ties loosened and brows still knitted, aftershave just a little stale by now. Nigel held a slim file in his hand and as they parted company, said, "Do nothing until I've managed to speak to Fritz and find out what's happening on his side. I'll buzz you as soon as I know any more." As he walked past Amy's desk he said, "More coffee please, and after that I don't want to be disturbed, not for anything OK?"

"OK Mr Lamington-Krill, I'll be in with the coffee right away." As Amy stood by the replenished coffee machine waiting for the jug to fill, she saw from the window a familiar pinstripe-suited figure walk briskly across the road with a briefcase, and hail a taxi. She moved swiftly to her desk and e-mailed 'Fin Dir doing susp runner, poss taxi airpt,' then returned to the coffee machine in order to take Nigel's requested refreshment to him. She knocked on his door then went in to find him sitting once again at his desk with his head in his hands, but this time looking down at the slim file open on his desk. She could only get a glimpse as she put the coffee on his desk and all she could see was three columns of figures, some of which had been highlighted. "Thanks," he said without looking up. "No calls or visitors."

"OK," said Amy and left his office. When the door had closed Nigel rang the Fischbacher Korporation again, and much to his relief, managed to speak to Fritz this time. His relief however was short-lived. "Where have you been? Things are getting a bit sticky this end, I need to know if our funds are securely out of sight and I think we should freeze all transfers for the time being at least." Things, it transpired, were even stickier for Fritz who had been comprehensively quizzed by the German financial authorities only that morning, hence his absence from his desk. "Oh shit," said Nigel "how much do they know?"

"They have been in contact with the European Commission regarding regeneration grants and they want documentary proof from us."

"Oh we can produce something convincing, that's no big deal."

"I don't believe you are aware of the nature of the body with whom we are dealing. Forgery is not an option my friend."

"Oh christ, this could turn nasty. I wonder whether they've been in touch with our lot over here?"

"That is a strong possibility. I need time to think. I will contact you - on your mobile - I don't believe any other contact is wise."

"Yes, yes I can see that, OK Fritz, we'll be in touch. Auf wieder sehen." Nigel sat back in his chair, with a horrible, uneasy feeling of panic beginning to take hold. He leant forward and pushed the intercom button. "Get Fallowburton up here again would you." Amy felt it best to go through the motions and in due course buzzed through and told Nigel that Mr Fallowburton's assistant said he had left the building, and didn't know when he would be back. "What does he mean," exploded Nigel, "left the building?"

"Er, exactly that Mr Lamington-Krill, he's not on the premises apparently." Nigel replaced his handset somewhat tremulously as he had a nasty feeling, a very nasty feeling, that an unpleasant situation was inexorably getting much worse.

Meanwhile Mr Fallowburton was relaxing in the departure lounge at the airport with a stiff whisky to help steady his nerves. His forehead was gleaming with moisture. He was, however, now safely in possession of sufficient company funds to be able to establish himself outside the jurisdiction of the British financial authorities and anybody else who might see fit to pursue him. He had rung his wife to say he had an unexpected business trip but not to bother packing anything as he could claim new clothes on expenses. She found it a little odd, but the prospect of having the house to herself for a few days was sufficiently enticing for her not to pursue the matter further. The police would be doing that in due course, but of this at the moment she could not be aware.

"But how is this possible?" Nigel was asking Louis Carmichael incredulously, having now established that Mr Fallowburton had absented himself from the employ of Lamington-Krill International accompanied by a large slice of company funds. The CEO, rubbing his temples, replied, "Well a loophole, loose accounting procedures I suppose. One just doesn't expect..."

"What, one's bloody company to be robbed? Oh do me a favour. We're in the shit and sinking. I can't call the police, they'll want to know too much." Then, a little more calmly and quietly, Nigel lowered his voice and steering Louis to the window said, "Look old man, the only way I can see that we're going to salvage anything from all this is to split the rest of *all* available proceeds, loopholes and loose accounting procedures allowing, and get the hell out and right away."

"What, today you mean? But what about all the staff, I mean there are all the assets ..... I, er ...."

"Bugger the staff, sorry, but they'll find other work, somebody might take it all over, but we need to be absent and pretty damn' fast. I mean just think of it man, everything we've worked for, it'll all be taken away, we might be sent to prison. I don't know about you, but I can't countenance that. I intend to carry on enjoying life, just looks like it won't be in this country."

"But the family, I... this is all so sudden ...I don't know..."

"Look, would your family rather be visiting you in prison, christ, we all know what goes on in prison too, or with you somewhere else out of reach? Come on man, we're both signatories, this is no time to go all ethical on me. The minute that bastard Fallowburton's misdemeanour becomes apparent on top of questions about European grants I would imagine there'll be a clamp-down on company funds tighter than bloody thumbscrews, then we will be well and truly stuffed and no hope of a get-out. Can you think of any alternatives?"

"Well, no, what you say is true, but this is just such a shock. I mean, we've actually had Fallowburton to dinner..."

"Yes, well, social gaffes aside, we'd better see what's available and go about extracting it. I'll come down to your office in, what, an hour? For god's sake make sure none of the staff get an inkling of what you're doing." Louis Carmichael nodded and left Nigel's office. The intercom buzzed and Nigel jumped. It was Mr Hockley wanting to speak to him with great urgency regarding The Bullrushes. Knowing now that he would not be present beyond today, Nigel surprised Amy when he agreed to speak to Mr Hockley, having studiously avoided doing so thus far. "Ah, Mr Lamington-Krill, you are a difficult man to get hold of." Nigel certainly hoped so. "Pressure of work, I've been overdoing it. What's the problem?"

"The problem, sir, is that the local planning authority is becoming a little too interested in The Bullrushes and the nature of the land upon which it is built."

"Why now, I thought that was all safely tied up at the beginning?"

"I have a dossier of complaints from the residents about cracks appearing, ill fitting joinery and generally questionable workmanship. They seem to be rather too well organised and got the local authority involved. This could be seriously damaging to Harmony Homes and I thought you should know."

"Oh we can get it fixed, get the builders back."

"Subsidence is being mentioned, it may take more than the builders. Do remember that the land never was drained properly and our friendly building inspector has unfortunately now retired. I think this one's coming back to bite us frankly."

"Look, leave it with me will you," said Nigel, who found the prospect of irritated residents and querulous authorities merely irksome. He had rather bigger fish to fry.

Nigel buzzed Amy and said "I'm taking Isobel for a surprise break. Book me a couple of tickets for Rio would you, leaving tonight. Leave it open ended." That was all the information Amy required to alert her colleagues who were already observing from afar some interesting financial manoeuvres taking place. The wonders of modern communication techniques and the perils of holey accounting systems were proving an invaluable combination.

Nigel then picked up the telephone and dialled Hake Hall. Isobel answered breathlessly, having run downstairs.

"Darling, we're going away. Just pack a few things, it's a surprise. I'll be home about six. Book a taxi to get to the airport for, say, nine thirty."

"But where, I mean what should I pack? Oh darling, I wish you'd given me a bit more notice, I've invited the Goldsmiths for supper on Friday, I can't just cancel."

"Sorry darling but I can't put this off, trust me. Please, just be ready with whatever's handy."

"But who's going to keep the house? How long are we going to be away? You've sacked Ron and Turtle's gone, I ought to give Cook a bit of notice at least. I don't know what Mrs T's plans are. We can't just go like that!" Nigel was becoming irritated with this domestic trivia and snapped, "Do you want to come or not? The place isn't likely to fall down is it?"

"There's no need to be like that. I'll just have to see what I can sort out."

"OK, I'll see you at about six then. Trust me, it's going to be exciting darling."

Louis Carmichael came back into Nigel's office looking worried and said, "Look old man, the banks are a bit suspicious and I'll need your counter-signature on these," as he handed several documents to Nigel. One of them would transfer an artificially large surplus from the pension fund, which did trouble Louis, but Nigel signed it off, smiling at him and saying, "Hey, the government will cushion this lot, don't worry about it!" Believing they had successfully secured the necessary funds, Nigel and Louis shook hands, bid each other goodbye and good luck and left the offices of Lamington-Krill International for a very interesting future. Amy could not resist wishing Nigel and his wife a lovely holiday in Rio as she confirmed that the tickets could be picked up at the airport.

Nigel really was in holiday mood as he sped towards Hake Hall. He sang along with passages from the Marriage of Figaro but faltered momentarily as his thoughts turned to India and how she was to be provided for if they couldn't come back. He would transfer a substantial sum into her account before they went and then try his best to explain their sudden departure to her via e-mail. Oh dear, this was something he hadn't allowed for, but she was a very spirited and self-sufficient girl and really didn't need her parents necessarily to be in the same country, he told himself.

Thus it was in rather more subdued mood than hitherto that Nigel swept into the drive of Hake Hall. He frowned when he saw a silver-coloured saloon car parked at the front of the house. "Damn' we really don't need visitors right now," he said to himself. Out of habit he abandoned his own vehicle, forgetting that Turtle was no longer present to deal with it and ran up the steps to the front door. As he went in he smiled at the sight of two large suitcases standing ready in the hall and called out "Hello Izzy, where are you, I'll just take a quick sh ......" His voice trailed off as two men emerged from the kitchen behind Isobel who had clearly been crying. "What the bloody hell...." said Nigel in disbelief, "Who the bloody hell are you? Isobel, what's happened?"

"Perhaps you could tell *me*. What have you got us into? How could you do this Nigel?" said Isobel plaintively, as one of her minders showed Nigel his official identity card.

"Serious Fraud Office? Oh *shit*. No, this is all wrong, it should be Fallowburton you're after...". The officer duly read a pale and disbelieving Nigel his rights and invited him to accompany them for further examination of the facts. Isobel elected to stay behind and stood in the hall watching as the silver saloon car drove away.

Chapter Eleven

As Helena Ruby awoke in her new lodgings she was momentarily disorientated, then winced as a sharp pain reminded her of her knee injury. She was amazed to see that the bedside clock said it was 10.30 a.m. She sat up in alarm, almost unseating Denholm from his position on the bed (letting him stay with her was the only way to stop his pitiful whining last night). She checked her watch with bleary eyes to ensure that the clock was correct, and it was. Her knee was sore and stiff, so she got carefully out of bed then put on her tired old dressing gown which she had hung on the back of the bedroom door. With Denholm close by her heels, she limped slowly downstairs, calling "Hello, is anybody in?" and feeling rather foolish. Her enquiry was greeted with silence. She went to the telephone mounted on the wall by the kitchen door in order to call Isobel and apologise for being late for work, but all she got was the answering machine. "Oh, er, hello. I, er ...this is a message for Mrs Lamington-Krill. This is Mrs Tremble. I am *so* sorry but I shall be late in to work today. I will be with you as soon as I can, and explain when I see you. Sorry, er, goodbye."

As Helena Ruby replaced the handset she saw a framed photograph of Cook (or Denzil as she supposed she might now need to start addressing him) standing with his arm round the shoulders of somebody she supposed to be a relative or maybe old friend. They were both grinning broadly and Helena Ruby found herself smiling back at them despite her present slight discomfiture at her new surroundings. She looked down at Denholm and said, "We've done it, we've actually done it! Come on, let's celebrate with a cup of tea. Then we must get a move on." Helena Ruby put down Denholm's bowl of water for him then located a mug and tea. She was unable to close the cupboard door properly, but shrugged and boiled the kettle, noticing how very clean and well organised everything was.

She supposed it was his training as a chef, but it was unusual for a man, she thought. She even found milk in an elegant jug in the refrigerator and smiled. This was going to be so different.

The previous evening, Helena Ruby had been most anxious to agree how best to organise her temporary stay as a house guest, for she was fully aware of what an imposition it was. Cook had been very kind and most accommodating, and it was agreed that Helena Ruby would contribute towards household bills and if she was happy to keep the house clean and look after the laundry, then that was more than fair. Cook had observed that it was a bit of a busman's holiday, but Helena Ruby was more than happy to repay his kindness in any way she could. Having drunk her tea, rinsed and dried the mug and returned it to the cupboard, Helena Ruby returned upstairs with some difficulty, for her knee was now throbbing with pain. She took her towel and sponge bag to the bathroom and pursued her normal routine, but now in rather more stylish surroundings. She examined her knee and it was very hot and swollen. Cook had been able to give her an ice-pack to put on it the previous evening, but it had only provided temporary respite. "Ron's revenge," she said to Denholm who was sitting at her feet. "What are we going to do with you, anyway? I suppose you'll have to stay in the car."

Helena Ruby dressed then went slowly and painfully downstairs again, taking her handbag with her, having checked to ensure that she had her car keys. She also had the spare front door key given to her by Cook yesterday (she still had difficulty thinking of him as Denzil). "Come on then," she said to the Dachshund, "let's see what's going on." Helena Ruby slammed the door hard behind her, as instructed by Cook, then went to the car and let Denholm hop in. He was very pleased to be going out with Helena Ruby and his bony little tail was waving energetically to and fro. Helena Ruby was just aware out of the corner of her eye of curtain movement from the downstairs window of the adjoining house, and couldn't help but smile. It took her about twenty minutes to reach Hake Hall. It felt strange driving to work and she wasn't sure where to leave the car. These were all details she hadn't considered, but as she came slowly up the drive, she saw Cook's car parked in a corner against the garage block wall, so she left her car beside it. It wasn't as if it was in anybody's way. She saw Nigel's car left at the front of the house and wondered what he was doing home. Helena Ruby fondled Denholm's velvety head and said, "You're going to have to stay here. I'll come and let you out and give you a drink later, be a good boy." She opened the car window a fraction then locked the door and walked slowly round the side of the house to the kitchen door, which was ajar. She entered a little hesitantly. Cook was taking some meat from the refrigerator and he turned on his heel when he heard Helena Ruby clear her throat.

"Ah, Mrs T, I don't know where everyone is today - the place is deserted. Did you sleep well? I thought it best to leave you to your own devices."

"Yes, thank you, I think I slept too well. I didn't hear the alarm. Hope you don't mind, I borrowed your telephone to apologise to Mrs L-K, but I got the answering machine. Have you seen her?"

"No, like I said, I've not seen a soul, and remember you've got to stop asking me if I mind. It was agreed, remember?"

"Oh yes, sorry......"

"And the apologising!" Helena Ruby smiled and said "OK it's a deal, but I might slip up now and then, this is all very strange for me you know."

"I know, I know, just relax. Now I'm just wondering ....." at which point Isobel came into the kitchen looking absolutely terrible. Her eyes were puffy from crying and she clearly hadn't taken the normal amount of care with her appearance. She didn't even seem to have brushed her hair. Both Cook and Mrs Tremble looked at her, momentarily speechless, then Helena Ruby said "Oh, Mrs L-K, are you not well? Can I get you anything?"

"I, ah, no thank you, oh god, something really awful has happened and I don't know what to do. I ....." and Isobel started to cry again. Helena Ruby's mothering instincts made her go to Isobel and put her arm around her shoulders. She pulled out a chair for her and sat her down. Cook passed over a kitchen towel in the absence of any immediately available tissues and Isobel pressed it to her face. "Thank you, I'm sorry, I...well, it's Nigel. Oh this is so awful. He .... he was arrested last night. Serious fraud. He was going to take me to Rio, a surprise holiday he said. They set him up, I just don't know what's going on. They've frozen our bank accounts, taken our passports. Oh this is so dreadful..." and Isobel started sobbing again. Cook frowned. This did not sound good. Frozen bank accounts meant no pay as far as he could tell, but now was not the best time to enquire.

"Did the police give you a contact number?" enquired Helena Ruby. "You could at least find out how long they're going to keep Mr L-K. I'm sure it will all get sorted out, it must be a mistake."

"Er, yes, yes, I have a card somewhere." Isobel got up, sniffing and dabbing her nose, glad to have something to do, and walked to the dresser, pulled open several drawers and at last located the card. She pushed the drawer closed with her hip and as she turned, put her hand to her forehead and said, "Oh dear, I've got the most dreadful headache."

"I'm not surprised," said Helena Ruby. "Here, have a couple of these" as she put a box of painkillers on the kitchen table. Cook had already put a glass of water on the table as ladies in distress always had a sip of water at some stage in the proceedings. With unsteady hands Isobel took two tablets and gulped them down with the water.

"Thank you Mrs Tremble, Cook. I'll, er, go and make the call from the study I think. I .... need to concentrate." Isobel took the card from the table and went to

Nigel's study, while Cook and Helena Ruby looked at each other.

"Jeeze, I knew he was a bit sharp, but not downright crooked," said Cook.

"It could be a mistake."

"I don't think they go this far unless they're sure of their ground, and a sudden trip to Rio - doesn't that sound a bit sus to you?"

"Just a romantic gesture perhaps?"

"Er, no I don't think so. Anyhow the point is, where does all this leave us. If their accounts have all been frozen, how are they going to pay us? If this all goes belly up we're going to be unemployed. I suppose we could sell our stories to the tabloids!"

"Oh dear, I didn't think of that. They must make allowances, surely? I mean, how will Mrs L-K get by?"

"Social security perhaps," laughed Cook. "Anyhow, that's not our concern is it?"

"I suppose not. Oh dear, where do we go from here? This is all a bit embarrassing really, I mean, should we stay and carry on as normal, or what?"

"We have a cup of tea and wait for Mrs L-K to tell us what's going on." Helena Ruby was grateful to sit down and rest her knee which was showing no sign of improvement.

"Um I noticed that one of your kitchen cupboard doors won't shut properly," said Helena Ruby, gently rubbing her knee as she idly watched Cook making two mugs of tea.

"Yea, I noticed that too - just another symptom of shoddy workmanship. It's been added to the list. Neville at Number Five has amassed a pretty big file of complaints and now the council building people have become involved. Didn't you say that Mr L-K was something to do with the developers come to think of it? Hah, not that that's going to get us anywhere now I suspect."

"Mmm, I found a card saying he's chairman of Harmony Homes. You don't suppose it's connected do you?"

"Wouldn't like to say," said Cook as he put two mugs of steaming tea on the table. "I ......" He trailed off as Isobel came back through the kitchen door. She looked at them both and said, "Well, er, they were quite helpful and it looks like Nigel will be home by this afternoon." Isobel looked down at her feet in embarrassment, really wishing she hadn't imparted Nigel's disgrace to the staff, and said, "Look, would you both mind taking the rest of the day off, I don't know what arrangements I'll have to make or anything, I just can't think straight at the moment."

"Of course," said Helena Ruby Tremble obligingly. "Should we come in tomorrow morning?"

"I, I don't know. Can I telephone you?" Helena Ruby went pink and said, "Er, just leave a message with Cook, that'll be alright." They drank a little more tea and Isobel went upstairs to bed to rest her aching head.

"So I wonder just where this is going to leave us," said Cook.

"I really don't know, it's all a bit awkward really isn't it? Um, is it a problem if I come back to your house, only my knee is really sore and I could do with resting it really. I just can't face going into town or doing anything energetic."

"Remember what we agreed, Mrs T, you must relax. I'm hoping to meet a friend so you can have the place to yourself. Perhaps you should start looking at situations vacant!" As he said this he was sending a text message on his mobile phone.

"I really wonder whether I ought to get one of those," said Helena Ruby, mindful that she couldn't miss any contact from the girls, and the thought of Jolyon did linger deliciously, she really did want to see him again, "but I really wouldn't know where to start."

"Easy Mrs T, I've got a spare one you're very welcome to use - you just need to top it up and you'll be away! I'll show you what you need to do when I get back later. I think it's in one of the kitchen drawers."

"Oh thank you, if you're sure ...."

"Yes I'm sure," said Cook smiling broadly as he received a message confirming his rendezvous. "So I'll see you later. Just feed yourself, do whatever you'd normally do. I will already have eaten."

Helena Ruby took a plastic bottle of water out with her for the dog who was delighted to see her and with his front feet up against the window, started barking and wagging his tail vigorously. "Denholm, be quiet," said Helena Ruby as she let him jump out of the car to drink his water. He ran about pushing his nose into flower beds and bushes, delighting in his freedom. "Denholm, come here, come on, we're going," called Helena Ruby as quietly as she could, conscious of the fact that Isobel's bedroom overlooked the front. She was not really able to pursue the dog because of her knee but eventually he did come to her, gratefully slurped at the water bowl, then jumped as bidden into the car. "Oh dear, we're going to have to sort something out for you aren't we? I didn't really think about all this." Helena Ruby got into the car and manoeuvred out to the drive. She could not help but glance towards the Lodge on her way past and was struck with a dreadful pang of guilt. She was grateful not to have encountered Ron today however, but realised she would have to speak to him soon. Perhaps she would pluck up the courage to ring him later now the day was hers. However, more pressing than that, she also wondered whether she had enough confidence to call Jolyon too. The last day or so had been so tumultuous that her longing to see him had been somewhat obscured, and then of course the old familiar feelings of inadequacy began to creep up on her. As she drove towards The Bullrushes she began to get terrible nervous butterflies in her stomach at the very prospect of ringing Jolyon. She pulled up outside her new lodgings and could not help but notice some large earth-moving equipment parked by the railings at the back of the development, and scaffolding was being put up around two houses. However, her painful knee and preoccupation with calling Jolyon meant she didn't linger. She opened the front door by leaning on it having inserted the key, and went inside with Denholm at her heel. He was still not feeling settled in his new home.

Saying, "Well there's no time like the present," (talking out loud always helped) Helena Ruby took the telephone to the sitting room where she pulled off her shoes, sat down on the sofa and then put her feet up. It was a relief to rest that knee. She must have bruised it badly, she thought. She found the now battered business card in her handbag and just looked at it for some time, quite unsure as to whether she was going to make a complete fool of herself (it felt like it was somebody else who had shared such intimacy in the cloakroom), or whether Jolyon was sincere and really would like to hear from her again. Her heart started thudding and she became light-headed. "Helena Ruby Tremble, what are you doing?" she said out loud. She was feeling decidedly odd but supposed it was nerves, and dialled Jolyon's number. She couldn't not do it now. She was breathing heavily as she heard the ringing tone and was about to change her mind and cancel the call when, "Jolyon Urquart's phone," answered a familiarly velvety female voice.

"Hello, is ... I ... ah..." The telephone slipped from Helena Ruby's hand as her ears began to buzz and she became very cold and started gasping for breath, then darkness descended upon her. She passed out. "Hello, hello," persisted the voice on the telephone, but now all they could hear was the sound of whining as Denholm licked Helena Ruby's flaccid arm.

Helena Ruby awoke in a hospital bed with a tube in her arm and a monitor wire stuck with a patch to her chest. And her knee, what had happened to her knee? Her whole leg was packed in what felt like an inflatable bandage. She put her hand to her forehead while she tried to assimilate all this and immediately a nurse was by her side saying "Hello Helena, is it Helena, can you hear me now, can you see me alright?"

"Er...yes, yes,......I....oh.. what happened?" Helena Ruby Tremble barely recognised her own voice and she had a terrible sore throat.

"You've had a very lucky escape, Helena. That wound in your knee has gone badly septic. You could have died of blood poisoning. How did you do it? Is there any member of the family we can contact?" She was trying to gather together the words to respond, but Helena Ruby Tremble started to cry instead and just could not stop. She was overwhelmed. What family did she have, who really cared?

"Oh don't cry Helena, here try to drink some water, don't worry, you'll be alright now, this is all a terrible shock," said the nurse kindly. That just made it worse and Helena between sobs said, "I'm ...... sorry....I just, just feel.......so miserable..."

"That's a perfectly natural reaction my dear, you mustn't worry, you'll soon feel better." Helena Ruby Tremble didn't see how. Eventually however her misery subsided and the pain in her leg began to make itself known. "So is there anybody we can call to let them know you're here?" asked the nurse again as she gave Helena Ruby some painkillers and checked her blood pressure.

"Um, well, my husband I suppose..."

"Oh well that's alright, of course, do you have his number?"

"But I left him yesterday," murmured Helena Ruby, unaware that she had been unconscious for longer than that, as the tears began again. "Oh dear, I see, but surely ...."

"I just don't know what to do, I'm in a complete mess ... and, oh, what's happened to my dog?" sobbed Helena Ruby. "Well shouldn't I at least just ring your husband to let him know what's happened? Surely he can look after the dog," persisted the nurse. Helena Ruby was feeling weak and helpless so gave in, told the nurse the telephone number of the Lodge then lay back with her eyes closed. She was in pain and felt terrible. She wanted to contact the girls but didn't have their mobile numbers with her. Oh god this was such a bloody awful mess. Tears still rolled down her cheeks from under her closed eyelids as she dozed and tried to blank out her sadness.

"What have you been doing my dear?" came a voice gently from the doorway. "You gave me the most awful fright." Helena Ruby Tremble opened her eyes to see Jolyon walking to her bedside with an extravagant bouquet of flowers. Oh my god, he couldn't see her in a state like this, and in a dreadful hospital gown too. "Oh how did you know, I .... those flowers .... it's..." and she started to cry again. "Now you're not to worry my dear, I can take care of you. You've been seriously ill and I can see I'm going to have to keep a close eye on you and make sure you look after yourself."

"But I'm such a mess, please, I ...." Jolyon leant forward and kissed Helena Ruby on the forehead.

"So who's this?" said Ron as he came up to Helena Ruby Tremble's bed, holding a drooping bunch of lurid orange carnations. Jolyon twisted round, slightly nonplussed but ever the gentleman, said, "Oh hello, I'm Jolyon Urquart." He proffered his hand which Ron chose to ignore.

"And what are you doing here, what's with the bloody flowers? I'm her husband."

"I, er...."

"Ron, please, there's no need ...." Helena Ruby Tremble was not feeling at all well again. Guilt and utter misery welled up and she could see desperation in her husband's face.

"So is this what you left me for? You dreadful old tart, can't think why anybody would take a second glance, look at the state of you."

"Ron, please don't, I didn't mean.......you can't....." The nurse came in having heard Ron's raised voice and said, "Please, this lady isn't at all well, I think it best that you leave sir." Ron flung the carnations on the floor and kicked them under the bed. "Never was good enough for you was I? I was going to ask you to come back but you obviously can't be trusted. How many others? You can both go to hell." And with that, Ron elbowed his way past Jolyon and strode angrily out of the door. The nurse said brightly, "Shall I put these lovely flowers in water for you?" not really knowing what else to do, and picked up the bouquet resting on the side table, leaving Jolyon and Helena Ruby alone to consider events. Neither said anything for a few minutes, but Jolyon stood and held Helena Ruby's hand gently as he gazed thoughtfully out of the window. Helena broke the silence. "I, er, I know you'll think this is stupid, but do you know what's happened to the dog? Is anybody looking after him? Poor Denholm, he won't know what's going on, what if he hasn't had any food or water?"

"Ah, that's not a problem my dear. You can stop fretting, it's all taken care of. My business associate is looking after him, she knows all about dogs. She got the emergency services to you - astonishing how they can track down phone calls these days!"

"Oh, what, I didn't realise .... d'you mean ... er, well, so you, er, you know I've left the Lodge?"

"Yes, yes I know you were elsewhere. It was she who picked up your call, I'd just popped out for a minute. Your timing is second to none!"

"Oh god, that's such a relief, I feel so stupid, I thought...." and Helena Ruby started crying again.

"Come on, come on, dry your eyes, I know what you thought and you're wrong, it's all going to be alright, trust me," said Jolyon gently. "But what about Ron, he's so angry, so hurt, I shouldn't have hurt him, I feel so bad. What's he going to do now?"

"That my dear I don't know, but what you have to do now is concentrate on making a full recovery."

"I suppose so, I do feel dreadfully weary. I can't think straight at the moment. This is all so .... weird."

"I'll leave you to sleep now my dear, but I'll come and see you again tomorrow, and you are not to fret, as I said, everything can be taken care of."

"But what about Cook? (she still couldn't bring herself to call him by his real name). Does he know what's happened? He's been so kind you see. It was his house that ...." Jolyon held up his hand. "All taken care of, so will you now please rest and get better?" Jolyon kissed Helena Ruby's forehead gently, squeezed her hand then walked from her bed to the door. There he turned and said "I'll see you tomorrow my dear, have a really good night's sleep won't you."

Helena Ruby Tremble gratefully lay back on her pillows, hardly daring to believe what was happening.

Chapter Twelve

Whilst idly browsing the cookery book shelves in Vere Moleditch & Hartspring's *Reading Matter for the Discerning* in the old market town of Whiting-en-Croute, Sonia de Souza glanced up and saw Isobel Lamington-Krill studying the shelves of the economics and business law section. Sonia had come in search of a birthday gift for Trevor. Obviously not a cookery book, that was for her enlightenment, but she was sure she could find a suitable leather-bound historical tome which if nothing else would look fine on the mellow oak library shelving in the study at Lamprey Manse. She would also seek out cufflinks, perhaps from Gurnard & Persimmon Gentlemen's High Class Outfitters, for Whiting-en-Croute did indeed cater for the more discerning purchaser. Sonia had an appointment in Herring le Parterre at Follicles for a manicure, pedicure and Tasmanian chalk scrub in the afternoon. She had read about it in Speditia Bliss's column only last week and it was thoroughly recommended for detoxification and rejuvenation of the epidermis. Sonia sauntered towards the alcove in which Isobel was engrossed. "Isobel?" she said with a touch of devilment, as it was fairly plain from her general demeanour that Isobel was not in the mood for socialising. Sonia had the impression that she hadn't expected to see anybody, for her general appearance was not as polished as usual and she did look awfully tired. There was a suggestion of grey around her eyes and her complexion looked pale and dull. "Oh, er, hello Sonia, how are you? What a surprise to see you in here."

"Yes, I'm just looking for a birthday present for Trevor. He's *so* difficult to buy for and they have such a fantastic selection of really unusual stuff in here, and such a lovely atmosphere. Are you after anything in particular, I didn't think economics was your thing. More Nigel's I should have thought?" Isobel smiled wanly. "Oh, I, er, I promised India I would try to get her a book for her coursework."

"Gosh, serious studying then?"

"Mmmm. Well, I can't see the title so I'll try somewhere else. Nice to see you," lied Isobel, and she turned to leave. "Oh, goodbye, but look, wouldn't you like to join me for a coffee? We could try that little place in the high street in the converted buttery, you know, opened not long ago by the Bentwood lad. I don't know where he got the money from, but it's supposed to be very avant-garde, interesting celebrity snaps on the walls and some amazing speciality coffees."

"No, really, thank you. To be honest I'm not feeling too well." Isobel could feel the threatening tears rising and even Sonia could see that she was best left. "Oh, OK, I *am* sorry, hope you feel better soon."

"Yes, thank you. Goodbye."

"'Bye then." As Sonia watched Isobel leave the premises she noticed a small, discreetly labelled section in an alcove entitled 'Erotica'. She smiled and sauntered over to investigate. That would be more fun than an illustrated analysis of the Boer uprising or early missionaries' adventures in the South China Sea. After a lot of perusing, Sonia chose a leather-bound volume of saucy line drawings with explanatory text. Yes, Trevor would like that and hopefully share his appreciation with her. She took the book to the till which was arranged on a leather-topped oak desk. Sonia smiled expansively at the gentleman as he took it from her and wrapped it in burgundy-coloured tissue paper, before placing it reverently in a bag. "That will be £52.60 please, Madam." Sonia passed over her titanium card. "If I might suggest, Madam," he continued in lowered tones, "if you have access to the internet, you may be interested in an associated site we operate for our customers with similar interests." He handed her a card from his top pocket with the internet address *www.saucystuff@bloater.com* on it. Sonia looked at it and was not slow to realise its significance. This was no site for those with culinary interests, she thought. "Oh, yes I do, er - thank you. I say, there's nothing at all questionable, I mean legally about it is there? Everybody seems to know what you're up to these days, one has to be so careful."

"Oh no, madam, it is all bona fide legal, tasteful material for connoisseurs, you understand. Nothing photographic."

"Well thank you, thank you very much." Sonia smiled. "A pleasure, Madam. We look forward to seeing you again."

With her thoughts now attuned to things not even loosely associated with culinary matters, nor historical volumes, Sonia wondered what that lithe young mechanic was up to at the moment as she walked to her car with her purchase. She locked it in the boot, checked her watch and decided she did have plenty of time for a visit to Gurnard & Persimmon. What fun it would be if she could find some complementary cufflinks for Trevor. She took from her handbag a bottle of *A Day in the Life* and sprayed her cleavage before entering the premises. "Hello Madam, may I be of assistance?" enquired a man whom Sonia assumed to be considerably younger than her. She smiled appreciatively as she surveyed his tall, broad shouldered frame, upon which hung a beautifully tailored dark suit. His sandy hair, greying at the temples, was brushed back to reveal a distinguished hairline and his piercing blue eyes engaged hers instantly. "I wonder if you can," breathed Sonia. "This may be a little unusual, but ...."

"We specifically cater for unusual, Madam." A knowing smile from the gentleman caused a hot tingling sensation to run deliciously through Sonia's own frame.

"Ah, well, um, look I don't even know your name."

"Miles, Madam, Miles Persimmon at your service."

"Oh, well, er, Miles, you must be Persimmon the younger, surely?"

"Oh, several generations down the line Madam, we were established in 1857 you know."

"Hah, yes, of course, silly of me......It's so nice to see some of the old school still in business."

"Oh yes, we pride ourselves on our service and attention to detail. Quality is ageless Madam, I think you will agree." There was something about the quality of Miles' voice and the subtle humour suggested in his delivery that Sonia found mesmerising. "Undoubtedly, Miles. Um, anyway, the thing is, I have just purchased a volume of, um, well, prints, sort of, well, erotic prints …" Sonia looked into those smiling blue eyes and momentarily lost her concentration. There was electricity in the air. "- and, oh this sounds so silly, I shouldn't have....."

"Not at all Madam, may I know your name?" enquired Miles Persimmon. "Oh, yes of course, it's Sonia, Sonia de Souza, *delighted* to meet you," and she held out her hand which was grasped by Miles' cool, firm grip as they lingeringly shook hands. "So these erotic prints," continued Miles. "Well, you see, I wondered whether you might possibly have any, er, cufflinks, perhaps, in a similar theme ……oh this sounds so stupid," said Sonia as she blushed and gazed at the floor. Her chin was lifted by Miles' index finger and he gazed straight into her eyes, then running the same index finger softly down her cleavage said quietly, "I think I might have just what you're looking for if you'd care to accompany me, Sonia."

"Oh my god, yes please," she gasped. Miles took her by the hand and led her past the beautifully presented silk ties, cotton shirts, a display case of watches and a rack of gleaming leather shoes, ushered her in to an oak-clad fitting room and locked the door. Miles bent his head to kiss Sonia who rose on tip toes to reach him. They remained locked in a passionate kiss for some time then buttons were undone, zips unzipped, hooks unhooked and clothes gradually removed as they explored each others' bodies breathlessly. "Would you care to dress my gentleman?" said Miles hoarsely in Sonia's ear as he passed her a small foil sachet. "Oh, er, crumbs, yes, of course, oh bloody hell...." said Sonia as she fumbled trying to tear it open. "Here, let me," said Miles as he ripped it open then offered it back to

Sonia. "Oh, *Miles*, I say," cooed Sonia as she applied the prophylactic.

Miles suggested Sonia face the floor-to-ceiling length mirror and lean forward which she willingly did, supporting herself across a balloon-back chair with ornate carving which dug in to her ribs, but she didn't care, for she was being transported to a different plane of existence as Miles clasped her not insubstantial hips and thrust his not insubstantial manhood. She urged him to beat his mount and cried out in delight as his belt stung her buttocks.

As Miles and Sonia hurriedly re-assembled themselves, laughingly she asked whether she could at least look at the cufflinks they had. After checking their appearance in the mirror and Miles having shaken Sonia's hand and expressed his pleasure in having met her, he unlocked the door of the fitting room, placed the chair back in the corner and ushered Sonia to a case holding a large array of gold and silver cufflinks. "These would be for your husband, would I be correct?" asked Miles, glancing at the glittering gem and carved gold band on her wedding finger.

"Um, yes, it's his birthday, just wanted to try something a bit different."

"Indeed."

Sonia chose two pairs of silver cherubic buttocks in the classical style, but she did find it very hard to stay focused on the matter in hand with Miles standing close beside her. She could almost feel his magnetic aura, it gave her goose pimples. As Miles gift-wrapped the box Sonia gazed longingly at his deft and elegant fingers. He had a positively electric touch, and such beautifully manicured nails. "My card, should you need any future assistance with gentlemen's outfitting," said Miles as he handed the purchase to Sonia, flashing her a dazzling pearly smile, his eyes creasing exquisitely at the corners. "Why thank you, Mr Persimmon, it has been a pleasure, a real pleasure to become acquainted with the finer points of the trade I must say....."

"Tell me, Sonia, do you enjoy equine pursuits I wonder?"

"Well, yes, I ride a little," said Sonia, "but why do you ask?"

"I have a very good friend who owns the saddlery in Blenny-cum-Whitlow and I think he could accommodate your, um, riding requirements most satisfactorily, should you need anything in that line, Sonia." She began to wonder if there was something in the water at Whiting-en-Croute and whether she shouldn't perhaps bottle some for Trevor. She smiled, blushed a little and said, "I see, well thank you, I shall bear it in mind. As a matter of interest, what is your friend's name, in case I should call by?"

"Purvis Mallard."

"Sounds vaguely familiar, isn't he something to do with hunting?"

"Yes, he does have interests in that direction, but he does have a *very* well stocked shop, catering for all tastes and inclinations."

"I see, well thank you, Miles and I shall recommend Gurnard & Persimmon to all my friends. Your service is without rival," and Sonia floated out of the shop, with just enough time to get to Herring le Parterre for her appointment.

Later that evening she stood chopping courgettes, still glowing either from her encounter with Miles Persimmon or her invigorating Tasmanian chalk scrub. (Tina, who had just qualified to administer same at Follicles, knew better than to enquire after the red marks on Sonia's generous rear for it only ever lead to embarrassment on all sides.) Sonia hummed along with Frank Sinatra flying her to the moon and took an occasional sip of white wine. She kept re-running a mental video of her visit to Gurnard & Persimmon and could not help smiling. She did however put her hand to her bruised ribs but said out loud "Ah, but boy was it worth it!" Apart from everything else, she was really excited about having found Trevor something other than a cashmere sweater and toning socks or his favourite cologne, Musk Mood. A thoroughly successful trip viewed from any angle, with mirrors or not.

In a moment of understandable inattention, Sonia caught one of her newly manicured nails with the chopping knife and said "Oh damnation" crossly as she could see the lustrous coating now chipped and a nick in the otherwise perfect curve of her nail. "Something wrong darling?" asked Trevor as he came through the door.

"Oh hello darling," said Sonia, "I've just caught my nail, that's all, but it's *so* annoying as I only had them done this afternoon."

"So no real harm done then. You're looking very, um, well, healthy. Had a good day?" It was unlike Trevor to pay such attention normally. "Oh thank you darling, I had a Tasmanian chalk scrub at Follicles too while I was there, it's amazing and really invigorating. The cold douse at the end really makes you tingle."

"Jolly good, pour me a Scotch would you while you're there darling. Heard some pretty interesting stuff on the grapevine today." Sonia passed him his drink in a large cut glass tumbler. "Oh, do tell," said Sonia, losing interest in the vegetable preparation as she picked up her wine and joined Trevor at the table. "Thank you. Seems like old Lamington-Krill is in major trouble. Detained by Serious Fraud, assets frozen, the whole works. Rumour has it he was going to scarper to Rio but they had him rumbled. Of course nobody will touch him with a barge pole now."

"Oh that's interesting, I saw Isobel in Whiting-en-Croute only this morning and she did look awful. Oh poor thing, I wonder if she had any idea?"

"She will have now. Don't see how they can hang on to that pile either. He could go to prison you know, been upsetting the EU chaps. I think this will wipe them out. Thank god we're at a safe distance."

"Thank god indeed," agreed Sonia, reflecting upon the day's events and sipping her wine, glowing.

Chapter Thirteen

Neville Martin Painswick was finding more and more of his time taken up with collating building defect reports from residents of The Bullrushes and negotiating with local authority inspectors. He did, however, find it surprisingly rewarding and it was a good way of getting to know one's neighbours and their decorative tastes very well indeed. Donna was a little put out by the amount of attention the whole sorry situation was receiving from her husband, but she could not help but admit that it was she who goaded him into action at the outset. She was also agitated at having been informed that it was pointless spending any more money on decorating the nursery or anything else, for it seemed as though the house would at the very least require major underpinning, having been built as it was on inadequately drained marshland and insufficient foundations. This was not how Donna had pictured her impending motherhood and domestic idyll.

"Look I'm sorry love, but it was you who insisted we move here," responded Neville Martin to a complaint from Donna as she learnt that for the sake of her health and wellbeing they may have to move out. "Oh don't use that excuse," snapped an unhappy Donna, "you can't hold me responsible for the bloody cowboys who stuck these houses here."

"I'm not holding you responsible for anything love, and you won't be doing the baby any good by getting worked up. You know your mother is more than happy for you to stay with her while we get all this sorted out."

"But this isn't what I wanted, I wanted it all to be perfect, I..." and Donna, easily disposed to tears, started to cry. "Oh come on love, it's not the end of the world, you've just got to concentrate on yourself and the baby," said Neville Martin Painswick as he drew a deep breath, put a pile of paper on the sofa beside him and got up to comfort his wife. "Look, this is obviously upsetting you, I know it's not ideal, so why don't we get you and what you need over to your mum's so you can relax there, she'll look after you a treat and you can enjoy some peace and quiet. I know you don't like all these visitors to the house and stuff."

"But I wanted you .... I ..... it's not ....." and Donna started to cry in earnest. However, when she had stopped being upset for long enough they did agree that a sojourn with her mother was sensible and probably for the best so Neville Martin Painswick started gathering together everything Donna thought she might need while she rang her mother to make arrangements.

Now that the full extent of the problem with the Bullrushes development had been revealed, it was inevitable that the legal profession would become involved. Denzil Fitzpelican at Number Eleven had told him, in confidence, that Nigel Lamington-Krill, chairman of Harmony Homes at whose well-appointed door the responsibility for all this ultimately lay, was under investigation by the serious fraud brigade, which shed an interesting light on proceedings. Neville Martin Painswick liked talking to Denzil, he was a thoroughly entertaining fellow and not one to become embroiled in estate gossip. Denzil had seen no harm in relating Nigel's present unhappy circumstances, for it was now apparent that he could no longer be employed at Hake Hall. Isobel had been through agonies in trying to explain to him but did reveal that she had a small savings account in her own right and as soon as she had persuaded the authorities that it was in no way connected with Lamington-Krill International, she promised she would pay him and Mrs Tremble what they were owed. She was genuinely sorry to hear of Helena Ruby Tremble's misfortunes too and asked that her best wishes be conveyed. Denzil actually felt sorry for Isobel, but was surprised at just what an unenquiring mind she had.

Denzil went to visit Helena Ruby Tremble in hospital and whilst appreciating that the poor woman was not in the best place to receive the news, he felt she should know as soon as possible so she could perhaps begin to make plans. She was very pleased to see him and felt far more presentable now she was wearing a nice crisp white bedshirt and she had managed to get her hair washed. Jolyon had been very kind in sorting it all out, in fact Helena Ruby still couldn't believe that people were inclined to be so kind to her. Denzil had brought her a sort of picnic, knowing what hospital food could be like, and was sure that even now Isobel and Nigel would not miss a few morsels from their gargantuan refrigerator. "Oh thank you, Cook, er, Denzil, oh I don't know what......"

"Denzil, please, and I'll call you Helena OK? How nice to have your own room - you must be in a bad way!"

"Um, yes, I'll explain. Anyway, it's awfully kind of you, how nice of you to visit. So what news then?"

"Well, you certainly had the curtain twitchers in a frenzy, that's for sure, but I trust you're on the mend now. Do you know when you're likely to be coming out?"

"About a week or so I think, blood pressure needs to stabilise and the wound's taking a long time to heal. But I'm feeling so much better now."

"Ah, well, that's great, but, er, well, sorry to be the bearer of bad news, especially in your current situation, but Mrs L-K can't employ us any more, no funds, Nigel really is in big trouble. She sends her best wishes by the way."

"Oh no, what will you do?" asked Helena Ruby, frowning.

"Can't say at the moment, but equally, Helena, what will *you* do?"

"Oh dear, we're both rather, well, up the creek, but look, I said I'd explain," said Helena Ruby Tremble, blushing and looking down at her hands. "Um do you know who called the ambulance?"

"All I know is it was some woman, very handsome creature. She put me in the picture and said she'd look after the dog."

"Ah well there's a bit more to it than that. She ah, well I was.... well you see, she's the ..."

"What are you trying to say Helena Ruby Tremble?"

"Oh, well, what I, um, oh this has all happened so fast, but, well, you see ..."

"Yes, we've got that far, now what about the rest?" Denzil was laughing now, recalling the sight of a slightly dishevelled Helena Ruby with a daisy in her hair.

"OK, Jolyon Urquart and me, he was at the German do, we've sort of rather, well, how do I put it … um … taken a shine to each other, and he's sorted all this out for me. It was his business colleague you met. I was on the 'phone when......is she terribly gorgeous?"

"To some eyes, yes, but I wouldn't worry about that. Well I'm really pleased for you Helena, but I wonder what's going to happen to Ron? Did you know that he was sacked after his performance at the do?"

"Oh dear no, I had no idea. Oh that's really terrible. He, er, came in when Jolyon was here, he was terribly angry, it was horrible, he didn't really give either of us the chance to say anything. Oh dear I am worried about him, I wonder what he'll do, how will he cope? I do understand that he must be terribly hurt, the timing of all this is just awful. This is certainly not how I saw things working out. Don't know what I expected really."

"I'm sure he'll get by. It's unhappy, I know, but frankly Helena, forgive me for saying it, I don't really understand how you two came to get together in the first place, I mean, you're such completely different people."

"Ah, yes well you see, there's something you don't know. I, um, I've never really spoken about it, silly really, nothing to be coy about in this day and age, but well, you see, I've, um, I've er, got twin daughters." Denzil sat back and raised his eyebrows, smiled and said, "Well, well you are full of surprises, so how come I've never met them? You've kept them very secret, Helena." Helena Ruby Tremble looked down at her hands, twisting her worn wedding ring. "Well, er, you see, back then we were obliged to get married, our parents insisted, it never occurred to me there was any other option. I was far too young and just had to do as I was told. They don't get on with their father, he's never had any time for them. They never even visit. But don't get me wrong, they are lovely girls, it's not their fault...." Tears began welling up as Helena longed for her girls and Denzil took her hand. "Hey, come on, don't get upset. Do they know you're here, shouldn't someone tell them?"

"I, I was going to ask Ron but that didn't work out. Oh dear, I miss them so. This is all too much." Helena choked back tears and Denzil, feeling rather awkward, got up to fetch her some tissues from the bathroom. As he came out, he almost collided with Jolyon coming in to the room. "Oh, I say, er hello. Um, Jolyon, Jolyon Urquart. You must be Cook. Pleased to meet you old boy, Helena has mentioned you a lot." They shook hands.

"The poor old thing's feeling a bit down, perhaps you can cheer her up." Denzil gave Helena Ruby the tissues, winked at her then held up his hand and said, "Goodbye then, I'll let you know of any developments and if you need any help, you know where I am."

"Oh thank you," said Helena Ruby as she dabbed her eyes and mopped her nose, "thank you so much, you're a good man."

"Don't know about that Mrs T. Cheerio then!" And he made his exit. As he walked to the car park, smiling he said to himself, "Well, well Helena Ruby, I never thought ..."

Ron happened to know that Hake Hall was unoccupied. Nigel had gone up to town to engage the expert assistance of Messrs Stickletrent Poodle & Crevice, specialist business lawyers to the gentry, and would stay up there for several days in a doomed attempt to negotiate with erstwhile business acquaintances and old family connections to shore up his plummeting fortunes. Isobel could not bear to stay in Hake on Spinach and had gone to stay with her sister in Sturgeon Fields, a cosmopolitan town developed in sympathy with the very latest socio-geographic thinking, and a world away from the grandeur and solitude afforded by Hake Hall. It was something to which Isobel was going to have to get used.

Ron, understandably in light of all that had befallen him, was still nursing a festering grudge against Nigel for the cavalier way in which he had been treated. Who did he think he was, arrogant, unfeeling bastard. And to have encountered his wife with a new man, bold as brass in the hospital, that really had knocked him sideways. As there was very little food left at the Lodge he intended to go and explore the kitchen at the Hall while it was unoccupied, and generally investigate the place. He had nothing to lose and he was driven by the vague need to get even, but he wasn't sure how just yet. He certainly wanted no further encounters with the local constabulary.

Ron knew how to gain entry via the conservatory and the security number to the alarm, and having satisfied himself that he was safely within Hake Hall, turned off his torch and turned on a few lights. Nobody would see them. His hand trembled a little as he pushed open several doors, just to make sure he was alone, and when he saw several bottles of spirits on the shelves in the morning room, he smiled and said out loud "Well just a small one then." He poured himself a single malt whisky, held the glass aloft and offered the toast "Up yours Lamington-Krill!" He grimaced as he took a swig, but as the warming spirit percolated through his system, Ron relaxed a little and sauntered to the kitchen, turned on the light and walked to the vast refrigerator to see what lay within.

Good god, there was an ice-maker, drinks dispenser, cheese humidifier, salad crisper, spillage sensor, internet connection, temperature alarm, yoghurt fermenter, meat isolator, but where was the real food? Ron opened both doors wide and did find an array of unfamiliar foodstuffs. Where was the bacon, the half tins of beans, the cold custard and last week's chicken carcass? He gathered up smoked salmon, cherry tomatoes, pesto sauce, something creamy in a pot, sliced cold rare beef (he supposed it was safe to eat), a wedge of blue cheese (ditto), various green lettuce-like leaves in a plastic bag, and some cold German sausage. It took several trips to the kitchen table, then Ron went about looking for a plate and some cutlery. He was quite unable to comprehend the purpose of most of the equipment he encountered in drawers and cupboards, but eventually found what he was seeking and sat down at the table with a grunt. Eating should never have been this hard work. Salt, he needed salt to make any of this edible, so he got up again and started looking for the stuff. He was unaware of the purpose of the salt grinder but eventually located some highly refined ionised Siberian culinary rock salt in a slim cupboard adjacent the range cooker, and showered his assembled collation with it. After a couple of mouthfuls he decided it needed bread too, but was able to find that with ease in the large crock marked, helpfully 'B R E A D'. He was nonplussed because it wasn't ready-sliced, and did make an untidy job of removing a chunk with an inappropriate knife, but now he had bread and he could continue with his supper. After a few more mouthsful of his exotic fare he needed a drink (not least because of the amount of salt he was consuming), and had noticed some bottled beers in one of the cupboards. "Ronald Arthur Tremble, you deserve it," he said as he opened a bottle of the Fermenting Fish Brewery's legendary Samphire Ale, and took a swig direct from the bottle. He wiped the back of his hand across his mouth, belched and smiled to himself as he walked back to the table and sat down to continue with his meal.

After the traumatic time he had recently endured, exhaustion coupled with alcohol meant that Ronald Arthur

Tremble awoke four hours later with a dead arm and a stiff neck from his slumber on the table. He sat up, groaned, shook his arm back to life then held his neck which was still not fully recovered from his recent mishap. He felt awful. He was so weary, his head hurt, his neck hurt, he was cold and very depressed. At two o'clock in the morning nobody was likely to be returning to Hake Hall, so Ronald Arthur Tremble left the remains of his supper on the kitchen table, went upstairs to Nigel and Isobel's sumptuous bedroom, relieved himself in Isobel's en-suite bathroom, then fully clothed, fell gratefully into their soft, warm and inviting bed, and fell into a deep sleep.

When he awoke in strange surroundings with sunshine streaming through the big windows opposite the bed, Ronald Arthur let forth an expletive as he sat up suddenly and wrenched his neck. His heart was pounding and his mouth was dry. He got out of the bed and straightened his clothes, went to the door and listened nervously for any signs of occupation. There were none. Silence cloaked the place. Calmer now, Ronald Arthur walked surreptitiously down the stairs and into the kitchen. He was desperate for a cup of tea, but nowhere could he find a recognisable kettle, so in an effort to remove all trace of his meal last night, he threw the beer bottle, whisky glass, plate, cutlery and remains of food into the bin, which he had discovered during his search for a plate the night before, cunningly concealed as it was within a mock tea chest. He wiped his hands on his jacket then made for the conservatory from whence he intended to slope out and return to the Lodge for a cup of tea and reappraisal of his situation. However, as he passed the great front door, fate had seen to it that at that precise moment, Patrick Hurst-Peachstone, managing director of Harmony Homes, would be calling, having failed to make contact with Nigel any other way. Nigel was not answering his mobile phone and something very strange was happening at the offices of Lamington-Krill International. Upon returning from an extended holiday in Bermuda, a tanned Patrick had heard from Mr Hockley, amongst others, all manner of very unpleasant rumours circulating and wanted to know what the hell was going on.

Ronald Arthur Tremble froze mid-stride as Patrick rang the bell and knocked on the door too for good measure. He was in full view. With heart pounding, he turned to face the door and went to open it, sliding back the vast iron bolt before turning the key. He held the door only slightly ajar, completely at a loss to know what he would say. "Oh, hello my man, is Mr Lamington-Krill at home?" enquired Patrick. "Er no, he's not here, there's no-one here," responded Ronald Arthur. "So what are you, some sort of caretaker, and where are they?" Here was Ronald Arthur Tremble's opening. "Er, yeah I'm the caretaker and they didn't tell me where they were going."
"Well I'm going to leave a message for Mr Lamington-Krill, will you make sure he gets it please. Look, are you sure he didn't he give you contact details?"
"Yeah."
"OK well can you let me in please and I'll write him a note." Ronald Arthur shrugged, stood aside and let Patrick through the door. He put his briefcase on a side table, opened it and removed a notepad, donned a pair of reading glasses from his top pocket and proceeded to write leaning on his briefcase.

' Nigel, what is going on? Have heard ugly rumours since my return and I hear Bullrushes is going down the pan. Am told we're not covered by insurance and must fund alternative accommodation for residents. Is becoming legal nightmare. Imperative you contact me urgently.

Paddy'

"Do you have an envelope?"

"Er, no, I'm the caretaker," said Ronald Arthur , emboldened by irritation. "Well where's the study, surely there's one in there?"

"It's locked," lied Ronald Arthur , not actually sure which room it was. "Oh very well, just make sure you pass this on as soon as Mr Lamington-Krill gets home, OK? It's imperative." Ronald Arthur Tremble took the folded note and simply said, "Yeah." This was one of his most infuriating traits.

Chapter Fourteen

Helena Ruby Tremble made a good recovery and would be allowed out of hospital as soon as it was established that she would not be alone. She couldn't expect Denzil to be responsible, and it looked as though he might have to vacate Number Eleven shortly in any case. She really could not return to Ron, who in due course would have to vacate the Lodge anyhow. Helena was to all intents and purposes homeless, a not altogether agreeable feeling. "My dear, you must come and stay with me," said Jolyon, "it is the obvious solution."

"That is *so* kind of you, but I couldn't possibly accept. I'd feel I was encroaching on you and ..... oh this sounds silly, but I do believe we should, well, get to know each other better first. I mean, this has all happened out of the blue almost and I need time to adjust, I don't know if I'm on my head or my heels at the moment. And of course, there's the girls - I'm not sure how to go about telling them what's been happening, I don't know what they'll think. Oh, look, I hope you understand." Jolyon smiled, shrugged and said, "Of course I understand. Well OK, let me think," (he tapped his nose with his index finger). "How would it be if you stayed in a flat I have above a jeweller's in Mackerel? It would be good to have it occupied, you could be my caretaker, give the place a good airing! It's furnished, so you don't have to worry about any of that."

"Oh you're too kind, but I still feel it's a terrible imposition, and I'm not supposed to be on my own for the next few days. Oh god, I'm such a pain in the neck, you're so kind, you shouldn't have to be dealing with all this."

"Oh no you're not, and I think I have the solution. I'm sure that my business associate, you know, Roberta, she's looking after the dog, would be happy to keep an eye on you for a couple of days and I bet the little fellow will be delighted to see you again my dear."

"But I can't expect her to ...." Jolyon held up his hand and said, "I happen to know she would be happy to help out, she's really kind hearted and would probably welcome a break from her digs above the off-licence quite honestly."

"But I thought she ... well, must have a boyfriend at least." Helena Ruby blushed and looked down at her hands. "I mean, she sounds gorgeous, I just didn't expect her to live in digs somehow I suppose."

"She is gorgeous, but she is my business associate and that's all, if that's what you're thinking, Helena my dear. There's something you don't know, perhaps I should have told you sooner, but two years ago she was known, quite properly, as Robert."

"What, d'you mean she, er, he's, I mean, are you saying Roberta's, oh, well, what I mean to say is...."

"What I am saying is that Roberta had a sex change and I saw no reason why that should be grounds for unpleasantness, which is why I offered her a job. People can be so nasty and narrow-minded you know."

"Yes, I do know. Heavens, what a surprise!"

"You will get to know her much better and I see no reason why you two won't become good friends. The dog adores her already."

"But will she mind, I mean it's still............"

"Enough, you need some TLC and that, whether you like it or not, is what you are going to get my dear. Should I telephone Mr Fitzpelican and arrange to collect your stuff and get it over to the flat, and is there anything else you'll need?"

"Oh I don't know, I can't really think.... it's all been so....." and Helena Ruby Tremble began shedding tears of gratitude. Jolyon put his arm around her shoulders and said, "You must dry your tears and start enjoying life my dear. Now what about clothes? What should we get you to travel in?"

"Look, I'll ring Cook, er, Denzil," sniffed Helena Ruby. "It's only fair that I let him know what's going on. I feel I've messed him about rather."

"Whatever you feel is best my dear. Well, you make that call and I'll get over there. Number eleven, isn't it?"

Jolyon arrived at Number Eleven, The Bullrushes and was taken aback to find scaffolding, striped tape, danger notices and traffic cones liberally applied about the place, and earth moving plant parked in the cul de sac. He knocked on the door and Denzil opened it with some effort. "Ah hello again, I believe Helena has rung to warn you of my arrival?" enquired Jolyon. "What on earth is going on here? Since when has this become a building site?"

"More of a demolition site I think you'll find," laughed Denzil. "Anyway, come in, I think it's safe! This is the result of, shall we say, an unscrupulous developer's turkeys coming home to roost!"

"That's bad. What will happen, I mean to you and the other residents? I presume you can't stay here with all this going on?"

"Well that's the problem. It seems a certain Mr Lamington-Krill" (- Jolyon raised his eyebrows but said nothing -) "has made himself unavailable and it's his company that's responsible for this. The whole place is literally sinking into a bog. We can't get hold of anybody from Harmony Homes, huh, that's a bit of a sick joke, who's prepared to give any assistance. The local authority people have been as helpful as they can, and if all else fails, it looks like it's bed and breakfast for some of us. Getting lawyers involved is just beyond our means, but it'll be bloody galling if that money-grabbing bugger escapes and leaves us all with this, I can't deny."

"I see," said Jolyon . "Hardly fair is it? Look, give me your mobile number, I'll see what I can do. I've got some contacts who might be able to pull some strings, stir things up a bit for old Lamington-Krill."

"That's uncommon kind of you. Hey, Francis!" he called into the living room, "what's my mobile number?" Francis emerged and smiling, said, "Gee you're hopeless man!"

"Oh, hey, Jolyon, meet Francis, my partner." They shook hands.

"Delighted old boy," said Jolyon. "So are you a master of the culinary arts too?"

"Er, not noticeably. I'm more of a gardener, bit of landscaping, some interior design, that sort of thing."

"Well that's great, it's a pleasure to meet you. Now I'd better collect Helena's stuff and get her installed in Mackerel. Poor old thing's been through a tough time, although it doesn't look like you'll be faring much better!"

"Don't you worry about us, we've been offered temporary lodgings with Francis' sister, I'm sure something can be worked out."

"Well look, here's my card and if you do get stuck, give me a call."

"Thanks, man, that's really good of you," said Denzil.

"Not at all, you've been really decent providing Helena with a bolt hole when she needed it, besides which, I hear you make a mean clam chowder!"

As Francis and Denzil watched Jolyon leave with Helena Ruby Tremble's few belongings, Denzil said, "Well, well, the old thing really seems to have fallen on her feet this time. Good for her! Hah, I wonder what the curtain twitchers must be making of all this!"

"Mmm, nice bloke, who'd have thought, eh!" said Francis.

"But not as nice as you," said Denzil, winking. "OK, so what shall we have as our last supper at Number Eleven?

"Simple and filling. Until you get another job, we're on rations I guess."

"I suppose so, god that Lamington-Krill has got a lot to answer for. Look, before I do food, I'm just going to see if Neville Painswick's in - tell him about Mr Urquart's kind offer."

"OK, but don't be long as this may be the last time we have a place to ourselves for some time. Man, what a way to get to know the neighbours."

"Be back in a flash, promise. May as well open that Fitou and let it breathe, we should dine in style while we can!"

Denzil Fitzpelican rounded the corner and saw Neville Martin Painswick talking to a man wearing a hard-hat and holding a clip-board. He smiled and called out to Neville, "Hi there, I may have a small bit of good news."

"Oh hello Denzil, this is Mr Swelling, from the Housing Inspectorate, he's come to assess the situation."

"Yes, hello, and I have to say, er Mister...?"

"Fitzpelican, Denzil Fitzpelican, I live, or lived, at number eleven. Does this mean progress is being made?"

"Ah, only of an administrative kind I'm afraid Mr Fitzpelican. From what I've seen of the state of the foundations I suspect they are probably beyond repair."

"So what does that mean?"

"It means," said Neville Martin Painswick, "that the whole bloody lot's probably got to come down."

"Oh my god, so who pays, where are we all supposed to live? I mean, who....." Denzil's attention was caught by the sight of Ronald Arthur Tremble walking slightly unsteadily through the main entrance to The Bullrushes. "Hello, what's he doing here?" Denzil said quietly. "Who is it?"

"It's Mrs Tremble's old man, you know, they were employed by the Lamington-Krills at Hake Hall until very recently. I suppose he's still living in the Lodge. Oh dear, I hope he's not come after Mrs T, I ...."

"Hey, you," called Ronald Arthur Tremble as he walked towards the three men who had now all turned to observe him. "Oh you live *here* do you, Mister la-di-da Chef?"

"Hey, come on man, what have I ever done .... I've lost my job too...."

"Yeah, whatever, anyhow I got this and that bastard Lamington-Krill deserves to be knocked off his bloody throne," and he handed over the note from Patrick Hurst-Peachstone.

"Where did this come from?" asked Neville Martin Painswick after reading it through and handing it to the others to see.

"Some bloke who came to the house, pushy bastard, thought I was the caretaker, said it was really important I give it to his lordship. I thought bugger that, so here I am. Hope it will do some damage."

"I think it will certainly help our cause," said Neville Martin Painswick. "Thanks very much, er Mr Tremble isn't it?"

"Yeah, that's right and if anyone's homeless, Hake Hall is empty - pair of them have gone missing and there's plenty of room."

"Hey, now that's an idea," said Denzil, "we could get squatters' rights, live the life of luxury! After all, they made us homeless." It suddenly seemed a far more appealing prospect than sharing a back bedroom in Francis' sister's house, for he just knew that she didn't entirely approve of them.

Mr Swelling declined to offer his opinion, being a servant of the government, and having seen all he needed to see, departed, leaving Ron, Denzil and Neville animatedly discussing the practicalities of invading Hake Hall. Denzil, remembering he had promised he wouldn't be long, said he had to go and get himself a meal so it was agreed that they would re-convene at Neville's house within the hour. Donna was now safely installed at her mother's so he saw no problem, and would get a few beers in.

"Hey man, you'll never guess what!" called Denzil as he shouldered open the front door of Number Eleven.

"That miserable old bugger Tremble has come up with a great idea. How d'you fancy living at Hake Hall - it's empty!"

"Are you serious?"

"You bet, Lamington-Krill is obviously a crook and can't have a legal leg to stand on. It seems the company's got no insurance to cover this current, shall we say, structural oversight. What d'you say?" Francis was standing in the kitchen and poured two glasses of wine for them then said, "I say let's have some cheese on toast, you know, the special way you make it, and talk this through." Forty minutes later Denzil Fitzpelican walked over to Number Five and found Neville Martin Painswick and Ronald Arthur Tremble in expansive mood, having refreshed themselves with Neville's beer. Denzil realised he had not told Neville about Jolyon Urquart's offer of assistance, but bearing in mind present company and Jolyon's relationship with Ronald Arthur Tremble's wife, he felt it best to leave it until some other time. "OK, so what do we think then?" asked Denzil. "We think ..... we think we should move in tonight while we have our chance," said Neville Martin Painswick, with Ron nodding in agreement. "Ron here can let us in, er, legally, you might say, then tomorrow a mate of mine who's got a removal van can move any of our stuff we want to get out."

"Fantastic!" said Denzil. "D'you want a beer?" said Neville Martin Painswick. Not quite knowing how to introduce the subject of Francis in front of Ron, Denzil accepted, although it didn't go down so well after a particularly fine Fitou. "OK, is there anyone else left we ought to include?"

"Don't know, shall we go on a recce now?"

"Er, yes, I guess so, no time like the present and all that!" said Denzil. Ron thought he'd stay put and see what was on the TV, although reception was poor due to the angle at which the aerial was now hanging from the mock chimney. He'd wait until they were ready to go then let them in to Hake Hall. It felt like he'd found some friends at last.

As they picked their way through cones and striped tape, Denzil said, "Look Neville, it's not just me who'll be going up to the Hall, you see, I've got my, er, partner with me."

"Hey, makes no difference to me, sounds like there's plenty of room."

"Yeh, great, but, well I know it shouldn't make any difference, but, well, I'm gay, man."

"Blimey, are you? Oh, sorry mate, I didn't mean it to sound like that. Hey, why should I care?"

"It's just that I know there are some, well, less enlightened people about places like this."

"Yeah, well, they can mind their own bloody business can't they."

"I guess so."

By the end of their recce, Denzil and Neville had signed up three more residents who up until then had been at their wits' end, not knowing where they could go. Neville said, "OK, so let's get on with it then, I suppose. Crikey, this feels weird, but then I suppose it's not every day that your house falls down. Yeah, definitely weird."

"Too true," replied Denzil as they approached Number Five. "Look, before we go in, I meant to tell you, I've met a bloke called Jolyon Urquart, you'd think he was a bit of a hooray Henry but he's actually not bad at all when you get to know him. Now he and Mrs Tremble seem to have become, er, a bit of an item, you see, she's just left him" (he pointed towards the part of Neville's house where he supposed Ron was sitting), "so I couldn't really mention it earlier, anyway, he's got some 'contacts' and is going to see if he can pull some strings for us at least on getting compensation or something. I suppose he must mean solicitors and such like, but I think they're the sort of people you need on your side."

"Great, I'd be pig sick if that arrogant bugger got away with this, knowing all the right people and all that stuff."

"Oh trust me, he is in the unpleasant stuff up to his neck, but that's no reason why we should cop it." Denzil Fitzpelican and Neville Martin Painswick went in to find Ron dozing in an armchair whilst a slightly fuzzy presenter urged everyone to get fit on a bicycle. He started as they came in and clutched his neck as a sharp pain reminded him of his previous recklessness. "Oh, aargh, hello, must have dropped off," said Ron as he gingerly sat forward and turned off the television. "Well I think we're all ready if you are," said Neville. "We've got five more people coming along, oh and Denzil's mate too." Easy-going though he was, Neville Martin Painswick could not bring himself to utter the word 'partner' in front of Ron, and shot an apologetic sideways glance at Denzil. "Many as you like, I don't care," said Ron.

"OK, let's get going then." As Neville Martin Painswick let Denzil out of the front door, Ron took the opportunity to drop a can of beer into each pocket. Denzil narrowly escaped being severely dented by a desiccated hanging basket whose bracket had loosened and was finally dislodged by shock waves from the opening of the front door. "Bloody hell!" exclaimed Denzil as he leapt out of the way. "That's a sign, see," laughed Neville, "- time to get out!"

"Right, we'll meet you and the others in twenty minutes - we'll have us a convoy!"

And so it was that the new residents of Hake Hall arrived with various clothes, toiletries, personal stereos, and any other personal belongings they could carry at short notice. A rather less expensive collection of cars than hitherto was now parked on the gravel in front of Hake Hall. Neville Martin Painswick had gone on ahead with Ron, and after a seamless entry through the conservatory, having nervously established that the place was indeed still empty, they opened the front doors to allow the new lodgers in. Everybody assembled in the hall and were all talking excitedly at once. "Hey, guys!" shouted Denzil. "We'll have to sort out rooms and things. Shall we have a look around?"

"Yeah, great," said Neville, "let's have a look upstairs. Hey, this is like being on holiday, where's the porter!" There was laughter, and supermarket carrier bags, holdalls, dusty suitcases still bearing the labels from long-forgotten holidays abroad and other bits of luggage were left in the entrance hall while their owners went exploring. Lights were turned on, doors were opened and there were exclamations of "Wow!", "Bloody hell!" and "Will you take a look at *that*!" as the lodgers took in the grandeur of the place. Everybody congregated some time later at the head of the main staircase, some still grudgingly marvelling at the scale of the place. Denzil, who seemed naturally to have taken charge being a little more familiar with his surroundings, asked if anybody had any preferences, but apart from the ex-residents of Number Eight taking a particular shine to the wallpaper in one bedroom which they were duly assigned, nobody else was particularly bothered, thus they all went downstairs to collect their luggage and just took the first available room they came to. Ron offered helpfully that the bed in his lordship's room was bloody comfortable, for he was rather enjoying some company and didn't feel inclined to return to the Lodge just yet.

"OK, so who's for the big room then?" asked Denzil. Neville Martin Painswick shrugged and said, "Well there's only me so I'm happy with a smaller one, so why don't you guys have it?" It took several moments for the implication of this invitation to register with Ronald Arthur Tremble, but when it did, he announced bluntly that he was off back to the Lodge as he couldn't stay in a house 'with a couple of queers, and darkies at that.'

"Oh come on," called Neville down the stairs after an affronted Ron, "you can't ....." but Ron marched unhearing out of the front door and stamped back to the Lodge, unable to comprehend the ghastliness of Cook's vile habits. My god, he handled food too.

Upon getting back to the Lodge, Ronald Arthur Tremble felt he needed to regain his composure and took one of the beer cans from his jacket pocket. It had of course been quite severely shaken during its ill-tempered trip back to the Lodge, and as he plonked himself into his armchair and pulled the ring, it showered Ron with malty yet refreshing Barbel Budget Bitter. He uttered a particularly ripe expletive and went to bed in disgust.

Before retiring to bed at Hake Hall, Denzil, Francis and Neville ensured as best they could that the place was secured from inside, for apart from anything else, Francis was particularly nervous about Ron returning to do them harm in the night. "Blimey, what a day!" said Neville Martin Painswick, dreading the prospect of informing Donna about what, in some lights, could be regarded as his reckless decision. He had run through several imagined conversations with her, all of which inevitably ended in her demanding he stay with her at her mother's. It was a truly depressing prospect and he was having so much more fun with his newly-found friends at Hake Hall. And it was so much handier for work too. "How about a night-cap lads, I think we deserve it don't you?" said Denzil. "Good idea, man," responded Francis who was still distressed at Ronald Arthur Tremble's vituperative outburst. They followed Denzil into the kitchen and sat at the table sipping brandy, getting to know each other a bit better and reflecting upon what lay ahead for them all.

Chapter Fifteen

As the new residents at Hake Hall awoke to their new surroundings, so Helena Ruby Tremble awoke in the flat situated above Elfinstone and Goldfarb, High Quality Jewellers. She hadn't slept particularly well due to some pain from her injured leg and being in strange surroundings herself, but it was nice to be in a large, comfortable bed without the inescapable smell of anti-bacterial gel and all the early morning clatter and bustle associated with hospital. Helena Ruby picked up her watch from the side table and after a moment taken to focus on it, saw that the time was 8.45. She yawned and stretched her arms. Jolyon had left a small bell for her to ring if she needed anything, but she just couldn't bring herself to use it. She smiled at the thought of his solicitousness as she slowly sat up then pulled back the covers in order to get out of bed. There was a walking stick propped against the side table which she used to take her weight and she took a moment just to steady herself before going to the door. "You may as well be ninety," she said to herself as she unhooked her dressing gown, of which she was growing less and less fond by the day, and slipped her arms into it. Leaning again on her stick, she opened the door and had to take a moment to get her bearings. The bathroom was just opposite, but before going in, she felt she should alert Roberta to the fact that she was up and about. (As Jolyon had anticipated, she was delighted to be able to assist.) "Er, hello, good morning!" called Helena Ruby softly.

"Oh hello, did you sleep well? How are you feeling?" said Roberta as she came out of the sitting room door to the right.   "Ah, fine thanks, it's so nice not to have plastic under the sheets!"

"Great! So what can I get you, tea, coffee? Would you like some breakfast? Come and sit down, you know you've got to keep that leg up as much as possible!"

"Ooh, just a cup of tea would be lovely for now thank you, I'll just pop into the bathroom first." As Helena Ruby stood washing her hands she looked at herself in the mirror and grimaced. Her hair was in a terrible state and she had large, dark rings under her eyes. Her shabby dressing gown did nothing to enhance her appearance either. The only thing she had noticed during her sojourn in hospital was that she had lost a little weight, but so what? How was she going to pull herself back into shape, and apart from anything else, what was she going to do about money? She had about a hundred and fifty pounds left in her own account but that was all. She knew that Jolyon would give her anything she needed, but her pride and independence wouldn't allow her to become a kept woman.

With all this going around in her mind, Helena Ruby came out of the bathroom and went to the sunny sitting room where Roberta was waiting with a cup of tea for her.
"Oh dear, I look such a fright, you must think you're living with a convalescing bag lady!" said Helena Ruby as she sat in a faded tapestry-effect arm chair. "Not at all, may I call you Helena?," said Roberta as she passed Helena her tea, and Helena could not help but notice the elegantly manicured and polished nails. How strange to think they used to be a man's. "Look, as part of your, er, rehabilitation, would you like me to do your hair, bit of a manicure? I can even stretch to a facial! I used to work in a beauty salon a few years ago, and I'm sure I can't have lost my touch."

"Oh," said Helena, blushing, "that would be *so* nice, I just feel so, well, *shabby*. I mean, apart from anything else, look at this awful dressing gown - it's only fit for a dust sheet, and probably big enough too! I have to admit, this all still seems so weird, I mean, what can Jolyon see in me? Why is he being so terribly kind, I don't deserve all this."

"Jolyon has always been most adept at seeing below the surface Helena, and I know he thinks the world of you.

He's a very unusual man under that exterior," Roberta laughed in those silky tones of hers, "rather like me!"

Helena was beginning to take to Roberta more and more and any initial discomfort soon evaporated. It had been agreed that Denholm would be brought over later that day once Helena Ruby had settled in. She was so looking forward to seeing him again, and hoped he would hold no grudges. "OK, so the first thing I need to do is pay a quick visit to the pharmacy to pick up your prescription and I can get some shampoo and stuff while I'm there. I'll be back in twenty minutes. This is my mobile number - ring me if there's anything at all and I'll be straight back."

"Oh well let me give you some money," said Helena Ruby, feeling uncomfortable.

"Don't worry about that, we can settle up later," said Roberta. "Jolyon has left me a kitty."

"Look, tell me honestly, what should I do? I've got no job any more, I have about a hundred and fifty pounds to my name and that's all. I just feel such a, well, a freeloader. I can't live off Jolyon, it's just not right."

"I know how you must feel, really, I've been there myself, but trust me, the minute you're back on track, Jolyon will give you every opportunity to, how should I put it, re-establish yourself. He gets so much out of helping people, and in your case, it goes rather deeper than that as I'm sure you know. Trust me Helena, you will get ample opportunity to repay his kindness if you feel you need to, but he doesn't expect it. Get yourself fully recovered and I guarantee, your life will be transformed. You've got to learn to relax and enjoy yourself now. What's the point of doing otherwise?"

"Oh, thank you," sighed Helena as she felt those tears welling up again. "I just can't..." and she started to cry, mopping her eyes with the cuff of her dressing gown.

"Hey, come on, I know it's all a bit much at the moment and you're still recovering. Here, have a tissue - it's probably more absorbent than your sleeve!"

"Oh dear, thank you," sniffed Helena Ruby, "you're so kind. Sometimes I wonder whether I'm menopausal. I never used to grizzle like this."

"Ah, now that's something I can't advise you on!"

"Lucky you, I say," said Helena, managing a smile. "Now that's better. So, no fretting while I'm away and when I get back we'll make a start on restoring you to your former gorgeous self. You've got a good bone structure you know."

Whilst Roberta was out on her errand Helena Ruby took the opportunity to wash as best she could, as she was not supposed to get her injured leg wet, then dressed in a floral blouse and loose trousers, which were easier to get on. It was quite an effort and Helena Ruby was thankful to sit down again. She idly picked up a glossy magazine from the table beside her chair. Having leafed through articles about how to keep your husband faithful, interesting ways with window treatments, slimmers' alarming tales, giving your kitchen a facelift which need not cost the earth and hints for successful dining, Helena Ruby decided that she was going to have to find something useful with which to occupy her time, or she would rapidly become dreadfully bored. As she sat looking at photographs of bathroom accessories for a dazzling new look, the telephone rang, making her jump. She dropped the magazine back on the table and having got out of the chair, walked towards the sound of the ringing phone. It was in the kitchen. Helena Ruby picked up the handset and said hesitantly, "Er hello..."

"Hello my dear, so you're up then?" came Jolyon's reassuring voice. "I trust you're being well looked after?"

"Oh, hello, it's so nice to hear from you, yes, I couldn't ask for more. Roberta is *so* kind."

"Good, and I trust you're feeling well. How's the leg today?"

"Bit stiff, but not so bad. It's just so frustrating being an invalid. I feel so useless. Look, is there anything I can do to help while I'm like this? I want to be of some use."

"Now that will take some consideration, but if you overdo it you won't be doing yourself any favours will you?"

"No, I suppose not."

"Anyway, I thought it would amuse you to learn that some of the residents made homeless at The Bullrushes have moved into Hake Hall whilst the Lamington-Krills are elsewhere. That splendid fellow Denzil is one of them! Now, you want something to do, and he is currently unemployed. Might I call round later to run an idea up the flagpole and see if you think it worthy of salute?"

"Good grief! What, d'you mean they're, well, squatting I suppose?"

"To all intents and purposes my dear, but it doesn't seem an unduly inequitable move to me, after all, it is Lamington-Krill who's ultimately responsible for their houses sinking into a bog, as I understand it. As Denzil so eloquently put it, his turkeys are coming home to roost!"

"Sounds like they are. Well, well, well. Anyhow, you know I would love to see you. Will you be able to bring the dog too?"

"Certainly, I believe he's desperate to see you both. I'm clearly a poor substitute. Look, I have a business lunch so I'll be over to see you after that. If you're feeling up to it, would you like to dine out this evening? It wouldn't be too late."

"Oh I'd love to, but shouldn't we invite Roberta too? I'd feel so, well, mean leaving her behind after all her kindness."

"Of course, and depending upon how things pan out, we might include Denzil too, and why not his partner as well!"

"Oh I'd love to meet her, what's she like, have you met her?"

"Um Francis, yes I have, it's actually, well, *he* was at the house when I went to collect your things." Helena Ruby was distracted as Roberta came through the front door and didn't catch the end of Jolyon's last sentence. "Oh,

Roberta's back, she's going to do my hair for me, so I should look a bit more presentable when I see you at least."

"Ah, excellent, well I'll leave you two to get on with things and I'll be along later complete with the dog."

"Oh thank you, thank you so much."

"Goodbye for now then my dear."

"'Bye."

"I still can't believe how kind everybody is being," said Helena Ruby Tremble as she put down the telephone.

"You'll get used to it. Right, the first thing I need to do is wash your hair, or would you be better off doing that? Oh, and I got you this while I was out," and Roberta handed a bag over to Helena Ruby. It contained an emerald green silk dressing gown. "Oh I can't .... you shouldn't have .... it's gorgeous!" said Helena Ruby as she removed it from the bag and held it up. "Consider it a gift to cheer you up and set you on the road to recovery and your fantastic new life!"

"Oh thank you, thank you so much," and Helena Ruby put her arms around Roberta's neck and kissed her surprisingly soft cheek.

"You're really most welcome, now this hair ......"

By the time Jolyon appeared at the flat, Helena was feeling nervous about how he would react to her polished appearance, which she was having some difficulty relating to herself. She was acutely self-conscious and had to keep looking in the mirror, which gave Roberta much cause for amusement. "OK, he's here," said Roberta, "stand by to repel boarders!" Helena Ruby Tremble was actually sitting by with her leg up on a footstool, as instructed by the nurse. Roberta brought Jolyon in to the sitting room and said, "Here she is, resting her leg as instructed."

"Well hello my dear," said Jolyon smiling expansively and revealing a set of even, white teeth. "You look sensational!" Helena Ruby blushed and looked down at her Etruscan Rosebud nails. "Thank you, it's all Roberta's handiwork," said Helena Ruby, looking up and into Jolyon's twinkling blue eyes. "I don't think so, but anyway, if I can concentrate for long enough, I have a proposition for you, a business proposition."

"Ooh sounds exciting," said Helena Ruby, her confidence growing. "But before that, sorry, did you bring Denholm with you?"

"Yes of course I have, he's in the car, just wanted to make sure you were prepared."

"Look, shall I take him for a walk first?" asked Roberta, whom Jolyon sometimes thought must be telepathic. "I'll pick up some food for the little fellow while we're out too."

"Splendid idea, don't you think, Helena Ruby? Here are the car keys. Thank you, Roberta."

"Ah, yes, I'm sure he'd appreciate the exercise, yes, thank you."

"A pleasure. See you both in about, say three quarters of an hour, then hopefully Denholm will be sufficiently worn out and will settle down without too much trouble. 'Bye for now!" And Roberta left the flat.

"Oh my darling Helena Ruby," breathed Jolyon as leant down to kiss her, "come to bed, I can't resist you!" Helena without demur, allowed Jolyon gently to help her up and, resting on his arm, accompanied him to the bedroom where he undressed her tenderly, kissing her on her shoulders and back as she attended with trembling fingers to the buttons on his shirt, and they made love on the bed, taking care not to cause her leg any further injury. Breathless and blissfully happy, Helena Ruby lay cradled in Jolyon's arms, for the first time not feeling the need to say or explain anything. Jolyon glanced at his watch and said, "I say my dear, I suggest we put our clothes back on, Roberta is likely to be back soon."

"Oh good grief, of course, I forgot." Helena Ruby sat up and ran her fingers through her hair. "Oh dear, have I undone all Roberta's marvellous handiwork?"

"Hardly, and no need for panic my dear, let me help you." Helena Ruby just loved Jolyon's caring and gentle touch. As they stood looking at each other holding hands, now fully clothed, kissing Helena Ruby, Jolyon said, "You have got the most beautiful, expressive eyes, Helena Ruby. Do you *really* want to stay here? Please, come and be with me." He kissed her on her forehead then said, "You go and sit down and I'll make us some tea while you have a think about it."

Helena Ruby walked serenely to the sitting room and sat on the sofa, just as the sound of Roberta's key in the door could be heard. She smiled as she heard the scrabbling of Denholm's small feet as Roberta put him down, and she called to him. Denholm came rushing in to the sound of his mistress's voice and almost squealed with delight. His wagging tail was a blur as she scooped him up on to her lap and hugged him. Roberta put her head around the door and smiling, said "Well that didn't wear him out did it!"

"Oh, thanks everso much, it's so lovely to see him again!" Jolyon came in with tea for all of them and said, "So, about this business idea of mine. In a nutshell, I have recently acquired a restaurant premises in Herring le Parterre, lovely little place, but it needs a major overhaul and I think a rather more inventive menu. The whole thing needs livening up. At the moment it's just far too ... twee and unadventurous. There'd definitely be demand for such a venue in that neck of the woods. Do you think, Helena Ruby, that Denzil Fitzpelican might be interested in such a project and would Helena Ruby Tremble be prepared to do a little project management on my behalf? It also occurred to me that Denzil's partner might do some interior design work for me, that being his line of expertise."

"I didn't know he had a business partner," said Helena Ruby, "he's never mentioned him before."

"He hasn't," said Jolyon, "Francis is his, I believe it's called, life partner. I mentioned him on the telephone earlier."

"Oh, oh, no, how stupid of me," said Helena Ruby, blushing slightly, "I just assumed ... I didn't hear.... I wasn't .... hmm, well, well, I shouldn't ever make assumptions should I?"

"Ah, we've all been guilty of that in our lives my dear. Anyway, would you be inclined to help me out with organising it all? I've got a pretty hefty workload coming up, several major projects and I may have to be abroad for a bit." Helena Ruby Tremble was assailed with self-doubt again, but she wanted to do something useful so she said, "If you think I'm capable then of course, I'd be delighted. Will you need to be away for long?" Helen Ruby Tremble suddenly realised how much she would hate Jolyon being abroad and how badly she wanted to be with him. "Marvellous. No firm travel plans yet my dear, all depends upon how business goes. Anyway, don't trouble yourself about that now, should we get in touch with Denzil and see if he's free for dinner this evening, and of course, ask Francis along too?"

"Yes, why not!" said Helena Ruby "It would be lovely.... but... I... ah, but, where would we go, I haven't got anything decent to wear." Helena Ruby's cheeks coloured up again and she felt suddenly most terribly drab. "Tell you what," said Jolyon, "I'll ask Roberta to sort it all out while I take you into Mackerel centre and we'll get you something that'll make you feel good. My project manager needs to look the part!" Jolyon held up his hand to signal that he would hear no arguments. Jolyon winked at Roberta and said, "Make sure you book a seat for yourself too. We'll be back in about an hour or two I should think."

"D'you mind having Denholm?" asked Helena Ruby as she got up from beside a slumbering Dachshund. He merely sighed deeply and rolled over as she moved.

"No problem, looks like he's worn out at last!"

"Thank you," said Helena Ruby, smiling.

When she was safely installed beside Jolyon in the car, she said, "When you said you would be going abroad..."

"Only might, my dear, only might."

"Yes, well, I can't deny that the thought of being apart from you... well, I can't bear it. If you really want me to come and stay with you, I, I will, it would be perfect. It's just that I can't ....."

"Helena Ruby Tremble you have just made me immeasurably happy, you need say nothing further." Jolyon leant across and squeezed Helena Ruby's arm affectionately.

"Yes, but I intend to pay my way. I need to be able to account for myself, if you know what I mean. I... it's... oh I don't want you to think.... "

"Whatever makes you happy, will make me happy, now let's find you something smashing!"

Helena Ruby emerged hesitantly from the changing rooms of Messrs Finial & Turnstile's Fashion for Discerning Women. She had never been in quite such an establishment before. She was wearing a flattering chocolate brown linen trouser suit which had been chosen with the help of a sniffy shop assistant, whose attitude mellowed following Jolyon's intervention. "Why that's simply splendid my dear, suits your colouring. Yes, we'll have that. I think a couple of blouses too while we're about it, don't you?"

"But it's ..." started Helena Ruby, then looking down at her tired floral blouse, couldn't help but smile as Jolyon imperiously held up his hand. "OK, I'll choose a couple." While Helena Ruby Tremble was leafing through racks of blouses, Jolyon found a rather eye-catching silk scarf which he passed to the shop assistant and told her to add to the purchases. "So is there anywhere else you'd like to visit while we're here?" asked Jolyon. Helena Ruby's leg was beginning to complain from too much exercise so she said, "Oh no, really, I must admit, I know I sound like a ninety-year-old, but I wouldn't mind a bit of a rest before we go out later. I need to take the weight off my leg for a while. Doctor's orders you know!"

"Righto, let's get back to the flat and see what Roberta has managed to arrange." The shop assistant archly observed Helena Ruby and Jolyon leave, not quite able to work out quite what might be going on there. Jolyon put the bags into the boot of his car having helped Helena Ruby into her seat first, then got in and said, "You don't have to prove anything to me you know Helena, I know what's genuine, believe me."

"Oh I know, Roberta said….. well, anyway, I, er, I suppose I just want to repay your kindness. I can't just sit around and absorb your generosity you know, it just goes against the grain – I might get splinters! And I suppose I want to be, well, part of a team, not just someone along for the ride."

"And part of the team you shall be my dear, now let me take you for a ride back to the flat at least!"

"Yes, home James and all that! You know, I still can't believe …."

"Well believe it you must my dear, you are about to embark on a most rewarding chapter, and I hope I shall be with you until we reach the endpaper."

The meal later with Roberta, Denzil and Francis proved most successful and Jolyon could not help but congratulate himself on having drawn together an excellent team, quite by chance. But most of all he congratulated himself on having persuaded Helena Ruby to come back and live at Elver Place with him. Helena Ruby had had the best (or possibly second-best) evening of her life and she was so tired when they returned from the meal that Roberta agreed she would stay the night with her in the flat, and that tomorrow she would help Helena Ruby Tremble take her belongings to Elver Hall. Denholm was so pleased to see them that he was allowed to sleep on the bed that night.

Chapter Sixteen

Neville Martin Painswick returned gratefully to Hake Hall after being obliged to spend the week-end with Donna and her parents. As he had predicted, Donna was deeply unhappy about his decision to take up his alternative residence and was barely prepared to countenance what he considered an eminently sensible solution to their current travails, being so much more convenient for getting to work.

The Spratley family, of whom Donna was the second-eldest child, lived on the outskirts of Great Roach, which was a good fifty minute drive to Neville's workshop. Currently Donna's eldest brother Ambrose was living there too until he found further employment as a mortuary technician, so things were a little cramped in their three-bedroomed semi-detached residence with scope for improvement. His father, Kevin, called him 'rice pudding' not because he did bear a faint resemblance to that confection, but because his mother had chosen the name following her near addiction to the stuff whilst she was pregnant with him. It seemed appropriate.

It was actually Mr Kevin Spratley who came to Neville's aid and did agree that it made sense for his son-in-law to live nearer his work, especially as they were a bit short of space and surely he couldn't sleep on the sofa every night. There followed an animated discussion about the feasibility of putting a double bed in Donna's room, but the swift application of a tape measure put paid to that idea. Added to which, somebody ought to be keeping an eye on The Bullrushes, and Neville did seem to have the right contacts on that front. Neville Martin Painswick could have kissed Kevin Spratley. Hazel Spratley asked Donna why she didn't go to Hake Hall with Neville if there was so much room, but to his relief, Donna proclaimed that she was not prepared to share a house, however big it might be, with strangers and weirdos, especially not in her condition. Thus it was that Neville Martin Painswick had kissed his wife goodbye, bidding her to take great care of herself, and headed back to Hake Hall. Kevin Spratley had obliquely indicated that he wouldn't mind accompanying him as they walked to the car together. Neville felt sorry for his father-in-law, who did seem to have aged before his time.

As Neville Martin Painswick approached Hake Hall from Great Roach, so Nigel Lamington-Krill was driving home from the City. His mission remained unaccomplished inasmuch as erstwhile business acquaintances weren't available to see him, or the one who did deign to have lunch with him, having been unfortunate enough to walk into the reception office just as Nigel was standing there, did offer the opinion that once entangled with Serious Fraud, he was pretty much untouchable, but it had been good to make his acquaintance again. God, the bastards could be so fickle. Fair weather friends and all that. Nobody had any moral fibre or loyalty these days. Still, Messrs Stickletrench Poodle & Crevice felt they could probably mount a defence sufficient to keep him out of prison at least and as that was the only straw available, Nigel was going to cling to it.

Neville arrived first, parked in front of the Hall and bounded up the steps to the front door. What a difference! Light, air, and sufficient space for the items of footwear, luggage awaiting dispersal, rescued pot plants, electrical appliances and odd furnishings which needed to be kept quite dry, to be hardly noticeable. It wasn't possible to get any of their cars in the garage because that now housed two containers which held the remainder of the displaced residents' chattels. Neville Martin Painswick unlocked the front door (for they had all agreed at their first residents' meeting that it was wise to keep it locked regardless of who was present) and, tripping over a pair of wellington boots, went to the kitchen to see if Denzil was there. It would be the natural place to find him as the residents had also agreed that he was best placed and better qualified than any of them to produce meals for the assembled throng, most of whom tended to eat at about the same time. This seemed equitable as he wasn't really in a position to make much financial contribution in his present circumstances, and he was happy to be kept occupied for the time being. The best bit was being able to sound the ancient dinner gong which had been idle for a good twenty years. Mrs Slingback from Number Eight had worked up quite a sweat polishing the thing, but now it gleamed like some celestial orb as it stood in the hall. She had had to re-stuff the head of the drumstick as it had been eaten by mice. She just knew that one day her attendance at evening classes for furniture restoring would prove useful, and that Mr Slingback would feel his bingo winnings not entirely mis-spent.

"Hey Denzil, is that you?" said Neville Martin Painswick to a pair of feet visible under the refrigerator door.

"It sure is." Denzil closed the door with his elbow and placed several large dishes of lasagne on the kitchen table.

"Wow, that looks good," said Neville.

"Not exactly feeding of the five thousand, but keeps my hand in!"

"Great, well I managed to escape being imprisoned with the Spratleys, but Donna isn't happy, she ......" Neville Martin's eye was drawn to the sight of an apoplectic Nigel appearing at the back door and rattling the handle. "Oh shit, bloody hell. I suppose we'd better let him in," said Neville, gesturing towards the door. "Oh christ," said Denzil, "this is going to be *bad*." As he was closest, he went and turned the key and opened the door, through which Nigel burst in a self-righteous rage. "Just what the fuck is going on?" he demanded of the two at volume, as they stood there rather like schoolboys outside the headmaster's study. "What are all those bloody cars doing, why is the front door......"

"What you should be asking, Mr Lamington-Krill," butted in Neville Martin, suddenly incensed and surprising himself, "is what the residents of the Bullrushes are supposed to do with their shoddy bloody houses sinking into the shit."

"That's not my concern. Who are you?" Without waiting for an answer and turning to Denzil, Nigel said, "Cook, I demand to know what's going on. I thought I could trust you at least. Betrayed by my own staff, bloody hell, I took you on when nobody else would....." Denzil drew himself up straight and squared his broad shoulders. Neville wondered whether he was going to hit Nigel. "Not being an employee any more, I don't believe I am answerable to you squire, however in the interests of clarity," (Nigel snorted with rage and banged his fist on the table, causing several items of cutlery to jump and clatter) "as the houses Harmony Homes so thoughtfully built for us, no doubt at a huge profit, on a bog are no longer safe to stay in, those without alternative accommodation," (Denzil paused to draw breath) "and in the absence of anybody from Harmony Homes shouldering their legal responsibilities, and you might refer to a certain Paddy Hurst-Peachstone for clarification, thought it only equitable that we camp out here for now. OK?"

"That's outrageous, I'm calling the bloody police!"

"If you feel that would be useful." Francis came through the kitchen door from the hall before Nigel had the opportunity to respond further.

"Hey, man, what's going on? Hey, guys, I've got a new commission!"

"Fant ......" began Denzil, before being cut short by another splenetic outburst from Nigel.

"Who the bloody hell is he?" spluttered Nigel. "Christ, what is this, an immigration centre?"

"Yes, we've got Home Office approval, didn't you hear?" said Neville. "The tents are going up outside next week."

"I'm not listening to this," fumed Nigel, "I'll have the lot of you evicted. Get out, get out of my house, all of you, " he yelled as he went into the hall, becoming even more enraged as he witnessed the scale of the invasion. He picked up a radio which was balanced on the back of an ornate Italian chair and hurled it at the stairs, kicked anything in his path and bellowed threats and expletives, enough to bring everybody present from their rooms. "Oh dear, he's not very happy is he?" said Mrs Slingback, always a keen observer of the human condition. "Hey, that's my camera!" shouted Mr Tickburn as Nigel flung the item at the front door, causing the thing to disintegrate.

"Get out, get out of my house, you parasites!" yelled Nigel as he launched a dusty pot plant after the camera. "What are you all looking at, you sheep? Want to see what a true man is made of?" With his audience gathered at the top of the stairs, Nigel unzipped his fly and proceeded to urinate on any shoes, bags or belongings within his range. At that, Mr Slingback urged his wife, agog at Nigel Lamington-Krill's outburst, to return to the room while he 'sorted this out'. He and Mr Tickburn ran down the stairs, grabbed Nigel by the arms and frog-marched him out of the front door before he had the chance even to close his flies. This was not the way for a man of property to be seen leaving his own premises. Denzil and Francis watched from the kitchen doorway and could not suppress their laughter at the sight. Neville Martin Painswick meanwhile, helpfully, ran out to the drive with the two suitcases Isobel had packed for their holiday in Rio, as he supposed it was better for them to be with their rightful owner, and if he had some clothes he might not come back. He dropped them by the car and fled back up the steps.

The sound of Nigel leaving at speed in his car could clearly be heard, as the two men came back through the front door saying, "Well I think he got the message," and "What a wanker!"

"He's unhinged," said Denzil.

"He's a bloody fascist," said Francis. Mr Slingback and Mr Tickburn were of the opinion that they could take care of him if he showed his face again. "Yes, well, er, that's great," said Neville Martin Painswick, "but d'you think that nutcase *will* come back, I mean, are we safe? He may try to burn the house down or poison the water supply."

"Look he's hardly likely to burn his own house down is he, he's already in big trouble."

"But he's clearly got a bit of a screw loose, I vote we all take turns to keep watch, just in case," said Neville Martin Painswick, now thinking that maybe sleeping on the Spratley's sofa, although uncomfortable, might be safer than squatting in Hake Hall with Nigel Lamington-Krill out for their blood. "Well let's see what everybody else thinks," said Denzil. "Dinner will be ready in half an hour, so we can talk it over then." Mr Slingback and Mr Tickburn went to the small sitting room for a pre-prandial stiff drink, for they could not deny that despite their bravado, they were a trifle unsettled by recent events, and a preoccupied Neville Martin Painswick went upstairs for a shower. It was not a particularly satisfying shower as the ageing hot water system of Hake Hall was failing to cope with the demands placed upon it by this suddenly expanded population.

"Anyhow, as I was trying to say before that lunatic started," said Francis to Denzil as he continued preparing a meal in the kitchen, "I've got a new commission. Out of the blue. Had a call from somebody by the name of, er, a Mrs Strang-Wellow – seems a straightforward sort of a woman. Anyway, she wants some major re-landscaping done *and* a bit of interior stuff. She said she's as hopeless as a myopic tree-frog and decided to get it done properly at last. Said she never did like her husband's taste, and now he's dead, well…. Clearly loaded, and I was recommended to her by our friends at the Mal de Mer."

"Fantastic news, as I think I tried to say earlier," laughed Denzil and he put his arm around Francis' shoulders and gave him a congratulatory squeeze and a kiss on the cheek. "I said I'd go and do a bit of a survey tomorrow, she lives in Bream, should be able to get there and back in a day quite comfortably, but I think she lives right on the outskirts, seems to be almost a small estate from what I can gather. Still, that'll be a good six months' work at least. Denzil, we're on our way!"

"Well praise the lord!"

"And all his seraphim and cherubim."

"Yeah, and everybody else who knows him, man."

"So why don't we open a bottle of the master's best vintage to celebrate. A bottle of sparkling stuff perhaps?"

"Yeah, why not man, cause for celebration!"

At dinner, the general consensus was that as long as the house was secured firmly from inside, there was little that Nigel Lamington-Krill could do to cause them harm. He seemed to be full of hot air and not much else from what had been witnessed, and they could always call the police, they supposed. It was a shame that the security lights didn't work. Neville Martin Painswick was not entirely convinced and elected to sleep on a sofa pulled into the hall, armed with a vintage walking stick taken from the stand by the front door, and a monkey wrench from his tool box. He did not sleep well because the sofa was particularly lumpy and not really long enough. However, he did dream fleetingly of Sonia and awoke in the darkness in no small state of excited anticipation.

He slept rather better than Nigel Lamington-Krill however. Nigel, his rage and bile having subsided a little (for it was a very exhausting state to maintain, and he had nearly driven into two fellow road-users already) realised that if he was to get to Sturgeon Fields, for nobody except Isobel's sister (and that was under sufferance) was prepared to accommodate him, he would need to put more fuel in the car as the gauge was now touching the red bar. He came to an abrupt halt on the forecourt of a petrol station situated on the outskirts of Mackerel, filled the tank then walked to the shop to pay, picking up a newspaper on the way. He presented his titanium credit card which was rejected, couldn't understand it and presented an alternative, also rejected. The dreadful, horrible truth began to dawn upon him. This was what it was like to have frozen assets. In an attempt to extricate himself from this abominable situation he shrugged and said, "Oh, I know what's happened, my current cards are in the glove compartment, haven't swapped them round yet!" The cashier however knew differently, for the fact that an unauthorised user was attempting to pay with a suspended card was indicated on her screen, and she had already followed procedure and remotely alerted the local constabulary. "I'll just go and get them, back in a tick!" The cashier remained impassive, having taken note of his registration plate as Nigel, although trying to look nonchalant, half ran to the Jensen, jumped in, started the engine then took off at high speed, ploughing through the corner of a pile of barbecue charcoal sacks and scattering the contents hither and thither. His one thought was to get away from there as fast as he could. The cashier was obviously stupid enough to have believed him.

"Good grief, I don't believe it," said Constable Berwick to the driver as they pursued Jensen Interceptor registration NLK 100X, the owner of which had knowingly driven away without paying for his fuel. "Oh fucking hell," shouted Nigel as they bore down upon him with flashing blue lights. He came to a halt and was now quivering with nervous rage as he leant his head on the steering wheel, not really being able to believe this latest turn of events. Constable Berwick strolled to the side of the car and knocked on Nigel's window. Nigel sat up, wearily wound down the window, and recognising Constable Berwick said, "Oh bloody hell it's you again. Come to gloat, have you? Look, I didn't realise ...."

"Sir, I must caution you," said Constable Berwick and he read Nigel his rights.

At the police station, Nigel sat tired and ill-tempered waiting for Isobel and her sister, Henrietta, who had been persuaded to stand bail for Nigel. He had attempted to raise the small matter of his house having been as good as stolen from him, place overrun by gypsies and bloody asylum seekers in the kitchen, but he was ranting, and it was suggested that when he was a little calmer and could decide upon the exact nature of his complaint, then the matter would be taken up further if it was felt there were legally justified grounds. When finally his two unwilling saviours arrived and the necessary paperwork had been completed in extreme bad humour, Nigel was allowed to leave. Not however, before having shared his unfavourable opinion upon the quality of the tea served at the police station, and now it was Isobel's turn to rant, ably assisted by Henrietta who was a good deal more shrill than her younger sister. "I just don't know how you could have been so stupid Nigel, you knew our accounts had been frozen."

"Look, I forgot, and how else was I supposed to get anywhere to sleep for the night?"

"Yes, well, that's another thing, why in the name of sweet reason are those people in our house, I just can't leave anything for a moment can I?"

"Isn't it something to do with those houses Nigel had built, not safe any more, did I understand correctly, Nigel?" asked Henrietta. "Well I suppose we'd better go and get your bloody car then," said an exasperated Isobel as they walked into the car park. Nigel at least could drive to Sturgeon Fields in peace. How could life have gone so horribly wrong for him? Constable Berwick, smiling, was thinking much the same thing as he watched Nigel walk out into the night. He was looking forward to his promotion in the next couple of months.

As Neville Martin Painswick went into work the following morning, he could not get the thought of Sonia de Souza out of his head. His dream had seeped into his consciousness. Melvin had three days off as he was moving out of the family home into rented accommodation. His mother was coming home for a trial period with the two new additions and he felt it best to make more room for them. He had promised her that he would be close at hand in case she needed him, for she had not maintained a robust constitution. As Neville Martin pulled on his overalls, his back and shoulders ached from the previous night's sleeping arrangements, and he swung his arms around and rubbed his neck to try to ease the stiffness. He stood waiting for the kettle to boil, reflecting upon the strange circumstances in which he had become embroiled, then smiled and said to himself, "Aah, what the hell, life's for living!" and, turning on the radio, picked up his tea and his tool box and walked over to the ramp to commence work on a vintage MG belonging to a dentist in Great Roach who had, coincidentally, been recommended to him by Trevor de Souza during a course of root canal treatment.

At midday Neville had finished working on the MG and was looking at his diary. Apart from having to collect Mrs Pippa Dent-Rokeby's Lancia from its MOT later that afternoon, he was free. Time for a little R and R perhaps? Had Sonia really meant what she said, or was she just teasing him? He still couldn't get the woman out of his mind after dreaming about her, so, wondering what on earth he thought he was doing, he called the mobile number on the card that she had given him and was already rehearsing what he would say when Sonia answered, "Hello, Sonia de Souza." He could hear the sound of conversation and glasses clinking in the background. "I, er, oh hello, it's, um Neville, Painswick, I...."

"Oh hello, is it time for another service?"

"Well, I suppose you could say, er, you see I'm free for a couple of hours and I've got the workshop to myself and well, you know, I just wondered, I mean, did you mean ...."

"Why yes I did. I'm just having a drink at the gym. My personal trainer is *very* pleased with my progress. I can meet you in, say, half an hour. Shall we meet at the Manse, it will be *so* much more comfortable? I could do with another work-out." Neville Martin marvelled at her voracious appetite and said weakly, "Of course, if, I mean, er, well, if you're sure it's safe, I, well, I'll um, meet you there."

"Trust me, it will be just fine. Ciao big boy, and bring your overalls!"

Oh my god, had he really just arranged what he thought he had? Trembling slightly, Nigel switched on his answerphone and went to the sink to scrub his hands. He splashed water on his face and mopped it dry with a paper towel. It would take him about twenty minutes to get to Lamprey Manse, and he didn't want to appear too eager, after all, he wasn't the woman's puppet. He paced back and forth rehearsing his opening line, then visited the toilet, washed his hands again and looked at himself in the cracked mirror above the sink. He ran his fingers through his hair then grinned at his reflection and said, "OK, let's do it!". He took a tube of mints from the top drawer of his desk and put one in his mouth as he couldn't risk stale breath, then locked the workshop door behind him, got into his car and set off for Lamprey Manse, not removing his overalls as instructed. "Well hello," purred Sonia as she answered the door to Neville, whose rehearsal had clearly been ineffective, for he just said, "Hi." Sonia was wearing a pale silk dressing gown, very loosely tied, and clearly nothing else. "Well come in why don't you, I was *so* pleased to get your call."

"Er, I've left my car behind yours, is that OK?"

"Perfect, now come with me," and Sonia pulled Neville through the door, locked it then having asked him to remove his shoes, led him by the hand upstairs.

"OK, everything off to start with you lovely feller!" said Sonia as she sat provocatively on the edge of the bed, with the top of her dressing gown now clearly exposing her very generous bosom. Neville Martin did as he was bidden and as he stood naked before her she stood up, let her dressing gown fall and proceeded to caress and kiss his taut body. Neville Martin could contain himself no longer and he grasped Sonia breathlessly and pulled her onto the bed. "So service me!" she laughed. It was the most rewarding service Neville Martin Painswick had ever carried out; one of several that day in fact, for the oily overalls could not be employed indoors and such sport was being had. Sonia had taught him how to shed his inhibitions amongst other things. And the swimming pool was so warm. The dog had to be shut in the study for he was not sure about Neville Martin Painswick being on his territory, but no matter.

Thus about two hours later, amazed and content, Neville Martin Painswick left Lamprey Manse and just could not help smiling to himself. He was whistling when unbidden grins allowed and did notice that his legs were less than steady when he got out of his car to pick up the Lancia from its MOT. Well he'd not done anybody any harm and life was for living. He felt great.

Chapter Seventeen

At Elver Hall Helena Ruby Tremble was gradually becoming accustomed to inhabiting such a place rather than cleaning it, although she insisted upon taking on responsibility for the laundry and making the beds at the very least. Mrs Larkfield had cleaned the place for the last fifteen years and could not kindly be usurped now, but Helena was able to supplement her efforts without encroachment. It seemed that her eyesight was not as sharp as perhaps it once was and she was not now blessed with the agility bestowed by youth. Helena Ruby also coaxed Mrs Larkfield into having a cup of tea with her regularly and little by little managed to dissolve her initially frosty carapace. Helena Ruby knew she had finally been accepted when invited to call Mrs Larkfield 'Myrtle'. "I have three sons, you know," she confided in Helena Ruby as they sat in the kitchen with Denholm sitting happily under the table by their feet. "They take after Mr Larkfield, god rest his soul, can never stay in one place for very long. Young Henry is working on an oil rig in the North Sea, but wants to go somewhere warmer. I can't say I blame him. Then there's Stuart, he's working with a travel company and never knows where he'll be next, but I can't see he'll ever settle down, after all it's not much of a life for a woman if she wants a family and all that, is it? Oh and then my eldest, Hilary, now he's a bit more settled I suppose. Must admit, I never really got on with his wife that well, but she's gone off with a dentist now. Between you and me, her teeth always could have done with a bit of work. She reminded me of a horse. I think he's seeing someone else now, I s'pose he'll tell me one day."

"Oh dear," Helena Ruby offered, "but I'm sure everything will work out OK."

"Yes, you're right. He's fine, got a publishing business and a lovely house and two girls going through university. He's a magistrate, you know."

"You must be very proud."

"I am! Anyway, do you have children?" enquired Myrtle. Helena Ruby cupped her hands around her mug and said, "Yes, yes I do. Two girls, twins. I, well, these days, I … I hardly ever see them. I've never really known why, but they, well, they …. never got on with their father, and moved right away as soon as they could. I've missed them terribly. It's been pretty miserable really if truth be told."

"But you must keep in touch, I mean, you're their mother."

"Yes, we do, a bit. Actually, I've written to them both to explain what's been happening and now I've parted company with Ron, er, their father," (Helena Ruby felt herself blushing) "I'm hoping they'll come and see me. I do so want to get to know them both well, know how they've turned out." Helena Ruby's voice started to tremble and Myrtle in kind tones said, "Of course you must, children are precious, but as for the men, well...." and she handed Helena Ruby a handkerchief.

Parts of Elver Hall dated back to Tudor times with the latest addition having been made during the Queen Anne period. Thus it was not at all a symmetrical building, but displayed great character and a particularly interesting roofline. It stood in an expanse of tranquil, partially wooded parkland and overlooked a large lake which was becoming rather overgrown with bullrushes, reeds and water mint but when the water lilies bloomed, the effect was magical. Jolyon was not one for manicuring his surroundings but did employ someone to mow the open expanses of grass and tend to the woodland, which provided ample supplies of fuel for the great open fire in the drawing room.

It was within the Tudor section that the kitchen was situated and Helena Ruby loved its smooth and slightly undulating flagstone floor and the substantial black beams in the low ceiling. She could see that the cupboards installed, from what she supposed would be around the 1970's, were completely out of character, but felt it was too soon to start suggesting any changes, and as cupboards they performed more than adequately. The ageing gas cooker which stood in the centre of the cavernous fire place also looked incongruous, but likewise it fulfilled its purpose and Helena Ruby saw no need to change the status quo for the moment, besides which, none of this was hers to change anyway. Although happier than she thought possible living with Jolyon, Helena Ruby Tremble never took anything for granted and fully appreciated her circumstances. Denholm, however, had completely taken for granted that this was his new home, full of fascinating smells and niches, and that the alcove beside the cooker was indisputably his space. His nervous skin complaint had completely cleared up.

Helena Ruby Tremble relished preparing meals in this huge kitchen. Until then, Jolyon had very rarely eaten any of his meals on the premises, and he did agree that it was a real treat relaxing and eating food prepared at home. It was most rewarding for Helena Ruby to have such an appreciative response to her efforts and, buoyed up with new-found confidence, her culinary repertoire expanded rapidly. She now sang as she prepared vegetables and hummed along with the radio as she made pastry. Jolyon took great delight in introducing Helena Ruby to the art of fine wine appreciation, and many a mellow evening was spent sometimes in the dining room or drawing room, but frequently in bed. Helena Ruby was now restored to complete good health and she was eager to start making a real contribution, thus she was delighted to be asked to accompany Jolyon to a meeting at the proposed restaurant premises. He wanted her opinion on how it might be improved and given the right image, for she clearly had an eye for such things. He also wanted her to meet the contractors because she would likely be liaising with them as work got under way. "Oh dear, what will they think?" asked Helena Ruby as they drove towards Herring le Parterre, as nerves began to get the better of her and she twisted the end of her scarf round and round her finger . "I mean, I've never done anything like this before, they won't take any notice of what I say, they'll laugh at me."

"They will not laugh at you my dear. I know the fellow in charge well. He is polite and co-operative and I know you will get on just fine. As far as they are concerned you are my business associate, for that is what you will be on this project. Now please relax and let your creative energies flow." Jolyon put his hand on Helena Ruby's arm and gave her a reassuring squeeze, and she twined her fingers around his. "You're so good to me."

"Because I want to be, and you deserve it my dear. I must say, that outfit really is most becoming. I do enjoy our shopping trips, may even update my own wardrobe! The ex Mrs Urquart hadn't the first idea, sometimes wondered whether she was colour blind." This was the first time direct reference had been made to Jolyon's ex-wife, and Helena Ruby found it rather unsettling. She had supposed there probably was one, but to hear Jolyon refer to her thus was a bit of a shock. "Oh, er, goodness, I see. That's, er, the first time you've ever referred to her. If you don't mind my asking, was it a long time ago?"

"Ask me anything you like my dear. We parted company, what, seven years ago now. I think I was lonely and she was after home comforts. We were completely incompatible, but were expected to soldier on. Family pressure and all that. We lived separate lives in the end, just polite to each other really, but the final straw came when I found she was operating a 'virtual one-woman brothel at the Hall. Very unpleasant carryings-on, most upsetting for poor Mrs Larkfield. Still, all behind us now, so you must stop fretting - I have no regrets on *that* front whatsoever."

"Oh dear, I am sorry. Funny what people put up with though, isn't it?"

"Yes indeed, creatures of habit, but you my dear, are one habit I do not intend to break."

"Me neither," said Helena Ruby smiling and rubbing his arm affectionately.

Jolyon parked the car in front of the restaurant then walked around to the pavement and opened Helena Ruby's door for her. She found this a charming touch every time he did it and smiled lovingly at Jolyon as he offered her his hand. "Thank you kind sir," she said, taking his hand and getting out of her seat. Jolyon had never been one for ostentation and drove an unremarkable car, although it was an eye-catching shade of green. He unlocked the main front door of the premises and Helena Ruby followed him through. She was immediately struck by how terribly dingy the whole place looked. It could have been an old fish and chip restaurant in some down-at-heel seaside resort. She almost expected to see the odd plastic crustacean on show. "So what do you think? First impressions please, Mrs Tremble."

"Needs a lot of lightening up doesn't it?"

"So cosy won't do then?"

"Um, cosy would do, but this, this is, um, retro seventies dreary." Jolyon laughed and kissed Helena Ruby. "Ah, your creativity is already coming to the fore. Let's go and have a look at the kitchens before Geoff arrives."

Geoff proved to be the gentleman that Jolyon had described and it seemed quite clear that he and Helena Ruby would make a good team, which was good news as Jolyon now knew that he would be obliged to travel abroad in the next month or so. He had yet to reveal this to Helena Ruby, for he knew it would make her unhappy. In the car on the way back to Elver Hall he broached the subject. "Well it looks like you and Geoff will have the project safely under way in no time my dear."

"Yes, you were right, he's a nice man and I think we've both got similar ideas. This is really exciting. I never thought, I mean, *me* ...... goodness, I must call Cook, er, Denzil - will he have a say in the kitchen?"

"He certainly will my dear, and it's marvellous that you're so keen. You have more than justified my confidence in you and I can see I can leave this to you," (he cleared his throat) "which is good, because I will need to travel to Germany and the States in the next month." He glanced across and squeezed Helena Ruby's arm. "Oh, oh I see," she said, looking down at her hands. "Please, don't let it make you unhappy. Next time you can come with me, we'll make it a proper break, it's just that this time I need ......"

"Please, you don't have to explain," cut in Helena Ruby looking across at him. "I'm not going to make demands, I've got no right, it's just that, well, I love you so much and it will be horrible being parted, but I'll have to be sensible about it won't I?"

"Oh my darling, I shall miss you dreadfully too and I promise that next time you're coming with me."

"OK, it's a deal. So is there anything you'd particularly like for dinner? I got some lovely salmon steaks from the fishmonger. Mrs Larkfield, well, I can call her Myrtle now, recommended them. She's been telling me about her family. She said her eldest, I think, has a publishing company but his wife has left him. He's a magistrate too!"

"Ah yes, the ghastly Hilary P Larkfield. I'm surprised his wife stayed as long as she did, and how he gets away with those magazines he publishes I really don't know. A magistrate, eh? How exquisitely inappropriate."

"Oh dear, what, it isn't, I mean.... surely, I can't, I mean...... you don't mean ...er, smutty stuff?"

"Yes unfortunately, that type of thing, bondage, sado-masochism, bit of bestiality, all most unsavoury."

"Good grief, but he, he's a magistrate."

"Indeed and what the poor old soul doesn't know, and must never know, is that her ghastly magistrate son paid several visits to Elver Hall when the former Mrs Urquart was 'entertaining'."

"Oh my goodness, that's dreadful, how horrible for you, oh dear, I'm so sorry."

"No need to be sorry my dear, he lost a lot of photographic equipment amongst other things and if I ever need to, I can make life excessively unpleasant for him."

"Oh but poor Mrs Larkfield."

"Yes, poor Mrs Larkfield. The departed Mr Larkfield wasn't exactly a paragon either. So, salmon for dinner, accompanied by a nice chilled Chablis, I think."

At Hake Hall Francis, returned from his trip to Bream, went into the kitchen to find Denzil, who was clearing up after the evening meal. "Any spare for a starving immigrant?"

"Hey, how did it go man?" Denzil turned round, grinning broadly.

"Huge place, I'm going to need some help, but boy, have I got some ideas and the old girl is happy to let me get on with it. I'll need to sort a few things out, get some sort of van 'though, and is that an open bottle I can see?"

"Sure is, care to join me?"

"Yes, I think a celebration is called for." Francis walked up behind Denzil and put his arms around his waist as he poured two glasses of Pouilly Fuissé.

"Been in the master's cellar again have we?"

"Yeah, why not, we've got things to celebrate and he hasn't!"

"Cheers!" They took their glasses and the bottle out to the conservatory. Most of the other residents were watching television in the small sitting room. Denzil and Francis sat back on a cane sofa and stretched out their legs. "So you're going to need help then?"

"Yeah, nothing particularly artistic, just heavy shifting and that sort of thing, but someone who could stick in a few plants would be good."

"Oh dear, you know who'd be ideal don't you?"

"Er, not sure I know where we're going here."

"Well there's a bloke, an ill-tempered fascist I grant you, who lives in the Lodge, who could do that, but could you bear to work with him?"

"No, I couldn't."

"OK, so how will you go about finding someone?"

"Job centre?"

"Oh yeah, I can just imagine what they'd send along."

"OK, so I'll advertise in the Hake Herald, stick some notices in newsagents' windows."

"Still a bit risky I'd say. Better the devil and all that.... Anyhow, d'you want to hear my news?

"You bet."

"Mrs Tremble, er Helena, rang me to see when I can get over to the restaurant they're re-vamping to see what I think needs doing in the kitchens."

"Brill!"

"Yeah, I said I'd go with them tomorrow. Here's to us!"

"Yeah, cheers!"

A very jaunty Neville Martin Painswick, hands in pockets and whistling, sauntered into the conservatory and said, "Hi guys, can I join the party?"

"Why not, maybe you can help us, come to think of it."

"I'll just get a beer I think, been working late," and Neville Martin went to the kitchen, unable to stop smiling. He had worked until about six-thirty when Sonia had called in with a trifling query regarding a part for Trevor's Aston and they had, after an initial flirting session and unable to contain themselves, made love on the back seat of the Mercedes upon which he had just finished working. Sonia was more flexible than her frame might suggest. "OK, so what's the problem?" he asked as he flopped down into a chair opposite Francis and Denzil, opened his can of beer and took a swig. "I need a sort of labourer to help me on this new job I've got at Bream."

"That's a fair old distance."

"Yeah, but the pay's above average and it really needs to be someone who has a basic understanding of planting and stuff. Anyway, there'll be a caravan on site, and bloody hell there's enough room at the place, in fact you could stick a whole caravan park in there and you'd hardly notice!"

"I'll ask Melvin if he's got any friends who might be interested. Then of course there's the miserable old git at the Lodge. Saw him this morning. Looks a real wreck. I almost feel sorry for him, he's in a terrible state."

Ron was indeed sinking into a depression of utter loneliness and rock bottom self esteem. He hadn't washed for days and only ate the occasional biscuit. He sat in front of the television for most of his waking day and often slept in the chair as he couldn't be bothered to move, but that meant that he had an almost permanently stiff neck, the discomfort of which served only to suck him further down. "Oh not you as well, what is he, some sort of charity case? You heard what he called us," said Francis. "I suppose you're right. Anyhow, when do you need your labourer?"

"Soon after I start, which will be next week. I've just got to get some rough plans done and a few things sorted out first."

"And *I* have a kitchen to design," joined in Denzil.

"Blimey, what an artistic bunch. Anyway, I think we need to get everyone together as a demolition notice has gone up on The Bullrushes and it looks like we can all get a claim in. What we need is a friendly solicitor. Better add that to the list!"

"Hey, I can ask Jolyon Urquart when I see him tomorrow, he said he had some good contacts, and he seems a genuine sort of bloke."

"Great, OK, so if we can get everyone together tomorrow and see what we're all going to do, that's a move in the right direction isn't it? I don't really want to live here for ever, the plumbing's bloody awful!"

"But the food's mighty fine," added Francis.

"You bet," said Neville Martin, holding up his can of beer as a toast, before emptying it. "And I need my bed now, tiring day. So we'll get everyone together tomorrow then?"

"Sounds like a plan, see you tomorrow," said Denzil. "Yeah, 'night." Neville Martin Painswick would no doubt be dreaming of Sonia that night.

As Denzil brushed his teeth, he wondered whether tomorrow he shouldn't just check if Ron was fundamentally OK before he met Helena Ruby and Jolyon. Regardless of having left him, he presumed that being the kind-hearted woman she was, Helena Ruby would not want to leave him neglected if he really was in a bad way, unendearing though the man was. As he climbed into bed he said to Francis, who was studying a book on landscaping, "Look, I know you think the man's dreadful, and I tend to agree, but I'm going to check on that Tremble bloke tomorrow before I meet Helena and Jolyon."

"Whatever. I just don't like being called a queer darkie, do you?"

"No, of course I don't, but the man's pretty inarticulate at the best of times. Anyhow, let's not talk about him, I've been thinking..." Francis looked up from his book over his gold-rimmed reading glasses and smiled.

"Oh yeah, about what?"

"Well this caravan you're going to have on site at Bream, we can't live here for ever and frankly I'm sick of cooking for this lot. I've got the restaurant project I'll be getting involved in, so why don't we move into the caravan and cut out all the travelling from here? Can't say I'll miss the place, and I could always give you a hand to start with - I could do with the exercise. We could manage couldn't we?"

"We certainly could, you're not such a dumb queer darkie after all are you!"

Next morning at breakfast everybody was notified of a house meeting that evening, but Mrs Slingback did have some difficulty coming to terms with the fact that Number

Eight was to be demolished. It was supposed to have been their dream retirement home and she'd chosen the carpets and curtains with such care. Denzil left the kitchen and walked down the drive to the Lodge and knocked on the back door. "Hey, Mr Tremble, anyone in?" he called as he pushed it ajar. The light in the hall beyond was on and he walked through the kitchen, not having got any response. There was a very unpleasant smell from several bottles of solidified milk stood on the draining board and the swing-top bin was overflowing. Encrusted plates, unwashed cups and cutlery were piled in the sink and several large flies buzzed lazily about the room. The smashed jar of marmalade still lay where it had fallen. "Hello, are you there?" he called again from the hall, then heard the sound of the television emanating from the sitting room. He gingerly pushed the door ajar and was overcome by the smell of grimy upholstery and unwashed body. Holding his hand over his nose and mouth he went in to the room and saw Ronald Arthur Tremble slumped in the chair in front of the television.

"Oh my god, hey, are you OK, can you hear me?" he shouted, convinced that he was looking at a corpse in the first stages of putrefaction. Ronald Arthur awoke with a start and with a shooting pain in his neck and faced with the sight of Denzil stood before him, shouted, "Aaagh, don't kill me!" as he held his arms up in defence. "Christ almighty," shouted Denzil as he jumped back, knocking over a dead pot plant. "I thought you were bloody dead!"

"May as well be," came the response. "How has this place got into such a state, man?"

"Wife's left me, got no job and no money, that's how."

"Can't you get some benefit or something?"

"What d'you care?"

"OK, if you're going to be like that, I'm off man."

"No, no. Don't … please don't go, I'm sorry, I'm sorry" said Ronald Arthur as he held his head in his hands and began to sob. Denzil was acutely uncomfortable and really did not know what to do or say next. There was no way he was going to touch the man, for sure. "Hey man, come on, you need to get yourself sorted out, cleaned up. You're just going through a bad patch."

"Oh god, I just don't know what to do. I, oh god, I know I treated her badly, I just can't ...." Denzil held out a handkerchief to Ron as he started sobbing again.

In an attempt to deflect some of the misery, Denzil said, "Look, we could get this place cleaned up for starters. I've got to go out in a bit, but when I come back, if you want, I'll help you, and maybe bring a bit of food too?"

"Why would you want to do that?" said Ron with his head bowed.

"Give you a bit of hope, I suppose," said Denzil, shrugging, and completely unable to cope with the wreck of a man before him. "D'you think you should go and see a doctor? Maybe you're ill."

"What, mental you mean?"

"No, ill, and you really need to drop the attitude you know, you're not doing yourself any favours. I don't have to help you out, just trying to be charitable you know."

"Oh bloody hell, I know, I'm sorry, sorry, sorry......" and he clutched his head in his hands again, rocking to and fro in the chair. "So, do I come back or will I just get more of the same?"

"Um, look, I ... I still don't know why you're bothering," said Ron as he heaved himself stiffly out of the chair, releasing a cloud of stale air, "but, yes, I must get cleaned up, even get working again, if anyone will have me. Maybe I will go to the doc's too. I can't... explain, it's weird, my mind thinks one thing but my mouth comes out with something completely different, then I just go and make it worse."

"Yes, well you get yourself cleaned up and I'll come back and help you get this place sorted out, but don't wait for me to make a start if you feel like it!"

"Look, thanks mate, and er, I'm really sorry for what I said, will you apologise to your mate for me? You're kinder than everybody else I know." Ronald Arthur Tremble held out his hand to shake Denzil's, which he felt obliged to take, for this was surely of monumental significance to Ron, and they shook hands. "OK, I'll be back later and look, why don't you come up to the Hall and have a meal with us all afterwards – I think you need a bit of company, and you can apologise to Francis yourself. I think he'd appreciate it." Ronald Arthur, dabbing his eyes with the handkerchief said gratefully, "Er, I, ah ….. that would be great, thanks mate."

As Denzil walked back to Hake Hall, absent-mindedly wiping his hands on his trousers, he said aloud, "Bloody hell, make way for Saint Denzil of the Bleeding Heart of Hake!" and started laughing.

Chapter Eighteen

Nigel Lamington-Krill was having a very bad time. Although he had now been granted sufficient funds upon which to subsist, it still meant he had to stay with Isobel and her sister because thus far the legal authorities were not exactly vigorous in processing his application to have the current residents of Hake Hall evicted. He was unable to visit family members in Germany because his passport had been confiscated. The Serious Fraud Office had gathered sufficient evidence with which to prosecute him and he was awaiting a trial date. Hugh Fallowburton had been only too keen to do everything he could to ingratiate himself with the investigating authorities and had provided them with documentation which had originally been destined for shredding. Mr Giles Blounce of Stickletrent Poodle and Crevice said it could be up to a year before Nigel's case surfaced. That was a dreadfully long time to be in a state of such ghastly limbo, and it would, he suspected, poison things between him and Isobel irreparably. She had become very shrill and sharp lately, ably encouraged by her sister, he felt. Thus most of his days were spent trying to stay out of the house. He had the proceeds from the sale of Isobel's car to cushion things a little, but did realise that with Lamington-Krill International no longer trading, he would have to seek some sort of alternative employment, for staying much longer with Isobel's sister was simply out of the question. At least he was not known in the Sturgeon Fields locale.

Isobel had, in the interests of maintaining an income and her wardrobe, taken a job in a colossally upmarket ladies' fashion house. She did find it rather difficult to remember upon which side of the counter she stood, and to adhere to that tiresome adage that the customer is always right. She also found that having to work all day precluded most other activities (not that she could now afford most of them) and she fumed at having to curtail her lifestyle thus. It all added venom to the cauldron of her simmering anger at Nigel for having brought them to such a pass. "Perhaps a larger size would hang better, Madam?" said Isobel to a stout creature emerging from the changing room. Edwina Braceplate was anxious to find 'something stunning' to wear to her son's wedding. "Oh dear, maybe, but is it my colour?"

'You look like a boiled bloater in that dreadful shade,' thought Isobel. She said instead with ill-disguised boredom, "Maybe you should try something a bit more demure from our 'Mostly Mature' range. It's very stylish and caters for every figure." Mrs Braceplate was not impressed and left the premises empty-handed.

Isobel, naturally, was not enjoying her job and going home to her sister's house every day was becoming a little wearing. It was a large, airy, open plan building and to Isobel it had no warmth and too many hard, shiny surfaces, and offered very little privacy. She was sure the neighbours in the close all knew of their circumstances and she hated walking back from the bus-stop almost as much as she hated travelling on the bus in case she encountered anybody and was obliged to make conversation. She had stopped asking Nigel what he had been doing during the day because it always ended in a bitter argument. In fact, she barely spoke to him at all and they slept in separate rooms. She was only glad that her parents were not still alive to witness their disgrace.

At Hake Hall red reminders were mounting up as bills went unpaid, but gradually the residents were finding alternative accommodation, as part-payment of the promised compensation had come through due to the diligence of Jolyon's legal contacts. Francis and Denzil had moved to their caravan on the Troutpool Estate in Bream and shortly, much to his uncharacteristic delight, Ron too would be taking up residence in the keeper's cottage on the estate as Mrs Strang-Wellow needed a groundsman and general factotum to look after everything, the previous incumbent having met an unfortunate end whilst pursuing wild boar. Having made his peace with Francis, he would also be labouring for him on the project. Ron had realised that this could be his last chance to make some sort of half decent fist of his life, and was so determined not to let himself spoil it that he sought medical advice. The pills he had been prescribed did help lift him from his negative rut and for the first time he could remember, he actually got up in the morning looking forward to his day. He was indebted to Denzil for having pulled him back from the brink, and of course, to Francis for giving him a second chance, and had to be asked to stop being so grateful, for neither Denzil nor Francis could cope any more with his frequent, earnest declarations.

Speculation spread fast amongst the residents on the fringes of Bream regarding the new arrivals at the Troutpool Estate and Amelia Strang-Wellow took enormous delight in indulging it, or at least took no steps to debunk the wilder stories abroad. She was stopped outside the post office one morning and asked how the visiting African princes were settling in. No doubt the ripples would be spreading for weeks. Amelia regaled Denzil, Francis and Ron with her tales over a meal at the Manor House one evening. "You should have seen the expression, wouldn't be surprised if somebody didn't send some welfare do-gooder snooping round the place!"

"I think Mr Lamington-Krill may be in need of some do-gooding welfare before long. By the way, these sausages are superb. Anyway, I hear he's awaiting trial on fraud charges and certainly isn't living in the style to which he is accustomed. Then of course there's the demolition of the housing estate his lot built. He seems to be seriously bad news for a lot of people, but I think his gold-plated quails are coming home to roost now," said Denzil. "Do quails roost?" asked Francis, and Denzil flicked him with his napkin. "Ah yes of course, Hake Hall, went there for some European evening or something with Peregrine, ended in chaos, lot of cars vandalised as I remember. Wild boar and cranberry, get them made up by a local butcher chappie, I can give you his details if you like. Didn't somebody drive a car into the pool?"

"Er, yes, it was me," said Ron, shifting a little uncomfortably in his chair.

"Oh I say, well done, quite a stunt. Must have put a few points on your licence!"

"Er, yes, I s'pose you could say that. Anyhow, I won't be doing anything like that again, you have my word."

"Jolly good, don't want the carp upset. Now Denzil, tell me about your restaurant venture. I know Jolyon Urquart well, sterling fellow, he's well respected in all the right circles. Bit of a socialist on the quiet you know."

"Er, yes, he's a good bloke." Now it was Denzil's turn to feel uncomfortable as he glanced across at Ron who just shrugged his shoulders and took a swig of wine. "So anyway, this restaurant of his in Herring le Parterre is being re-hashed, bit more upmarket, clever lighting and all that. My domain is getting a whole load of new gear installed too - it'll be brill!"

"Ah, Herring, sleepy little market town and all that eh. Do you think they're ready for you and your cutting edge presentation dear boy?" enquired Amelia with a smile. "I guess Jolyon has done his market research and the place seems to attract the right sort of people, commercially speaking," replied Denzil. "Including African princes, I shouldn't wonder!"

"A toast to the African princes," said Ron holding his glass aloft.

"Hey, not again, enough, Mr Tremble!" laughed Francis. "Yeah, yeah, I know. But I never thought I'd be sitting eating at Troutpool Manor. Blimey, how things can change."

"Yes, here's to change," said Denzil. "For the better!" added Francis. "Another bottle?" enquired Amelia, who was feeling particularly mellow.

Helena Ruby was delighted to learn from Denzil of Ron's employment and was eagerly anticipating the arrival of Josephine, one of the twins, who was coming to visit her mother in her new life. She had tried three different outfits that morning and wished she had Jolyon there to reassure her, but he was travelling abroad. He rang her every day and she kept him informed of developments at the restaurant. "You know it won't be long before we're going to have to think of a name," Helena Ruby had said during one of their conversations. "The kitchen is nearing completion and the decorators can make a start quite soon. Geoff has given me some colour cards and Francis has made some really excellent suggestions. He came over with Denzil a couple of days ago. It's nice to see them so happy. Seems they're really enjoying themselves with Mrs Strang-Wellow at the Troutpool Estate." Jolyon said he thought Helena Ruby and Denzil should choose the name, and that they would have a grand opening celebration when he got back. He was missing her terribly but they would have a lot to celebrate upon his return, for things were going well for him. Perhaps she would like to get herself something special for the occasion.

Thoughts of Jolyon circulated agreeably around Helena Ruby's mind as she gazed out of the sitting room window, having put a large vase of fresh white and yellow chrysanthemums on the window-sill. Josephine's car approached up the drive and Helena Ruby's heart began to pound. She knew she really had no need to be nervous, but seeing her daughter again and making it work was more important to her than anything else she could think of. Helena Ruby walked briskly to the front door, with Denholm at her heels, glanced at herself in the mirror, then opened the door and walked out to meet Josephine. A tall, slim woman elegantly got out of a low sports car, and she pushed her sunglasses onto her head, holding back long glossy locks of chestnut hair. She was wearing tight, faded jeans with a white shirt and fashionable pastel green jacket. "Oh sweetheart, you look gorgeous!" said Helena Ruby as Denholm rushed to greet Josephine. "Mum, you're looking pretty good yourself you know," said Josephine as she leant down to stroke Denholm. She stood up and they embraced, both unable to speak as they were overcome with emotion. "Oh dear, let's go indoors and get a tissue," sniffed Helena Ruby. "Mum, it's so good to see you, and I'm so glad things have worked out for you. I should have,..... well, it's not .... I mean, I.... er, oh dear, look at us!" They walked to the front door, Josephine with her arm around Helena Ruby's shoulders, and dabbing her eyes with the back of her sleeve. "Oh this is fantastic," said Josephine as they walked through the house to the kitchen.

"Hmm, as you can see, some of it needs a bit of attention, but it works. How about a cup of tea, or maybe something stronger to celebrate?"

"Oh Mum, a gin and tonic would be great, thank you. We've got so much to talk about. You did say on the phone that I could stay for a couple of days - if it's still OK I've got my bag in the back of the car."

"Sweetheart, of course it's OK, I really hoped you would. Oh this is so wonderful, I'm so happy...." and tears of happiness rolled down her cheeks.

Helena Ruby and Josephine sat in the drawing room sipping their drinks, having taken a precautionary box of tissues with them, and Denholm lay contentedly under the table. The conversation was ceaseless as mother and daughter got to know each other again. Josephine was an executive for a housing association and her boyfriend was away on business too. He ran an engineering company specialising in solar power generation, and often travelled abroad. Helena Ruby and Josephine agreed that their menfolk should meet, for they felt they would get on well. "OK, so what about Dad then? Maggie said I should ask." (Maggie was Josephine's twin sister.)

"Oh love, I know you two didn't like him and you never got on, and I know he's not been, shall we say, a happy presence in our lives, but looking back now I can see he's had, well, mental problems, depression I suppose, but he'd never open up, I just didn't think....."

"Come on Mum, don't blame yourself, but hey, it doesn't really matter now does it? You're happy, and that's all I care about."

"I suppose not, he's actually got a job working in Bream - now this *will* make you laugh - he's working for a gay fellow, and not only that, the fellow's black!" Helena Ruby and Josephine laughed until it hurt. "Oh Mum, Maggie will be so pleased when I tell her how happy you are. You just look like a different person you know. Tell you what, why don't you ring her now? She's in Italy at the moment, but she'll want to come and see you as soon as she gets back. This is all so fantastic." Helena Ruby rang Maggie who was, as predicted, delighted to hear from her mother. She was in Italy for the next week on a photographic assignment for an architectural journal, but would come and visit her mother as soon as she returned. "Oh what a fantastic pair of daughters I have!" exclaimed Helena Ruby, hugging Josephine. Denholm jumped up, tail wagging furiously as he tried to join in.

They had a candlelit meal together in the evening and then retired happily to bed, still with an awful lot to talk about the following morning. After breakfast, Helena Ruby was keen to take Josephine to see the restaurant, and to introduce her to Denzil whom she knew would be there at lunch time. As they drove to Herring le Parterre in Josephine's car, Helena Ruby was telling her about the plans for an opening celebration but that they had still to think of a name for the place, and she had to find something suitable to wear. "Sounds like the ideal opportunity for a mother/daughter shopping trip to me, Mum," said Josephine. "Oh that would be marvellous, and I can show you around the place," agreed Helena Ruby.

It was with enormous pride that she introduced Josephine to Denzil, who kissed her hand and declared himself *enchanté*. She was very interested in the works, Helena Ruby's decor plans and Denzil's menu plans and suggested they all have lunch together, if somebody could suggest somewhere good to eat. They had a bar meal at the Plump Pullet in a small village on the outskirts of Herring le Parterre, and toasted each others' success.

Denzil made his way back to Bream having satisfied himself that the kitchen installation was now successfully completed, and Helena Ruby and Josephine went in search of a celebration outfit, amongst other things. When they returned to Elver Hall, the small back seat of Josephine's car was piled with bags and boxes. "I can't remember the last time I've been in so many clothes shops," said Helena Ruby. "It's fun once in a while though, isn't it Mum?"

"Oh I've had a fantastic time, in fact I still can't believe that this is me, plain old Helena Ruby Tremble. I feel like I'm living someone else's life, but I'm *so* happy."

"You deserve it Mum, after all you've endured a lot in life haven't you?"

"Well I don't know about that, but.... oh it's just so lovely to see you again, and I've got Maggie to look forward to and Jolyon comes back next week. I don't think it's too early to open a bottle of something celebratory, what do you say?"

"I say great, and I never thought I'd hear that from you!" Thus Helena Ruby and Josephine sat in the drawing room sipping sparkling wine while they examined their purchases and discussed events. Denholm had great fun with all the packaging strewn on the floor. "Look, I know this is a lot to ask, but would you see your father before you go?"

"Ah, yes I wondered whether I should, although quite what we'll say to each other I don't know."

"I think you'll find he's a rather different character these days, from what Denzil tells me, but I don't want it to upset you love."

"Oh it won't upset me Mum, trust me. Perhaps I could call in and introduce myself on the way back. Bream's not that far out of my way, and I must admit, I'm fascinated to be able to meet this Francis fellow, after all, he must be pretty special!"

"Oh he is. Denzil and he are very happy together and they are lovely company."

"OK Mum, in the interests of family harmony and all that, and if it makes you happy, I'll call in and see the old bugger on my way back. I've had such a lovely time, thank you, and I can't tell you how happy I am that things have worked out for you."

"Oh thank you sweetheart, you've made me so happy..... I ..... oh come here and give me a hug!" The two clung together and when the tears had ceased, Helena Ruby said, "OK, so what shall we have for dinner then?"

After breakfast the next morning Josephine gathered together her belongings and threw them in the back of the car. "You'll look sensational in that outfit we chose Mum, don't you dare change your mind!"

"I wouldn't dream of it my dear, and I'm sure Jolyon will love it too. Anyway, you'll be joining us for the opening won't you, and I hope Maggie can be there too. It would make it just perfect."

"We wouldn't miss our Mum's big moment for anything, trust me!"

"And you will call in and see your father won't you. I could telephone Denzil and tell them to expect you."

"OK Mum, good idea, in fact, give me the number too just in case I get lost."

"Oh sweetheart, it's been so....."

"Don't start us off again! Look just jot down that number for me and I'll be off, but I'll ring you when I get home and report on Dad, OK?" Josephine bent down to pat

Denholm who had come trotting out of the front door while Helena Ruby wrote out Denzil's number on a pad that Josephine handed to her. "OK, goodbye and take care love." Helena Ruby kissed Josephine on the cheek and squeezed her arm. "'Bye Mum, and I'll see you again soon, promise!" Helena Ruby waved to the departing car until it was out of sight, then sauntered back into the house. "Ah Denholm my love, I couldn't have wished for better really could I? Come on, I'll put my boots on and we'll go for a walk in the woods."

As promised, Josephine rang her mother that evening and Helena Ruby was relieved to hear that her encounter with her father was without incident, and she did indeed confirm that he seemed an altered character with a slightly less negative slant on everything in life. He had not been very comfortable with Josephine and conversation was stilted, but she had done her duty, and although Ron was unable to demonstrate it, he was very grateful that his daughter had taken the trouble to visit him after so long, and he was proud of what Josephine and Maggie had achieved.

"Anyway Mum, I don't think you need to worry yourself about him. He seems to have found a nice little niche for himself on the estate. He's even developing a sense of humour of sorts! You will let me know as soon as you can when the grand opening is to be, won't you, so I can make sure I'm not doing anything else. I'm so looking forward to bringing Roger with me. Can't wait for you to meet him!"

What Josephine did not reveal to her mother was Ron's tearful plea to her to forgive him. When she was seven and before they had moved to Hake on Spinach, she had come home early from school one rainy afternoon to find her father on the sofa involved in sexual antics with the neighbour's cleaner, who had brought the tools of the trade with her. She had found a very novel application for the crevice nozzle of the vacuum cleaner. Caught as he was in an excruciatingly embarrassing situation, he had as a reflex reaction threatened that little Josephine would be sent away on her own if she ever revealed what she had seen to anybody. Maggie had known there was something wrong and eventually persuaded poor troubled Josephine to tell her, and it remained a shared burden for them throughout a significant portion of their childhood. Looking back now, Josephine couldn't help laughing as she recalled the scene, but it had been a terrible weight upon her innocent shoulders at the time, and she was only grateful that she had had Maggie with whom to share it. She didn't think for one moment that her mother would be concerned about Ron's infidelity now bearing in mind all that had come to pass, but she knew it would be intolerable for her to realise under what an unhappy cloud her girls had lived for a good few years.

As she sat sipping tea from a chipped mug, Josephine told her father that in her eyes, to threaten a young child in order to cover his sordid little misdemeanour was pretty much unforgivable, but it was pointless bearing him a grudge now she had grown up and shaken off that particularly unhappy chapter, and it was left at that. She did take the opportunity as she was leaving to ask Ron if Amelia Strang-Wellow had a cleaning cupboard and whether it was well equipped. It took him several seconds to realise that she was joking. "You asked for that Dad."
"Yeah, I s'pose I did. Well, thanks for coming over and p'raps I'll see you again."
"Maybe, if I'm passing, but I'm glad you've got yourself sorted out anyway. 'Bye," and she held up her hand in salutation, for she could not bring herself to kiss him. "'Bye," said Ron quietly, and as the tears welled up, he turned and walked back towards the keeper's cottage, wiping his eyes with the back of his sleeve.

Chapter Nineteen

Nigel wandered disconsolately through Hake Hall. It felt shabby although the former residents had removed most traces of their occupation, and apart from the odd scuffed skirting board, they had left the place in relative good order. Dust had settled everywhere, cobwebs were festooned in corners and around lamps, and the carpets and rugs looked dull and grimy. The electricity supply had been cut off which left the place in a permanent state of gloom. The building was chilled as the summer weather had been retreating, and naturally the heating system would not work without power. Neither would it work without fuel, which was also no longer on tap. Nigel walked unhappily into the kitchen which had been left clean, although there was the suggestion of an offensive odour lingering in the room. He absent-mindedly pulled one of the huge refrigerator doors open and was greeted with the smell of putrefying dairy produce and various other foodstuffs abandoned within, some of which had begun dripping through the racking. "Christ!" he said as he slammed the door shut, holding his hand over his mouth. The surveyor walked into the kitchen and said, "Something wrong?"

"Er, no, not really, just a bit, er, shocked to find, well, rotting stuff in the fridge, that's all."

"Oh dear, well I think we'll be getting this professionally cleaned before putting it on the market in any case. I pity the poor sod who gets to do the fridge though!"

"Mmm. Won't we have to get the power back on as well? People have got to be able to see what they're investing in, and you can't exactly clean the place with a carpet sweeper."

"Yes, I'll get Vicky on to that now actually," said Lance Jervis of Jervis, Parsloe and Rankine, property investment agents and surveyors, as he dialled then held his mobile phone up to his ear.

"Yes, Vicky, it's Lance. Look I need you to arrange getting the power back on at Hake Hall, I'm here now ......

Well I don't know, isn't Blake in the office? Can't you speak to the administrators? Oh I haven't got time now, it'll have to wait until I get back if you can't sort it out yourself. I'll be in later." He ended the call with a peevish gesture and said to Nigel, "Jeeze, I wonder what I pay these bloody women for, I really do."

"Yes, I know what you mean, no bloody initiative," said Nigel bitterly, having been the recipient of more initiative than he could usefully deal with. His real identity was unknown to Lance. Nigel, being of the right ilk and wearing the right sort of shirts (which he had had to learn to iron himself), had been taken on as an associate by Jervis, Parsloe and Rankine as he knew a lot about property markets. He had managed to sidestep the need for producing references or a CV, for this was not exactly a run-of-the-mill common estate agency was it, and he was known to Jervis, Parsloe and Rankine as Nigel Lamport so that he did not have to alter his signature radically, although it often looked as though he was called Nigel Lambswool as he momentarily forgot his new identity. Ingrained habits could be dangerous and Nigel had to think hard before speaking on anything of substance.

"Hmmm, this will be a dream for some interior designer," said Lance as he stood in the morning room. "I presume the administrators will be auctioning the furniture, although I don't imagine it'll fetch much, I mean, look at this!" he said, pointing to the marquetry-topped table depicting the stag at bay with more recently bestowed halo. "It's just so, well, naff!"

"Family heirlooms probably," said Nigel, silently wounded. He was ambivalent about accompanying Lance to Hake Hall, for he knew it would be traumatic, but he couldn't resist seeing the place again and at least now he had access to keys and hence the means to re-visit unaccompanied should the need arise. They went upstairs and Nigel had to remember that he did not know his way around. He opened doors and glanced in, wondering quite what horrors might greet him. In one bathroom there was a yellowing, scummy ring around the bath and hair in the plug-hole of the basin. "Oh my god, will you take a look at this!" called Lance. Nigel walked briskly to what used to be his bedroom, their bedroom, and was mortified to see the four-poster bed with a vast tiger-skin print cover on it. Francis and Denzil had forgotten to take it with them. It was their joke. The stuffed bear was standing at the foot of the bed with one of Isobel's fur hats on its head and sporting a studded dog collar. Worse than all this, there was a 'Gay Pride' poster hung on the wall - another of Francis and Denzil's personal touches. "Er, oh, yes, not really in keeping is it?" said Nigel. "Weirdos," said Lance. "I've heard rumours about what went on here you know."

"Good god, really?"

"Oh yes, odd bunch, some sort of Nazi connection I heard. Friend of mine from the golf club seemed to think there were arms involved. Lucrative business mind, in the right hands of course."

"Really?" Nigel said again, feeling slightly nauseous with alarm.

"Yeah, but that's what you get with the European Union isn't it?"

"Yes, I suppose so," said Nigel, wanting to learn more but not wishing to sound too interested. "I wonder if Mrs Jervis would like that tiger skin," said Lance to himself and Nigel walked through to his old dressing room in utter dismay. That too had an air of dusty dereliction about it. He did however spot the corner of a twenty pound note folded beneath a box of cufflinks on a small side table, which he deftly slipped into his pocket. He really did want to get away now but had to suffer being subjected to Lance Jervis's increasingly odious company as they walked around what used to be his home.

As Nigel Lamington-Krill said a silent, sad farewell to his old home, Neville Martin Painswick was taking his now heavily pregnant wife around the show home of a new estate nearing completion on the edge of Mackerel. Donna, not unreasonably, had said she really didn't want to bring their new baby home to her parents' house and Neville was forced to concur. Being apart so much was not an ideal start to parenthood and the compensation funds released thus far more than amply covered a deposit. Neville Martin, having had his libido awakened by Sonia, realised that this move would rather curtail their increasingly frequent and vigorous liaisons, but there was no way round it, and he did know that he had to take his impending responsibilities seriously. "Yes, I think this could look really nice in peach for the baby's room and we could put the changing table in the corner and the cot over there. What do you think?" Neville Martin was gazing out of the window watching a lithe young saleswoman with bleached blonde hair. She was wearing a short skirt which showed off her gorgeous long, slim legs. "Oh, er, yes, great, whatever you think's best."

"Neville, you're not taking this seriously, this could be our new home we're talking about."

"Oh sorry love, but you know me and decorating, I've never had much of an idea. Look, the important thing is, if you like it, then we'll go for it."

"But d'you think the lounge is big enough? I think the new suite might be a bit of a squeeze, then of course there's the TV cinema system. And what about the pram - that's not going to fit in the hall is it?"

"I don't know love, p'raps we ought to do some measuring-up but we can't hang around as there's only two left, and you've only got a month to go."

"OK, I s'pose we could maybe let Mum have one of the armchairs, that old one of Dad's is falling to pieces."

"Yeah, good idea, so shall we go for it then?" asked Neville, "Only I've got the Aston to get finished and I can call in to the wholesaler if I'm running you back."

Within half an hour, Neville and Donna had secured number four, Cobbler's Glade and in the car on the way back to Great Roach Donna chatted excitedly almost non-stop about decor and furnishing, babies' names and suitable fencing for the back garden, occasionally inviting Neville to feel the baby kicking. Neville Martin wondered whether his friend Dave, with whom he was temporarily sharing a house in return for help in rebuilding his vintage MG-C, was likely to be back, or whether he might have the place to himself for a while.

At Elver Hall builders were remodelling the kitchen and Denholm was perplexed. Helena Ruby was busy making up floral displays for the grand opening of the restaurant. She was standing at the dining table which she had protected with plastic sheeting, wondering whether to use lilies or roses for the main display, when Jolyon walked in. He came up behind her and put his arms around her waist, leaning into her neck and kissing her. "Mmmm, hello. Lilies or roses?"

"Roses, they remind me of you."

"Oh you're too kind!"

"Yes, soft, sweet and very desirable."

"I'm having my greenfly treatment tomorrow!"

"Oh Helena Ruby, come to bed with me."

"It's a lovely prospect, but I must get these finished before Roberta comes to collect them. You should see her outfit for tomorrow, it's stunning."

"Mmmm, I'm sure it is. I shall be surrounded by beautiful women. When do your daughters arrive?"

"Tomorrow morning. I can't wait to meet Josephine's Roger. She says she knows we'll all get on. But then it's difficult not to get on with you, Jolyon Urquart."

"But you won't come to bed with me Helena Ruby Tremble?"

"I will, later my darling, but I must get these done."

"I'll go and see how the builders are getting on then. Must admit, even *I* can see the improvement. Perhaps you can teach me to cook my dear. We could have fun in the kitchen." Helena Ruby laughed and flicked Jolyon with a stem. "Be gone, and let me get on!"

Next morning, Helena Ruby was so excited that she didn't feel like eating any breakfast. She sat at the dining table absent-mindedly picking up dry cereal flakes from her bowl. "Aren't you having milk with that my dear?" enquired Jolyon, looking over his newspaper. "Um, no not really," replied Helena Ruby. "Looking forward to the girls arriving, I bet!"

"Yes, oh dear I've got such butterflies, I'm just not hungry."

"Well never mind, there'll be plenty to eat later won't there?"

"Yes, yes, Denzil's done a fantastic job. Oh dear, I do hope it's a success, I mean not just this evening....."

"You are in charge my dear and I know you'll make it a success, now at least have some tea. Here, let me pour it for you." As Jolyon leant across with the teapot, Helena Ruby stroked the back of his hand with one finger and said, "You're so good to me, I don't deserve it."

"You can demonstrate your appreciation later my darling," said Jolyon winking at Helena Ruby, and they laughed.

Maggie arrived in a taxi from the station and as she paid the driver, Jolyon called upstairs to Helena Ruby, "Your first visitor has arrived my dear, and stunning she is too!" Helena Ruby came running downstairs in her dressing gown with a towel wrapped around her head, having just emerged from the shower. "Oh no, I'm not dressed, what will Maggie think?"

"She'll think she's got a lovely mother. Shall I let her in?" asked Jolyon, laughing. "Oh yes of course, yes please," said Helena Ruby with Denholm rushing around her legs sensing the excitement as Jolyon opened the door. "Ah, you must be Maggie, I am delighted to meet you," said Jolyon as he leant down and kissed her hand. Maggie laughed and responded, "And you can only be Mr Jolyon Urquart, my mother's saviour!"

Helena Ruby walked to the door and said "Oh Maggie, sweetheart, sorry I'm not dressed, I, er, oh, it's ....."

"Oh Mum, it doesn't matter, you look fantastic!" and they embraced, with Denholm frantically trying to join in. Helena Ruby buried her face in Maggie's dark locks as tears of happiness rolled down her face. "So who's for a cup of tea?" asked Jolyon, not quite knowing what he should be doing. "Oh, how about something a bit stronger?" sniffed Helena Ruby as she released Maggie and wiped her eyes with the sleeve of her dressing gown. "Oh dear, look at me. Sorry everybody, I must look a fright."

"Mum, why don't you go and get dressed and I'll start with coffee, then we'll have something to celebrate with when you come down. Here, have a tissue, you really shouldn't be using that lovely gown as a hankie!" Helena Ruby did as suggested and Maggie followed Jolyon to the kitchen. Denholm had followed Helena Ruby upstairs. "This is a fantastic building. Would you mind if I took a few shots?" Maggie asked Jolyon. "If you think it a worthy subject, I should be delighted my dear. As you can see the kitchen is having a bit of a spruce-up. Your mother has a real eye for these things you know."

"Mum's got all manner of talents, just a pity she's never really had the opportunity to use them to the full. Still, she's clearly very, very happy now, and that's all that matters really isn't it?"

"Yes, indeed. Making contact with you two after all this time has really buoyed her up. If I'm not being intrusive, I gather it was your father who was the problem?"

"Er, yes, me and Josephine didn't have a happy time at home with him around, but it wasn't Mum's fault. And it wasn't anything, well, you know, er........ um, well *bad* .. .... and I don't know, somehow we just never wanted to make the effort to put things right when we left home. I realise now it was very unkind on Mum, but, well, it's all behind us now. I'm just so pleased she had the guts to leave him, and d'you know, I'm really proud of her."

"Well you're clearly both very well balanced and accomplished girls and I know your mother is *immensely* proud of you. And I can't tell you how happy she makes me." Maggie and Jolyon toasted Helena Ruby with their coffee cups, then Maggie started quizzing Jolyon about the history of Elver Hall.

Denholm was the harbinger of Helena Ruby's arrival in the kitchen. "Aha, time to open something sparkling I'd say, what do you think?"

"Ooh, yes please, after all, it's that sort of day really isn't it!"

"I'll have a bit of orange juice in mine please," said Helena Ruby "I don't want to get squiffy too early in the day!"

"Oh Mum, your big night eh?"

"And Denzil's too, I mean a restaurant's no good without the food is it?"

"So what's it called then?"

"It's a surprise for Jolyon, we're going to unveil the sign," said Helena Ruby as Jolyon poured the champagne. "I wonder if we ought to wait for Josephine?"

"Don't worry, there's plenty more in the cellar. Can't think of a better reason than celebrating spending time with Helena Ruby and her two gorgeous daughters. Cheers!" As they sat chatting amiably in the sitting room the telephone rang. It was Josephine: "Mum, look I'm so sorry, I'm going to be held up. It's Roger you see, he's had to go into hospital. Now you're not to panic..."

"Oh but darling, what's happened, this is awful, I mean awful for you, for, well ...."

"Look Mum, there was something I didn't tell you. I know I should have but I, well, I didn't want to sort of take the shine off your day, and it's all under control but, well you see, Roger, he.....he's in a wheelchair. It's unlikely he'll be able to walk, spinal injury in a car accident a couple of years ago, but he's picked up a bit of an infection and they thought it best ...."

"Oh Josie, I'm so sorry, oh dear, I'm ...... look, talk to your sister for a minute would you, this is all ....." and Helena Ruby handed the telephone to Maggie as she fumbled for a handkerchief, unable to see through her tears. Jolyon put his arm around her shoulders, concerned at what he had heard. "Come on my dear, what's the trouble, look, Maggie doesn't seem too concerned, it'll be alright, I'm sure." Maggie handed the telephone back to Helena Ruby and said, "Mum, you're not to worry, really, and Josephine will be here."

"Oh sweetheart, you can't leave the poor man if he's in hospital, really, you need to be with him. I am just so sorry, it must be awful for you both. I wish you'd told me. Can't I do anything to help? Oh dear, poor you, I ...."

"Mum, they've only taken him in as a precaution and he wants me to be with you tonight. As soon as he's over it, I'll bring him down to see you - bit of R and R, eh?"

"Only if you really are sure sweetheart, I mean, it's only a restaurant and he's the man you love."

"Yes he is Mum, but I'm also enormously proud of you and I want to be there, OK?"

"OK darling, I'll see you later then, but if anything else happens...."

"It won't, I'll be there. Get that champagne on ice!" Helena Ruby put down the telephone. "Oh Maggie, why didn't you say?"

"Because it's up to Josephine, Mum. Roger is a lovely man and you'll get to meet him soon."

"I suppose so. Anyhow, what about you? You've been very quiet about your love life." Maggie took a sip of champagne and said, "Mmm. Where to start. I'm, well, recovering I suppose. Met a fantastic chap, journalist, and we were having a terrific time together and just when it looked like we might make things a bit more .... um, permanent, I found out quite by chance that the bastard was married and his wife was expecting their second child."

"Oh Maggie my darling, I'm so sorry, how awful for you."

"Yes it was a dreadful shock I must admit, and I can't deny that it hurts and I feel almost, well, soiled I suppose. But I'm getting over it now. I hate myself for still missing him, but hey, I'm here and I'm going to have a fantastic time. At least you've come out on top Mum!"

"I certainly have."

"A toast to the ladies!" said Jolyon.

Helena Ruby had made everybody sandwiches but she was too excited to eat much herself. The grandfather clock in the hall chimed five and Jolyon suggested that perhaps they go and start getting ready. Roberta was going to join them at six and had promised to help Helena Ruby 'do' her hair. Denzil had telephoned to confirm that all was prepared and told Helena Ruby that the sign had been put up, suitably veiled, and that it was 'brill', and he just knew Jolyon would love it. Helena Ruby took her outfit from the wardrobe and lay it on the bed. Jolyon walked in from their bathroom in his dressing gown. "I think a little hors d'oeuvres, don't you my dear?" he said as he embraced Helena Ruby and kissed her neck. "As long as we don't get crumbs on the carpet I suppose!" she giggled as she reached inside his dressing gown.

"Zip me up would you?" said Helena Ruby presenting her back to Jolyon, who was adjusting his bow tie in front of the mirror. Helena Ruby's outfit was charcoal grey linen with a low neckline and a softly fitted bodice which gently gave into a fairly full ankle length skirt. "My dear you look absolutely gorgeous," he said, pulling up the zip and stroking the back of her neck. "And so do you Jolyon Urquart," said Helena Ruby, turning around to kiss him. "Shall we go down then?"

"Just one thing first my dear," said Jolyon as he took from his jacket pocket an exquisite antique pearl and platinum necklace. "Here, this should complete the outfit." He fastened it around Helena Ruby's neck and she gazed, delighted in the mirror. "Oh darling, thank you, I don't know what to say, I ..."

"Say nothing my darling," said Jolyon as he kissed her tenderly and stroked her neck. "You are the most beautiful person I have ever had the privilege to be with, Helena Ruby Tremble. Just promise me you'll never go."

"I promise, oh dear, look at me, I...." and the tears welled up again. Jolyon smiled and pressed the handkerchief from his pocket into her hand.

"I'll go down and see you in a minute."

"Yes, yes, everybody should be here soon. You have booked the taxi haven't you?" asked Helena Ruby in an attempt to regain her equilibrium. "It's all under control my dear, all you have to do is charm the customers and enjoy your evening. I have no qualms on the first count, and I insist that you comply with the second."

Roberta arrived and declared Helena Ruby's hair perfect as it was, and five minutes before the taxi arrived to collect them all, Josephine arrived. She ran to the front door where Helena Ruby was waiting for her and they embraced. "Oh sweetheart, thank you so much for coming, I know you, I.... oh dear, here I go again...."

"Mum, your mascara!"

"Oh, never mind that, I'm just so happy, but how's Roger, I'm so ....I mean, it's......."

"Let's go in and get a tissue and get you sorted out Mum! Roger is responding well to treatment and sends you his very best wishes, OK?" They went inside, Josephine with her arm around her mother's shoulders. "Jolyon, Roberta, this is Josephine, Maggie's sister, in case you couldn't tell! Just give me two minutes to mop up my face and I'll be with you." Everybody shook hands and Josephine and Maggie hugged each other tight.

The taxi arrived outside the restaurant and Helena Ruby, the twins, Jolyon and Roberta got out, to be greeted by Denzil and Francis who looked dazzling, Denzil in his chef's whites and Francis in a stylishly cut suit which hung beautifully on his spare frame, and a very jaunty bow tie. Maggie took several photographs of the group, then they went inside, Denzil and Helena Ruby making one final check on everything.

Guests began to arrive and much greeting and shaking of hands commenced. A lot of the guests already knew each other and a cacophony of chatter gradually swelled within the quietly elegant confines of the restaurant. Maggie, Josephine and Roberta handed out glasses of champagne and drew many admiring glances. Helena Ruby Tremble felt as though she was floating in a bubble of happiness as she circulated with Jolyon, occasionally squeezing his hand affectionately. She slipped into the kitchen to make sure everything was well with Denzil. Sauces were bubbling and steam was hissing from saucepans, as his three staff stirred, sliced fruit and vegetables, checked the oven occasionally and wiped down surfaces frequently. Denzil was piping chocolate onto an astonishing dessert. "Looks like everything's under control," said Helena. "Anybody need anything?"

"I think we're just fine," said Denzil without looking up. Ready for the unveiling when you are, then everybody can eat."

"OK, Francis, would you be my MC?"
"Delighted!"
"Good luck, man," called Denzil.
"You've got it!"
"Yes indeedy!" rejoined Helena Ruby.

Helena Ruby Tremble and Francis walked out into the cheery throng and Francis knocked a fork on his glass and called for everybody's attention. "Ladies and gentlemen, if you would all care to step outside for one moment, we will now officially unveil the name of this fabulous new eatery, where we hope to see you and your colleagues frequently!" Helena Ruby took Jolyon by the hand and their guests followed them out onto the pavement. When everybody was assembled, she waved to Roberta who twitched a cord, pulling the covering to one side. Helena Ruby was beaming and Jolyon broke into laughter, as the guests all broke into applause.

The name on the sign said '***B R I L L***'.